A STORY OF JAPANESE INTERNMENT

IN LIGHT OF DECEMBER

Andrew Hayes Williams

Illustrated by
Nicholas McInvale

Copyright © 2019 by **Andrew Hayes Williams**

www.andrewhayeswilliams.net

Illustrations and cover art by Nicholas McInvale

Cover design by Germancreative.

Book Layout modified from © 2017 BookDesignTemplates.com.

In Light of December: A Story of Japanese Internment / Andrew Hayes Williams. —1st ed.

Paperback ISBN: 978-1-7340466-0-1
eBook ISBN: 978-1-7340466-1-8

IN LIGHT OF
DECEMBER

A Story of Japanese Internment

Part One:

OUR UNITY OF PURPOSE

CHAPTER ONE

SHIKATA GA NAI

Come on, Yoshi, he pleaded with himself. *You can't screw up. It all depends on this. It all depends on you.* He trembled. His heart pounded. He tried taking slow, deep breaths to calm his nerves, but the air entered his mouth in a series of little gasps, then sputtered back out again in a hot, quivering exhale. The sweat on his palms itched his blisters as he tightened his grip on the bat. Once he positioned himself in the proper stance (his feet a *tiny* bit more than shoulder-width apart, just like Father had taught him), he raised his arms and squinted at the pitcher. Across the field, a little off to the right, a giant scoreboard stared over the game like a king observing a duel. Yoshi struggled to keep his eyes from drifting over to it:

Guest—3; Jackson—2.

In the bottom of the ninth, with two outs and three empty bases, Yoshi knew he needed a miracle to hit a home run and tie the game. If he could manage to pull this off, he would add an extra inning, giving the Jackson Stallions one more chance to win the last game of the season. More importantly, Yoshi would finally prove that he belonged on the team. Everyone considered him to be the weakest player—and worst of all, he knew they were right.

Not anymore, he swore to himself. *From this moment on, you're Yoshi Yamaguchi: champion of Jackson High School. They'll cheer for you at graduation next month. They'll give you a special medal. In his speech, Principal Wilbur will thank you for saving the game: "Yoshi Yamaguchi turned out to be the greatest baseball player in the history of our fine school, and I can say, without a doubt, that he is the most important graduate of the Class of 1941."*

It had to come true. It had to…

Pitch.

Swing.

"Strike One!"

It's okay, Yoshi. Stay focused. You still have two more chances.

Careful not to adjust his stance, he gave a slight shake of the shoulders, hoping some movement would release a little tension. He wished he had been blessed with a more enviable athletic form. Unlike Father, who possessed broad shoulders and a muscular build, Yoshi had been called scrawny more than once in his life. Despite his average height, his slenderness made him look a little gangly. His sharp elbows and bony knees made his batting stance less than flattering, and he blamed his occasional clumsiness on his oversized feet. Beneath his bright red helmet, a couple inches of thick black hair felt hot and heavy on his head. Hats never suited him well. He never had a particular hairstyle (the barber always laughed at him for requesting a "normal guy cut," but Yoshi never asked for anything special because Father scoffed at lofty hairdos). Yoshi preferred to have his lazily side-swept bangs covering his face. With his hair pulled back, his dark bushy eyebrows stood out a little too much, and his nose, mysteriously, seemed extra flat and small.

Sometimes, he wondered if he was ugly. He certainly didn't feel very confident. And whenever someone told Sato that she looked just like her brother, she always seemed a little offended. He didn't take that as a good sign. At the moment, thankfully, the crowd couldn't see his face—nor could he see them. But the eyes of a hundred people seemed to tingle the back of his neck. Sweat stained the pits of his bright red Stallions jersey, and he saw the pitcher's arm fling forward...

Pitch.

Swing.

"Strike Two!"

Yoshi cracked his neck. For a second, he stepped away from the plate, sensing the crowd was studying his every movement. He glanced back at Mom, Grandma, and Sato, who all stood in the front row with their mouths covered in anticipation. Up in heaven, Yoshi liked to believe, Grandpa looked down on the game with his mouth covered too. And Father, who couldn't attend because he had to run the grocery store, awaited a tale of victory. Yoshi longed to bring one to him.

You can do this, he told himself. *You can do it. You can do it. You can do it. You can do it.*

Of course, his family would support him no matter what. The person he *really* wanted to impress stood a few rows back in the stands. His crush, Sarah Hassenger, with her bright blue eyes and blonde ponytail, popped a stick of bubblegum with the other cheerleaders. The girls'

coach required them to attend all major sporting events—
a school spirit policy that the cheerleaders met with countless eye rolls and grumbles. Nevertheless, Sarah was here,
she was watching, and she even leaned forward like she
was interested in the game. In the last four years, Yoshi
had never mustered enough courage to have a serious
conversation with her. He had one more chance to win her
over: this swing, this hit, this home run...

He got back in his stance. The ball rested in the pitcher's glove. Any moment, it would charge through the air.
Yoshi knew he shouldn't overthink. Last week, in the
game against the San Pedro Seahorses, he almost got
kicked off the team because he hit the ball, second
guessed himself, and then waited a full four seconds before starting to run. Only after the team shouted his name
did Yoshi drop the bat and sprint, turning what might
have been a double into a single. This time, as he held up
his bat, he vowed not to let self-doubt slow him down.

Come on, Yoshi.

He stared at the pitcher's hand.

*Don't worry about Sarah. Don't worry about telling
Father.*

The pitcher raised his knee. He flung back his arm.

Don't think.

Deep breaths.

Don't think.

Ball in the air.

Don't think.

Heart pounding.

Pitch.

Swing.

Hit.

The ball soared into the outfield.

The moment Yoshi felt the ball strike the wood, he dropped his bat and darted. Shocked cheers from the crowd swept over him. In the back of his mind, a voice insisted this moment couldn't be true. He refused to listen. After all those times he had slowed himself down, he couldn't handle making the same mistake again.

Right after his foot touched first base, he heard his name being called. The word came to him faintly, like a group of voices trying to shout him out of a dream: *Yoshi! Yoshi! Yoshi! Yoshi!*

A grin filled his face; they were chanting his name!

His foot touched third. All that mattered now was making it to home plate. He could practically see Sarah, bright blue eyes agape in anticipation, pumping her fist in the air with the rest of the cheerleaders to chant, *Yo-shi,*

Yo-shi, Yo-shi, Yo-shi. After the game, she would give him a huge hug. She would say, *Wow, I was wrong about you. You're just about the swellest guy I ever met.* He would finally impress her, he would graduate as a champion, and he would make Father prouder than ever before. Nothing would stop him. Nothing could take this moment from him.

Yo-shi, Yo-shi, Yo-shi, Yo-shi!

He did it. He reached home plate. He raised his arms in the air and shouted, "Yahoo!"

The chanting died out. Only the coach kept shouting his name: "*Yoshi*, dagnabbit. Your ears broke, son? They caught the ball. You're *out*!"

"What?" Yoshi said through a nervous laugh. Way out in the distance, the center fielder held up the ball in his mitted hand and tauntingly shook it. Yoshi's gaze drifted over to the stands, where Mom and Sato covered their mouths in shock. A few rows back, Sarah and the other cheerleaders were cracking up.

Yoshi took off his helmet and threw it on the ground.

After a cold shower to wash away the tears and red cheeks, Yoshi waited in the locker room until the crowd had time to leave. He slouched on the long, uncomfortable wooden bench that ran down the aisle of lockers. A musty, sweaty stench filled his nose.

"Hey, Yoshi. Nice work today."

The voice made him jump. Yoshi looked up and saw Freddy, the only teammate who was ever nice to him.

"I didn't know you were still here," Yoshi mumbled, quickly wiping his eyes to make sure no leftover tears remained.

"I forgot my bag. Hey, don't feel bad, okay? Happens to all of us."

When Freddy left, Yoshi wanted to hear the door slam. Instead, the hinges gave a long creak, followed by a gentle click. Somehow, this added to his disappointment.

The sun burned his eyes as he stepped outside. He hung down his head as he moseyed over to his family's spot. Mom pushed herself up when she saw him, causing her short black curls to jiggle.

"There he is. Great job," she said, with the typical warmth in her voice. To be honest, he sort of liked that his mom still babied him, even though he would never admit it to anyone. His peers all seemed so independent and mature. Part of him wondered if he had zipped through the time of his life when he was supposed to grow up. Deep down, he still felt like a little kid.

"It wasn't a great job," he grumbled. "It was a lousy job." Mom hugged him, and her shoulder muffled his voice as he leaned his head down onto it. "The lousiest job in the history of the school."

"Of course not, Yoshi. You gave it your best. I'm so proud of you."

Yoshi pulled away. "You shouldn't be."

Mom's thinly plucked eyebrows creased ever so slightly, and the corners of her ruby lips tightened. Yoshi knew what this meant. When Mom didn't know what to say, she became frustrated. Deciding not to push the subject any further, Yoshi waved at Sato and Grandma.

"Oh my, Yoshi-kun." Grandma let out a little groan as Sato helped her up. "How nice it is to get to see you play." She gave a giant, open-mouthed grin. Of all the wrinkles on her face, the crow's feet around her eyes looked the deepest—a result of countless smiles like these.

"Thanks," Yoshi mumbled, as Grandma wrapped her arms around him. He never understood why, but she always smelled like pepper.

"When I saw you out there," Grandma continued, as she pulled away. "When I saw you hit the ball, I said, 'That is my Yoshi-kun.'"

"When I hit the ball, sure." Yoshi looked down at the ground. "Hopefully you fell asleep after that part."

"Oh," Grandma laughed. She didn't seem to understand what Yoshi had just said.

"Don't worry," Sato told him. "I've seen worse. I mean it. One time, Timothy Stapleton lost his grip on the bat, and it went flying when he swung."

"I don't know who that is," Yoshi stated.

"Susan's little brother."

"I don't know who that is either."

"Sure you do. She's been to our house before."

"Her and your five hundred other friends?"

"Okay, you two," Mom said. "I think it's time for us to celebrate."

With a nod, Yoshi started dragging his feet away from the field. "Let's go celebrate Sato skipping a grade." Sato had just gotten the news that she could skip freshman year. After getting ahead in both seventh and eighth grade, she had advanced so much that she could enter high school as a sophomore next fall. Yoshi knew he should be a proud big brother, but he couldn't help feeling a little bit jealous. He may have missed the part of his life when he was supposed to become a grownup, but Sato acted mature enough for the both of them.

"You gave it your best effort, Yoshi," Mom insisted. "You did your best. That's all anyone can do."

"That's what people say when you're no good."

Mom sighed. Yoshi knew he shouldn't have said it, but he couldn't resist. He didn't have the energy to force a smile, and he dreaded the humiliation of telling Father about the game. As he shuffled toward the car, knowing he'd never set foot on the baseball field again, one thought ran through his mind: *good riddance.*

By the time they arrived at Ricky's Bistro, Father had already claimed their usual spot by the window to the left of the front door—an easy accomplishment, since no one was there but him. Despite Yoshi's enduring frown and low-hung head, he couldn't help feeling a little better as he stepped through the door and whiffed the scent of cheese and garlic. For years, Ricardo talked about wanting to remodel his restaurant, but Yoshi hoped the plan would never happen. Ever since he was a kid, the same four tables stood on each side of the narrow aisle, and the same two chandeliers hung from the ceiling, casting a golden light across the room. With so many birthdays and celebrations held here over the years, this place felt like home just the way it was.

Having snagged an extra chair, Father sat at the end of the table, sticking halfway out into the aisle. As soon as he saw his family, he shot up and pulled back the seats for Mom and Grandma.

Father looked like a giant. At least, something about him seemed gigantic, even though he was only a foot taller than Yoshi. He had a lean, muscular body, always covered by a white, short-sleeved button up shirt and a pair of black slacks. The skin on his face appeared as thick as leather, his wrinkles little more than minor indentations. Tiny black hairs prickled out of his head, with a thin, balding patch on the back of his scalp where the buzz cut had started receding. Bronze, wire-rimmed glasses pressed down his big ears, and the circular lenses covered the darkest brown eyes that Yoshi had ever seen. On the rare occasions Father smiled, he did so by slightly parting his lips, careful not to reveal his yellow and somewhat crooked teeth. Most of the time, Father's square jaw stayed locked in place, with a tiny scowl indenting his upper lip, as if he smelled something unpleasant but didn't want to say anything.

"Where did you leave your bike?" Mom asked him as she took a seat.

"At the store," Father said. "I left early, walked. Tell

me of the game."

When Mom saw Yoshi slouch in his seat, she changed the subject:

"Where's Ricardo? I would have thought you two would be talking politics by now."

Father shook his head. "He prepares the food. Tell me of the game."

Hanging his head, Yoshi shrugged.

"Yoshi almost hit a home run," Mom said.

Father's lips parted—another one of those toothless grins. He gave a satisfied nod.

Grandma closed her eyes and laughed. "Oh, Yoshi-kun, it was so good."

"You guys don't have to do that," Yoshi mumbled.

"You really don't have to feel bad about it," Sato chimed in. "Remember when Shannon Becker was on the softball team with me and—"

"Nope."

"You don't even know what I was gonna say."

"I don't know who Shannon Becker is."

"And there they *are*. All the *Yamaguchis*. Finally *here*." Ricardo was the size of the doorway. The kitchen's aluminum door squeaked as it flapped shut behind him. As he clomped forward, his giant belly knocked against

the tables on both sides of the aisle. His sprawling red apron complemented his giant ginger mustache. If the restaurant hadn't changed at all from Yoshi's earliest memories, neither had its owner. Somehow, even though he was in his mid-sixties, his shiny round bald spot hadn't expanded in the slightest, and the horseshoe of tufted red hair hadn't grayed at all. Even Ricardo's strange habit of emphasizing the end of his sentences hadn't changed. "How is *everything*? What's the *occasion*? Mr. Yamaguchi tells me there was a *game*."

"Yoshi played his very last baseball game today." Mom leaned forward, like she wanted to make sure Yoshi heard her encouraging tone.

Ricardo knelt behind Yoshi and Sato, putting a hand

on the back of each of their chairs.

"Oh my *goodness*," he said. "His last game *ever*?"

"No, no," Mom laughed. "Of high school."

"Ever," Yoshi muttered, before giving Ricardo a timid wave.

"And Sato just learned she can start high school as a sophomore next year," Mom added.

With a groan, Ricardo put a hand over his chest like he was having a heart attack. "Little *Sato*. Always so *smart*. Seems like just yesterday you were here for skipping *fourth*."

"Skipping third," Sato corrected, with a proud grin.

"Skipping *third*. Of *course*. Where does the time *go*?"

For as long as Yoshi could remember, a few things happened every time his family came to Ricky's: political talk, some old story, and the comment, "Where does the time *go*?" Usually, Ricardo told the story about the first time Mom and Father ate here. Yoshi still liked hearing the tale, even though he could repeat it word for word. His family's past fascinated him, and while he wished his father would tell him more, he did learn quite a bit from Mom.

For instance, soon after Father got back from fighting in World War I, he opened a small grocery store. One day, Mom came in looking for work. Finding a job as a woman was difficult enough, but being Japanese didn't make the process any easier. Father had been running everything himself, and even though he couldn't afford to hire an assistant, he offered her a job. He wanted to get to know her, and he wanted to help her out when she told him about her circumstances.

What happened was this: dreaming of a better life, Grandma and Grandpa immigrated to America in 1900, when Mom was an infant. Grandpa worked as a farmhand for eighteen years, until he fell from a ladder and broke his leg. The Hashimoto family moved into the city, hoping to find some sort of income. By chance or by miracle, Mom wandered into Father's brand-new store.

This backstory was Yoshi's favorite part of the tale. But for Ricardo, the story began when Mom and Father were looking for a place to have a date, and three other restaurants had already turned them away because of their race. "When your parents came *in*," Ricardo always began. "They seemed so *kind*. But they looked so *tired*. I said to them, 'Hey, you two, what's going *on*?' They said to me, 'We've been turned *away*. By three other *places*.' Can you believe *that*?"

Without a doubt, Yoshi would soon hear this story

again. But in the meantime, Ricardo stood back up and patted his belly.

"I hope everybody wants their *usuals*. I started *preparing*."

"I think someone needs a root beer." Mom raised an eyebrow at Yoshi. "How does that sound?"

Being offered his favorite drink *did* make him feel a little better, but Yoshi didn't want to look too reassured. If he gave the impression that a simple soda could take away his disappointment, then he would make his family think the game didn't really matter to him. He pursed his lips and scrunched his brow, then gave a tiny nod.

"Let's take a couple root beers." Mom glanced across at Yoshi and Sato. "For the athlete and the scholar."

"Two *root beers*," Ricardo exclaimed as he scurried back towards the kitchen. "I'll have everything out for you *right away*."

The aluminum door swung back and forth: *croak-creak, croak-creak, croak-creak, croak-creak*. As Yoshi leaned his elbow on the table and gazed across the room, the noise changed in his imagination: *Yo-shi, Yo-shi, Yo-shi, Yo-shi*. The chanting crowd started coming back to him. He was at home plate again, bat in hand. Ball whizzing toward him, he swung with all his might. His hit roared like thunder. The bat's reverberations tingled through his arms. Half the baseball's skin hung loose as the battered object soared toward the sun. Everybody stared in awe. Even the other team stood frozen, mouths hanging open as they watched Yoshi run from base to base. Once he reached home plate, he didn't stop. He jumped into the stands, wiped the sweat off his forehead with the back of his right arm, and stood beside Sarah Hassenger.

"Oh my goodness!" she exclaimed. "It's Yoshi Yama-guchi! He's the swellest guy in the whole school. Will you please kiss me?"

"Gee, I've never kissed anyone before!" he shouted back. "I'd sure love to."

"Yoshi will see." Father stared at him, awaiting a re-sponse.

With a gulp, Yoshi leaned back in his chair and looked around the table. His daydream had clogged his ears; he hadn't been paying attention to his family's conversation.

"Huh?"

"If he tries to buy oranges again," Father stated. "I will not let him. You will see."

You will see. Yoshi knew what that meant. Over the years, Father had built up a reliable clientele, so now he could easily afford to hire an assistant. Mom hadn't worked in the store since before Yoshi was born, and Father's dream was always to have his son work with him in the family business. As a result, he kept mentioning that Yoshi would work at the grocery store after graduation. Long before Yoshi even started high school, Father would throw out an occasional reference to this inevitable truth. For someone who never showed much enthusiasm, Father seemed ecstatic about it. This made Yoshi feel special. He only wished he had a little choice in the matter. Given Father's determination, working at the grocery store seemed like his only option for the future.

Yoshi gave a confused nod. "Wait...Who can't buy oranges?"

"A young man," Father answered. "He dropped them. He said they were damaged. He wanted a discount. I told him I would not sell to him again."

Sato nudged Yoshi's shoulder. "Are you asleep or something?"

"I'm just tired. Jeez." Yoshi rubbed his forehead.

"Look what's *ready*." Ricardo's hips knocked against the empty tables as he dragged his feet down the aisle, holding up a big black tray with his hairy right arm. Six plates and two glass bottles were squeezed together on the tray because Ricardo refused to take more than one trip to deliver anyone's food. He walked around the table and set down each dish. "For *Grandma*. For *Mrs. Yamaguchi*. For *Mr. Yamaguchi*. For Yoshi and *Sato*." Ricardo held the empty tray under his arm and pointed at Father. "Now Mr. *Yamaguchi*. I have to *say*. The world is falling *apart*. Tell me what you *think* about—"

Father held up a hand. "After dinner."

Ricardo gave an aggressive sigh, then smiled, nodded, and waddled off. The restaurant turned quiet as they all stared at their meals. Aside from the sense of community the Yamaguchis felt here, another perk of Ricky's Bistro was the diverse menu. The food, albeit not the best, had something for everyone. Most of the menu reflected Ricardo's Italian heritage, but a few classic American entrees could also be found, which Yoshi and Sato preferred. While Yoshi always ordered a hamburger with nothing but ketchup and mustard on top, and Sato got a grilled cheese sandwich, the rest of the family preferred items that more closely resembled Japanese cuisine. Mom and Father both took the rice-based *risotto*. Even Grandma, with her sensitive stomach, found something on the menu that agreed with her: *brodo*, an Italian soup that was similar to Japanese *dashi*, with its dried sardines and shiitake mushrooms.

Back when Grandpa was alive to join them, he ordered the *brodo* too. To this day, the smell of the broth made Yoshi think about how Grandpa used to slurp down the soup to make everybody laugh. As the fishy steam reached his nose, Yoshi gave a melancholy smile.

"Lord, thank you for food. Thank you for…"

When Yoshi heard his father's voice, he realized his whole family had already bowed their heads and folded their hands. He felt guilty when he didn't pay attention during prayer, but memories of Grandpa filled his mind. As a kid, Yoshi had a favorite gag. Grandpa would stick his spoon behind his own left ear, and once the soup was placed in front of him, he would look around for a utensil to use.

"Mr. Ricardo," he would say. "You forget my spoon. Always forget my spoon. How to eat my soup?"

Cracking up, Yoshi and Sato would shout across the table at him. "Your ear! Behind your ear!"

"Behind the ear? Behind the ear?" Grandpa patted the back of his head. "No, no. I find nothing. I have no spoon."

Yoshi and Sato both pointed across the table. "Right *there*. It's right *there*."

Grandpa took a peak under the tablecloth. "No, nothing. I do not see it." He picked up his fork. "Oh, here. Right here it is." He scooped up a mouthful with his fork, and the broth dripped through the tines. "Hmm…" Grandpa said, sliding the empty fork from his mouth. "This soup, it tastes of metal. Why is this?"

Sometimes, the gag stopped there. Other times, Grandpa kept going for another few minutes, and he ended up slurping down the soup. It all depended on how long he could keep Yoshi and Sato entertained. Once Yoshi turned thirteen, he didn't like laughing in public because he didn't like drawing attention to himself. By that point, Grandpa put less energy into his act, and he only directed his performance at Sato. If Yoshi had known, at thirteen, that these jokes would end for good in another two years, he would have kept on laughing through his early teens.

But now, it was May 1941, Yoshi was seventeen, and Grandpa's jokes were gone for good.

"…an end to the war in Europe," Father concluded. "An end to the bloodshed in Asia. Keep America safe. Amen."

"Amen," everyone mumbled.

As everyone ate, the words "war" and "bloodshed"

lingered in the air. England had been at war with Nazi Germany since September 1939, and the recent debates between Father and Ricardo were about whether or not America should join the fight. Since England was America's friend, Ricardo thought the U.S. needed to do more than just give money and supplies to its ally. Father disagreed. His personal experience with combat made him disdain all war, so he hated the idea of sending troops overseas, but he did believe that Italy and Japan were making a mistake by being allies with Nazi Germany.

Yoshi didn't know much else about the conflict, because politics never interested him. That stuff always seemed so tedious, and none of it really affected his life. The only time he paid attention to the news was last September, when President Roosevelt enacted the peacetime military draft. At that point, Yoshi felt a little nervous, but his anxiety didn't last long. Even though men could sign up for the military at eighteen if they wanted to, the draft was only for men aged twenty-one and older.

After taking his last bite, Yoshi washed out the leftover taste of ketchup and mustard with a sip of root beer. The chilly fizzes tingled his throat as he swallowed. He savored his favorite treat, and he couldn't deny that it succeeded at cheering him up.

"Thank you for the root beer," he said to Mom.

Mom grinned through pursed lips. She used to smile this way when Yoshi did something cute as a kid, and once in a while, that look of hers reemerged.

The kitchen door swung open and Ricardo stomped back down the aisle. "All *finished*?"

Father nodded.

"Then I have to *say*. The world is falling *apart*!" Ricardo grabbed one of the empty seats and plopped it down next to Father. Just like always, he placed the seat the wrong direction, so he could sit down backwards and lean his crossed arms against the back of the chair. The moment he sat down, the legs of the chair wobbled, and Yoshi had a feeling that one day the seat would break under Ricardo's weight.

"What's happening to our *countries*? What do you *think*? Will we go to *war*?"

By "we," he meant America.

"Japan is not stupid," Father replied. "It became arrogant. It should not have invaded China. But it could not win against the United States. It must know this."

Ricardo threw his arms up in the air. "But they side with *Hitler*! Think of all the places he's *taken*! Czechoslovakia, Poland, Denmark, Norway, the Netherlands,

Belgium, Luxembourg, France…" He took a deep breath. "Now *Yugoslavia. Greece.* I have to tell you, Mr. *Yamaguchi.* I think we need a war to put an end to all this *madness.*"

Father shook his head at Ricardo. "We should not go to war."

Ricardo's eyes widened. His bushy brows shot up, crinkling his forehead. "No *war*? No *war*? Then how does this *end*? We let the crazies keep running the *show*?"

"I know war like you cannot," Father stated. "It is useless. My son will have no part in this."

Ricardo jumped up. He stuck his index finger in the air and waved it around. "I will have you *know*. My son was on the front lines the last time we had a *world war.* I've heard the *stories.* I know the *horrors.* That war was *pointless.* It was *stupid.* It should never have *happened.* This one is *different.* Those leaders are *crazy.* They're *crazy.* They need to be *stopped.* The world is *on fire.* Our old countries have lost their *minds.* We have to *stop* them, because the *whole darned world is on fire*!" Ricardo's voice came close to a shriek.

With a chipper smile, he plopped himself back down on the chair. "Boy, I've missed you, *Yamaguchis.*" His gleaming eyes landed on Yoshi and Sato. "Do you two

know the place of your parents' first *date*? It was *here.*
I'm not *kidding.*"

Tonight, Yoshi couldn't focus on the story. He wasn't
in the mood. All he could think about was the way Sarah
Hassenger laughed at him. If someone as special as her
thought he was lame, then he must have been really, aw-
fully, horribly lame. Throughout Ricardo's shouts of
"seemed *impossible*" and "such a lovely *pair,*" Yoshi
turned his focus elsewhere. He clenched his fists to grip
an invisible bat, and he retreated into the comforting fantasy of being a baseball star.

By the time they left Ricky's Bistro, Yoshi wished he
hadn't moped quite so much. On the drive home, Mom
and Grandma kept bragging about how smart Sato was,
and they didn't mention Yoshi at all. He knew why, of
course. He had made his feelings about the baseball game
pretty darn clear, and none of their support seemed to
cheer him up. Even still, Yoshi wished they would keep
complimenting him. He shouldn't have been so dismissive of their encouragement.

Sinking into the backseat, he gazed out the window of
his family's old black Ford Coupe. They took the long
route home because they had to drop Father off at the gro-

cery store. There was no room in the car for Father's bike, so he pedaled his way home instead. Yoshi was envious of the alone time. He would rather ride a bike home than listen to his family gush about Sato's brilliance.

"You should start researching universities," Mom said, keeping her eyes on the road.

"What do you think most congressmen get degrees in?" Sato asked.

Yoshi rolled his eyes. Not only did his sister excel in school—she was already thinking about her future. She wanted to be the first Japanese American woman elected to Congress. Sato was smart and kind and popular and ambitious. To contrast, Yoshi had no idea what he wanted to do with his life, and he scraped through school with Cs. All he wanted was for Sarah Hassenger to like him, and he couldn't even have *that*.

"That's a good question," Mom answered. "Law, perhaps? Maybe that's something else for you to research."

"Oh Sato-chan." With a grin, Grandma shook her head. "You are so good."

Yoshi sank a little further into his seat. The grocery store was just over a mile from their house, and most of the trip was through residential area. The shop was on the outskirts of downtown San Pedro. The fun stuff, like the movie theater, was a little farther out.

As soon as they parked on the driveway at home, Sato hopped out of the car. The Yamaguchis lived in a small, two-story house. Two windows sat beneath the saddle roof, one for Yoshi's bedroom and one for Sato's, and the whole house was painted with a fading shade of yellow. A sidewalk ran over the grassy lawn and right up to the front door. To the right of the house, the driveway led to a one-car garage tucked away in the back. Because there were no bedrooms on the first story, and Grandma struggled with stairs, the Yamaguchis had converted the garage into a little room. Grandpa used to sleep there too.

Before Mom climbed out of the driver's seat, she looked over at Grandma. "Mama, would you like some tea or anything?"

"Oh no." Grandma let out a little laugh and patted her belly. "I won't want this now. With the dinner, I want nothing more. Just time to rest for me, I think."

Mom looked into the backseat. "Yoshi, will you take her?"

Before getting an answer, Mom disappeared into the house.

Yoshi took Grandma by the arm, and the two of them slogged along the driveway. Grandma walked carefully, silently, as if she needed all her focus to move each leg.

As they neared the garage, she finally spoke. "What a good day this has been." She gave a tired groan. "Oh yes, a good day."

"It's been okay." Letting go of Grandma's arm, Yoshi rushed to the side of the garage and opened the door.

"You at your baseball game." Grandma smiled. "And Sato-chan, oh she is so smart."

At least she acknowledged him again. Still, Yoshi sighed.

"Grandma, can I ask you something?" he said.

"Oh?"

"Do you ever feel real lousy? Like you're no good at all?"

She stared at him, mouth hanging open with concern. "What does this mean?"

"Do you ever feel like you wish you were special? Like you know you're not, and you know you can't become it...because that stuff's just born inside of you or something like that. But still you think you ought to change something, because some people just don't care about you." He said nothing for a few seconds, because he didn't think he was making any sense. "Do you know what I mean?"

"Oh, Yoshi-kun, of course you are special."

"But if those people don't care about you?"

"Then these are not the right people for you."

Sarah's face popped into his mind.

"But if you *wish* they were the right people?" he asked.

Grandma took a step inside and sat down on the double bed, which took up much of the room. Once he helped her sit down, Yoshi stepped back out and leaned against the doorway. As a little kid, he was supposed to stay out of his parents' and grandparents' rooms, and something about the old rule stuck with him. He still had a sense those places were off-limits.

"Yoshi-kun," Grandma said. "We cannot choose who will love us."

"But can I try really hard to make somebody love me?"

"The harder you must try, how much worse this person is for you. When you have somebody you are wishing will love you, this means in truth you seek to prove something to yourself. What is this you are wanting, Yoshi-kun? What are these things you need to prove?"

Yoshi shrugged. He didn't really know what his grandma meant. His eyes drifted to the empty side of the bed. "Do you ever get mad about Grandpa? That he's gone, I mean?"

Grandma smiled. "Oh no. Your grandfather lived such a happy life. I could not be mad by this. He grew old. This happens, Yoshi-kun. *Shikata ga nai.*"

Shikata ga nai. Grandma always loved that expression. Growing up, Yoshi heard it many times. The phrase meant, "It cannot be helped." If you couldn't change your situation, then there was no point in worrying about it. No matter how bad things got, Grandma always managed to utter those words and be at peace. Yoshi appreciated the idea in theory, but it never made him feel much better.

With a little nod, he started closing the door.

"Yoshi-kun," Grandma said. "When you realize you are special, maybe you will not need to seek these people."

Grandma had a way of making him feel better even when he didn't fully grasp her message. Whatever she meant, her words could fill the air with compassion. Sometimes, that was all he needed.

CHAPTER TWO

PLEASE AND THANK YOU

"Three! Two! One!" they all chanted, and everybody cheered as 400 graduation caps soared into the air. For fear of it getting lost in the jumble, Yoshi didn't throw his own too high. His square black hat spun a few feet above his head before twirling back down into his hands. The tassels swayed back and forth like the tail of an old dog. He tried to grasp that he would never be a student again. At the moment, he didn't feel any different.

All around, friends hugged each other. Sniffles filled the air. For Yoshi, there was nothing bitter about the sweetness of graduating. Quite the contrary: he couldn't understand why anyone felt sad to leave this place. While others saved a graduation cap as a souvenir from a fond past, Yoshi wanted to keep his own as a reminder that bad times eventually come to an end. If he could survive four years at Jackson High School, he knew he could get through anything.

Yoshi felt a pat on the back.

"Congratulations, bud!" his teammate Freddy said. "Listen, I just wanted to say it's been real fun playing ball with you. Maybe some of the guys can get together over the summer and keep at it. Whaddya say?"

Yoshi smiled and nodded, appreciating the invitation but knowing he would never touch another baseball in his life. After giving Freddy a wave, Yoshi put his cap back on and approached his family in the front row of the stands.

"We're so proud of you, Yoshi," Mom said, wrapping her arms around him.

Grandma embraced him next. "Oh, Yoshi-kun." As she pulled away, she pinched the fabric of his black robe. "How wonderful it is for this to happen."

"You actually graduated," Sato teased, as she gave him an obligatory hug.

Father didn't open his arms. He didn't give Yoshi a pat on the shoulder. He didn't even give one of his mild, toothless smiles. All he did was look at Yoshi and utter, "You can work at the store now."

Yoshi frowned. A clear expression of fatherly pride would have been nice to hear once in a while—especially on a day like this. Nevertheless, Father's expression remained stoic, his lips as tight as two bricks in a wall.

"I'm just glad it's summer vacation," Yoshi said with a shrug.

Then those tight lips parted: "You will work at the grocery store."

"After summer vacation." Yoshi looked around at his family for validation. They remained silent. "Right?"

"You became an adult today," Father stated. "You need work."

"But I *just* graduated! Don't I get a break?"

"You can take off the half-day Saturday," Father said. "We do not work Sunday."

"That's it?" Yoshi's mouth hung open. He stared at his mom for support.

Mom's eyes widened. "Why don't we let Yoshi take a little break?" She looked at Father and gave him an encouraging nod. "I think he's earned it."

Father clenched his teeth and sighed through his nose. "He can start Tuesday instead of Monday."

The graduation robe felt hot and heavy. Yoshi didn't want to wear it anymore. He dragged his feet as he followed his family to the car, and under his breath, he muttered, "I wish Grandpa was here."

With a root beer and a hamburger from Ricky's Bistro gurgling in his belly, Yoshi lay on his bed and stared at the ceiling. Sunlight shone through the window above his headboard. Normally, the golden light from a sunset would be splayed across the flat white surface above him, but this was the longest day of the year. On June 21st, the evening looked just like an afternoon, so the light through his second-story window remained bright white.

Yoshi had a tiny room, but he didn't mind. If anything, the smallness made the place feel intimate, adding to the comfort of being in his childhood bedroom. Little had changed throughout the years. He still slept on the same twin-size bed, which took up a majority of the space. To his right stood the bookshelf that Father had built over a decade ago, and to his left hung the closet doors. Just two framed pictures adorned the white walls, with one on either side of the bedroom door. The first, a movie poster for *The Frontiersman*, showed Hopalong Cassidy in full cowboy garb, sitting proudly atop his trusty white steed and pointing his pistol at a trio of bad guys; the other, a cover of *Life Magazine* from the previous year, showed a

U.S. tank commander on the training fields, posing for the camera.

Compared to being a cowboy or a soldier, working at a grocery store didn't seem too exciting. Even the name of the shop sounded boring: Yamaguchi Grocery. Maybe if it was called Super Swell Stuff or Food is Really Important, he would have been more excited. At one point, when the topic of working at the store first came up, Yoshi suggested changing the name. Father refused, saying he "disliked poetics." The name "Yamaguchi Grocery" got to the point.

While everything about the grocery store bored Yoshi, the thing that bothered him the most was that the job seemed unimportant. He knew he should feel grateful to be handed a career, but he wanted his life to have meaning. What would happen if he never accomplished anything that mattered? What would his legacy be? When he grew old, would he be known as the guy who stocked fruits and vegetables all his life? Or if he tried really hard, could he hope to become something more than that?

He closed his eyes. With a depressed sigh, he imagined himself at the grocery store. The property was tiny. Not as tiny as his bedroom, of course, but even as a kid, Yoshi thought the place looked small. The older he grew, the more cramped the store seemed. A planked, 20-foot walkway led from the front door to a shelf of Campbell's soup cans against the back wall. Both sides of the aisle were crammed with tables of goods. Even the counter for the cash register had a pyramid of cans waiting to be sold. The only place free of goods was the cramped little office in the back of the shop where Father kept his bike during the day.

As he pictured the place, Yoshi could almost feel a sack of potatoes in his hand, and he saw himself plopping one spud after another into the bucket—*thump... thump... thump... thump...*—every thud like a punch of boredom to the head.

Why couldn't he have a job that made him feel special?

"Gee whiz, it's Yoshi Yamaguchi!" In his imagination, Sarah Hassenger's voice made him tighten his grip on the potato sack. "I'm so glad I caught you while you're working. I wanted to let you know that your store has the best potatoes in the whole world. They were good before, but once you started working here, they got even better somehow."

Yoshi gave a confident nod. "I wrote a letter to the potato growers. I told them to make them extra good, because it's important to me."

"I'm sure glad you did. And that's not all. Every other grocery store has been taken over by outlaws. If not for you, me and my family would starve. You're a real hero for working here."

"It's a tough job, but someone's gotta do it." Yoshi winked.

Just then, the trio of mustached bandits kicked open the door and stormed inside, shooting their pistols at the ceiling. Sarah screamed, and Yoshi stepped in front of her.

"Listen up," one of the bandits shouted. "We're here to claim the last grocery store in town."

Yoshi faced the men. He planted his feet on the ground, shoulder-width apart. "Not on my watch."

As fast as lightning, his right arm dove into the potato sack, and he threw spuds, one by one, at each of the men's faces. The bandits dropped their guns and rubbed their heads, then ran out of the store.

Sarah rushed to Yoshi's side. "Golly, Yoshi. You saved my life." She gave him a big hug. "I think we're pretty swell together. Also, I want you to know that you're not too old to have silly fantasies. Oh, and I'm sure sorry I laughed at you during that baseball game. Maybe we can…"

Yoshi felt something softly press on his belly. He opened his eyes. Sato's cat stood on his chest, staring back at him. Yoshi had to adjust to being back in reality.

"Are you okay?" Sato stood in his doorway. "Your mouth was hanging open in this weird half-snore, half-smile thing."

"I was just napping." He wiped the drool from his chin. "Jeez. Haven't you ever heard of knocking?"

"I *did* knock. You didn't answer."

Yoshi opened his mouth to rebut her, but he realized he had no defense. Even worse, he figured his cheeks were probably bright red.

"Mom just gave me money so we can go to the movies tomorrow," Sato said. "What do you say?"

With a grin, Yoshi nodded. He tried sitting up, but Sato's cat wouldn't budge. Gulping, he looked at his sister for help.

Sato laughed. "You can pick him up, you know."

Yoshi shook his head. "He's always hated me."

"Come on, Rutherford." Sato picked up her orange companion and held him in her arms as she stepped back out into the hallway.

Alone again, Yoshi plopped his head back on his pillow and smiled. He always loved going to the movies. Even if he wouldn't get to have a real summer vacation, he decided to have as much fun as possible before Tuesday. After all, school had ended, and work hadn't begun. For the next three days, he had no responsibilities, and he vowed to savor every moment of it.

The long weekend couldn't have gone any better. After sleeping in Saturday morning, Yoshi and Sato went to the movies, where they got to see the latest John Wayne film and a brand new *Pippy the Pirate* cartoon. When they got home, they had the best family night in months. Father started a game of Scrabble by putting down the word "lamb" horizontally. Out of the first and last letters, Yoshi used up all his tiles by putting down two words at once: *lumpy butt*. The fact that nobody complained about him breaking the rules—or about him being vulgar—was the clearest sign the night was going well.

The good times continued into Sunday. At church, Yoshi and Sato struggled not to laugh. Pastor Branford had an unfortunate speech impediment, which caused him to whistle his s's. When he spoke, "savior" became "shavior," "sin" became "shin," and "salvation" became "shalvashun." In the proper frame of mind, his whistles posed no distraction from his message. But this Sunday, Sato suggested keeping tallies of how many s's they could count, which made composure much more challenging.

"Pleashe, be sheated," Pastor Branford solemnly said, taking the pulpit after the opening hymn. Everyone obeyed, sitting back down in the pews. "Thish morning, I would love to focush sholely on Shcripture. That shaid, I'm shure you all have read the newshpapersh by now, and I shimply musht addressh the newsh."

Yoshi had to bite his tongue—Father would be outraged if he saw Yoshi laughing in church.

"Yesh indeed," Pastor Branford continued. "Today, Hitler invaded the United Shoviet Shocialisht Republicsh."

As a laugh shot up his throat, Yoshi pretended like he had to cough. Saying Russia's complete title, the United Soviet Socialist Republics, was rather unnecessary. "Hitler invaded the Soviet Union" would have been much easier to spit out.

At any rate, the secret tally made church less boring than usual, and after the service, Mom suggested having a picnic at the park. Yoshi expected Father to shoot down the idea. But instead of saying, "Too hot" or "Go without me," he just gave a gentle nod, as if he didn't understand the invitation.

Father drove to the park without complaining. He sat on the blanket beside Mom, and he swallowed bites of PB&J without grimacing or griping about the taste. All day, he seemed distracted. His jaw still had the stern clench, but his eyes seemed more concerned than angry. Yoshi considered asking what the matter was, but he knew he wouldn't get an answer.

As Yoshi tossed a football back and forth with Sato, he tried eavesdropping on the conversation Mom and Father were having. They remained expressionless, but by the softness of their voices, they were clearly in the middle of a serious discussion. Yoshi remembered how, as a kid, his parents tried hiding arguments and bad news from him. This moment felt exactly the same. In a way, he appreciated their protection, but he wondered when they would finally treat him like an adult, and he wanted to know what they seemed so glum about. Ten feet from the blanket, Yoshi could only make out the words "Soviet Union" and "rising tides."

On Monday, Yoshi relaxed, trying to make the most of his last day off. He slept in late, read some of the Hardy Boys book that Mom had bought for him, and listened to the new episode of *The Lone Ranger* on Mom's radio. Before he knew it, he was lying in bed, feeling both nervousness and dread about starting at the grocery store the next day. Partly, he didn't want to mess up and disappoint his father. At the same time, he felt his life would never change after tomorrow. Day in and day out for the rest of his life, he would be stuck at the grocery store, stocking vegetables and wishing for a change.

He imagined it again. The potato sack in hand. The stocking of the bucket. The *thump thump thump* of painful boredom.

A knock came at his door.

"Come in," Yoshi mumbled. When the door squeaked open and Father stepped inside, Yoshi turned wide-eyed and sat up straight. In his entire life, he could only remember a couple of times that Father had ever come into his bedroom. The last time was right after Grandpa died.

Something awful must have happened.

Father sat on the edge of the bed. *What's going on?* Yoshi wanted to ask, but no words left his open mouth.

"Today," Father said, "the Vichy government gave French Indo-China to Japan."

Yoshi stared back blankly. He had no idea what any of that meant, and he *really* had no idea why Father felt the need to tell him about it now. Despite this strange behavior, Yoshi breathed a sigh of relief. He expected some sort of terrible news.

Seeing the confusion on Yoshi's face, Father took a gulp. He scratched his chin. "Vichy," Father explained. "The French government. France had control of many territories in Southeast Asia. Japan demanded to have this land. France agreed today."

Yoshi nodded, pretending like he understood why this mattered, but he knew his eyes remained wide with confusion.

"Japan grows more aggressive," Father said. "This cannot be ignored. America is concerned. All trade between the two nations will likely end within days. This comes after yesterday—the Nazis invaded the Soviet Union. We cannot say how this will end. But China is ruined. England fights alone." Father took off his glasses and rubbed the skin between his eyes.

Yoshi hated that he couldn't think of anything to say. For the first time, Father came to him for an adult conversation. Speechlessness didn't look very mature.

As Father put his glasses back on, he let out a heavy sigh. "I know war," he said, seemingly to himself. "I know what it does. I know how useless it can be." He looked Yoshi in the eye. "I do not wish this on anyone."

Yoshi didn't know how to respond.

Father kept staring. "Preparing for a war that might not come, this does not require many men. Fighting a war, this does. Rules change. Everything can change." Father lowered his head. He squinted, as if he were trying to read some tiny text on the tip of his left kneecap. "Have your summer vacation," he finally said.

The words made Yoshi gasp. He cocked his head to the side. "You mean…?"

"No need to start tomorrow. You can work soon enough." Father rose and headed for the doorway. "Goodnight," he stated, then shut the door behind himself.

Yoshi leaned back, put his hands behind his head, and smiled at the ceiling. He didn't understand what had just happened. All he knew was that his three-day weekend had turned into a summer break, and what could be more important than that?

CHAPTER THREE

O'ER THE RAMPARTS

Yoshi was a Nisei. Sato was a Nisei too. Mom and Father and Grandma were Issei. All his life, Yoshi knew these terms, but he never understood the logic behind them. Nisei were the children of Japanese immigrants. Issei were the immigrants themselves. Nisei were born in America, which meant they were U.S. citizens. Issei came to America from Japan, and the law prevented them from obtaining citizenship. Even someone like Mom, who had no real memory of Japan, couldn't become a naturalized American. The United States was the only home she knew, but because she wasn't born on American soil, she wasn't a citizen like Yoshi or Sato.

One day, many years ago, Yoshi inquired about this. Why did he and Sato get to be citizens just because they were born here?

When he asked his mom, he received a slowly spoken and carefully crafted answer:

"There was a time when even your birthplace wouldn't have made a difference. A hundred years ago, it wouldn't have mattered if you and Sato were born here. Then America decided to make things a little fairer. That's what happens, Yoshi. Progress is slow, and it takes lots of courage and hard work, but over time, it always wins. That's the way this country was designed."

When he asked his father the same question—why did he and Sato get to be citizens just because they were born here?—all he got was this:

"The Fourteenth Amendment."

Over time, Yoshi gave this dynamic less thought. He was a Nisei, so he was a citizen. Gradually, the how and the why stopped mattering to him. But once he started work, some of his old questions came back to him. Sure, he wondered about the law. And sure, he wished someone could explain why Japanese immigrants couldn't become American citizens. But something else stuck with him instead. What he really wanted to know, and what nobody could answer for him, was this: *What would I have done if I came to this country with nothing? What if I was an Issei too?*

These questions inspired Yoshi to cut his summer short. After a month of lounging around, with a few more trips to the movies and the park, he started thinking about how blessed he was. His father never had a vacation in his life. When Father got back from the war, he had to start a life in a country that didn't want him, and he had enough ambition to open his own store. Yoshi just struggled finding the drive to become an employee after getting out of high school, even though his job and his citizenship were handed to him.

Compared to his father, Yoshi felt tiny and talentless. At the beginning of August 1941, when he started working at the shop, he marveled at his father's ability to power through the day without losing any stamina. After five or six hours of stocking shelves, sweeping floors, and ringing up customers at the register, Yoshi started losing energy, but Father seemed as fresh as the moment they unlocked the door. What was his secret? What was his story? How did Father become such a great man?

Hopefully, the two of them would bond through work, so Yoshi could find out at last. Father wasn't *secretive* exactly. He didn't lie, but he responded with simple answers and never elaborated on anything. For instance,

Father immigrated to America by himself as a thirteen-year-old boy. There had to be some exciting stories about the journey, but Father shot down every question Yoshi asked. If normal conversations resembled a game of catch, then talking to Father felt like ping pong.

"Weren't you scared to leave your country?"

"At times."

"Did you worry the trip would be dangerous?"

"A bit."

"Was America what you expected?"

"In ways."

Not much personal history left Father's lips either. Yoshi knew that Father's parents were both dead (his mom died in childbirth, and his dad died in some random Japanese war that Yoshi had never heard of), but Yoshi didn't want basic facts. He wanted stories. Whenever the shop had a slow hour or two, he tried his hardest to make Father open up.

"How did your dad die again?"

"Fighting."

"Fighting who? Fighting where?"

"Russia. At sea."

"Why?"

"Conscription."

"What's that?"

"A draft."

"But why were they fighting?"

"Politics."

If Yoshi asked a tricky question, Father always responded with "politics."

"When did he die?"

"1905."

"Is that why you left?"

"Partly."

"Did you ever wanna go back?"

"No."

"Did you have to sneak in here? Did you go through Mexico?"

"No."

"Canada?"

"I did not sneak in."

"I thought Japanese people weren't allowed to come."

"I came in 1906. The ban came the following year."

"Why did the ban come?"

"America and Japan agreed on it."

"But why?"

"Politics."

As the weeks passed, Yoshi felt determined to start a

real conversation. He wondered if his father's hesitance to speak had something to do with the age difference. Being treated like a little boy was starting to bother him, and he wanted to find some way to talk man-to-man. Even though he didn't care about current events, he decided to use Ricardo as an example. Father always spoke during those debates at the restaurant.

"Boy, those Nazis," Yoshi said one evening, as he swept the floor. "They seem real bad, huh?"

Father was counting the cash from the register. When he nodded, he didn't bother looking up.

"Do you still think we should stay out of it?" Yoshi asked.

At this, Father froze. He pursed his lips. His nostrils flared. A full minute passed with no reply, and Yoshi went back to sweeping.

"Japan liked war," Father finally said.

Yoshi's head shot up. At last, he could sense he was on the verge of having a meaningful talk.

"Looks to me like they still do," Yoshi responded, trying his hardest to seem informed. He lowered his voice an octave, as if he sounded smarter by becoming a baritone.

"When I left, it was the seeds of this. Smaller fights, the seeds of empire. That would have been my life." Father's voice sounded soft, and he seemed to be talking to himself. He blinked a few times, like shaking off a trance, then went back to stacking bills.

Yoshi wanted to enjoy his first adult conversation with Father, but the pressure got the better of him. He felt desperate to understand what Father was talking about—and even more desperate to respond in an intelligent way. After a nervous gulp, he tried piecing together what his father meant.

"You'd be a seed...of Japan...if you stayed there?"

"Drafted in one of their wars," Father said. "I wanted no part of it."

Yoshi tried imagining Father's circumstances: being an only child, with no mother, whose own father died after being drafted to fight. All at once, Father's revulsion of war started making sense. If he felt like his only future in Japan would be as a soldier, then he must have felt the need for a fresh start. Everyone knew of America as the land of opportunity. But as Yoshi considered what happened once Father immigrated, he frowned. The thought of his father sailing all the way to America, only to be forced to fight in the First World War, made him pretty sad.

"Golly," Yoshi said. "Then you came *here* and got

drafted."

Father shook his head. "They only drafted citizens."

"You *volunteered*? But I thought…"

"America offered me something to fight."

Bitterness filled Father's voice. An awkward silence fell over the room. Suddenly, Yoshi remembered the fragments of a story he was told in the past. A few years ago, Father became one of the very few Issei to gain American citizenship. The occasion should have been filled with joy. Instead, Father acted like a man released from prison, whose innocence was proven twenty years too late. During World War I, the government made a promise: if immigrants signed up to fight for the U.S., they could petition to become citizens after the war. This turned out not to be true for everyone. Once Father returned from battle and applied for naturalization, his request was denied. He was told that, regardless of his service, Asians weren't allowed to become citizens.

In 1935, seventeen years after the end of the war, Congress passed a law to correct this injustice. Issei veterans could become citizens at last. After so much time, Father debated whether or not he should apply. On principle, he didn't like the idea of becoming a citizen when Mom couldn't become one too, since the law only applied to

veterans. But he ended up taking the offer—if, for no other reason, so he could vote.

Mom told Yoshi this story, a few years back, to explain the circumstances of Father's naturalization. Father
never spoke of it himself, and until now, Yoshi had kind
of forgotten about the whole ordeal. He gave a sad nod
and looked down at the floor. He almost apologized, as if
mentioning this unfortunate chapter from the past somehow made him complicit in the wrongdoing. In his
deepest, most mature-sounding voice, Yoshi tried giving
his analysis:

"Good thing it worked out in the end, huh?"

Father said nothing.

September 8th became September 9th. The 9th, in
turn, became the 10th. After working at the grocery store
for over a month, Yoshi started counting down the days.
He realized he had nothing to count down to, aside from
his day-and-a-half-long weekends. Even still, checking
off the dates somehow made his days go by faster—an old
trick from school he decided to hold onto. It's not that he
hated his job. Spending time with Father could be nice.
Overall, the customers had been pleasant enough. And
despite his old fears about disappointing Father, Yoshi

hadn't made any major mistakes. Everything had gone fine. Just fine.

He wanted more than "fine" for his future.

After such a hard and rocky life, Father's satisfaction with this place made sense. Stability must have seemed wonderful compared to war and serious labor. Yoshi never learned what jobs Father had taken upon first arriving in America, but they couldn't have been very pleasant. With boredom being Yoshi's biggest problem, he knew he shouldn't complain. But Father got to experience adventure in his life, even though the times were tough. If Yoshi had to settle for an uninteresting job, couldn't he at least make some wild memories first?

And so, the 10th became the 11th. It was another Thursday morning. Father went to the bank to get some change, so Yoshi stood alone in the store. He held a potato sack. He dropped the spuds into the basket, one by one. *Thump…thump…thump…* Either he had become more mature or more cynical over the past few months, but his old daydreams started seeming ridiculous. Reality could never be so fun.

That said, if a bad guy *were* to sneak into the shop, Yoshi knew what he would do. He'd somersault down the aisle and grab a Campbell's soup can off the back shelf.

He'd hurl the can right at the bandit's black bandana, and if the crook had the gall to come back for seconds, Yoshi would scare him off by twirling around the potato sack like a lasso and—

The bell rang. The door swung open. Yoshi froze, and he gasped at the person he saw.

It wasn't an outlaw.

It wasn't Father.

It was Gus Needaburger.

Yes, Needaburger. That was his real last name. For over a year, Yoshi thought this was a joke, until the two of them had a class together and the teacher took attendance. All through high school, Gus Needaburger had many titles: quarterback, prom king, captain of the wrestling team. Somehow, even with a last name that seemed ripe for mockery, Gus had managed to climb the social ladder.

Yoshi always hated him. He hated Gus's slicked back hair and beady green eyes. He hated Gus's button nose and tiny little lips. He hated the way Gus carried himself, with his chin turned up, his spine perfectly straight, and his constant arm flex under his ever-sported letterman jacket. Yoshi hated that letterman jacket. He hated Gus's nasally voice and twinkly white smile. And even though

Yoshi knew nothing about the Needaburger family, he hated Gus's parents for bringing someone so terrible into this world.

More than anything, Yoshi hated how much everybody loved the guy, despite the clear, extraordinary awfulness Gus Needaburger embodied. If Gus liked a movie, everybody liked that movie. If Gus bought new tennis shoes, the halls would be filled the following week with guys wearing the same pair. One time, Gus won a talent show by talk-singing his way through "Wrap Your Troubles in My Dreams." Before walking off stage, Gus exclaimed with a smile and a wink, "Look out, Bing Crosby. There's a new cat in town!" Somehow, most of the audience found this stunt charming and hilarious. The judges did too.

"Weh-heh-hell." Gus laughed through his big stupid smile. He punched Yoshi on the arm. "If it ain't *this* kid. It's—don't tell me—Yokel?"

As Yoshi clenched his teeth, he tried his hardest not to angrily purse his lips. He gulped, trying to swallow his rage. His fury only grew.

"Yoshi," he corrected.

"*Yoshi*. Okay. All right." Gus nodded with a squint, like he needed to think about this. He practiced the name over and over again, and he started pronouncing it "Yaw-shi." Gus shrugged. "I'll just call ya Little Yosh. I've never been good with foreign stuff."

In the past, Yoshi could quietly disdain Gus Needa-burger at a distance, like from the opposite side of a classroom. A one-on-one encounter like this had never happened before. He didn't know what to do. With everybody else in the world, Yoshi felt infinitely kind. Like spitting on a candle, Gus Needaburger extinguished that spark of goodness.

Yoshi squeezed past him and headed for the potato basket. He needed a task to keep himself occupied. If he looked busy, then maybe Gus wouldn't start a conversation.

"So, tell me, Little Yosh," Gus began. "Whatcha doing at a lousy job like this? Still bringing in some measly summer bucks till ya find something better to do?"

Yoshi just nodded. After dropping the final two spuds into the bucket, he held the empty sack and desperately looked around for something else to do. Feeling trapped, he started putting the potatoes back into the sack.

"Woah there, Little Yosh. Not to tell you how to do your job, but you should probably be leaving the goods *out*."

Yoshi froze. He took a deep breath.

"Think about it," Gus continued. "If you don't leave out the goodies, nobody will buy your stuff. You dig my wiggle?"

At hearing this question, Yoshi lowered the sack, stared at Gus, and raised an eyebrow.

"It's this new expression I made up," Gus explained. "It'll catch on soon. You'll see."

Yoshi wanted to run into the office behind the counter. He knew he couldn't leave the store unsupervised, but the cramped, closet-sized room started seeming like paradise. Instead, he headed for the back wall, where he rearranged the Campbell's soup cans.

Gus followed Yoshi down the aisle.

"So here's the deal-iosh, Little Yosh. Me and my girl-friend are celebrating our one-month anniversary today. I'm lookin' for some sweets to get her. Got anything here to help your buddy out?"

"We don't sell sweets," Yoshi stated, as he lined up all the soup cans.

"You joshing me?" Gus said. "Boy, you gotta be josh-ing me. Well, that's sure too bad. Usually my mom does all the shopping. She never liked this joint, but I was in here once or twice before, and I could've sworn you had some sweets. I guess I can go to the candy shop across town if I *have* to."

"You should probably go *now*," Yoshi said. "They might close or run out of everything. You don't want to disappoint your girlfriend."

Those beady green eyes widened. That mouth opened all the way like he was giving birth through his lips. Then, from out his esophagus, there emerged a high-pitched, wavering, breathy cackle.

"*Disappoint* her?" Gus exclaimed. He slugged Yoshi on the shoulder. "Good gosh, Little Yosh. She's *crazy* about me. She has been for years. I could stand her up for lunch, and she'd *still* be craving the Needaburger. And *that's* before I spring the news on her today. You ready for this?" Gus reached into his back pocket and pulled out a paper, thick from being folded into sixteenths. He unfolded the squares and showed off a poster for the air force. "Ta-da! This is *my* future, Little Yosh."

O'er the Ramparts We Watch, the poster said, above a towering soldier who had angel wings made of clouds.

"You carry that with you?" Yoshi asked.

"I wanna show her an 'aesthetic display,' if you dig my wiggle. I'm sure she'll be pretty crushed to see me go, but gals have a thing for men in uniform. Especially her.

You think she's hooked on me now? Just wait and see what it's like when I get back from serving."

Gus gazed at the poster in his hands, then pointed at the soldier in the sky. "This will be me, Little Yosh. Crazy missions. Zooming through the air. *Va-room*. Real hero business. But hey, not every guy is cut out for that kinda stuff. That's why girls are *so crazy* about it. Man, I can almost picture her drooling when I tell her." Gus panted like a dog. Then he chuckled and gave a dismissive wave. "Naw, she's a sweet gal. Sarah Hassenger, you know her?"

Yoshi's heart stopped.

"What am I saying?" Gus continued. "Everybody knows her. We got a good thing going, you could say. After sampling lots of different stuff, I finally started thinking about the future. And you know what I decided? I decided it's better to be with a gal who's a *little* bit less of a looker, as long as she's super into you. You know she'll stay committed. Makes for good marriages or whatever."

"Why are you here?" Yoshi snapped. He had to get away. He rushed to the other side of the store and ended up back at the potatoes.

Gus followed him. "I told ya, Little Yosh, I was

lookin' for some sweets."

"And I told you we don't have any."

"I thought I should double check. You dig my wiggle?"

"Ew. Please stop saying that." Yoshi raced behind the counter and gripped the sides of the cash register. "Just buy something or leave."

"Slow down, Little Yosh. I'm lookin', I'm lookin'." Gus picked up a few oranges. "Got any specials on these? Buy one, get one free or something?"

The bell rang. Father stood in the doorway, a bag of change in hand. Yoshi breathed a sigh of relief. He didn't know how, but he knew his father would fix this situation.

Father and Gus stared at each other. Nostrils flaring, Father gazed around the store, scrutinizing every detail like a detective at a crime scene.

"I will not let you buy oranges," Father finally stated.

Gus threw his arms up in the air. "What?!"

"You dropped them last time. You said they were damaged."

"Are you kidding me? That was like three months ago."

Yoshi vaguely remembered his father mentioning this incident. If he had known, at the time, that Gus Needaburger was the jerk in question, the story would have left a greater impression. Nonetheless, Father's memory was pretty impressive. How could he recognize someone on the spot after one brief encounter in the past?

"My parents warned me about this place," Gus said, shaking his head as he made his way to the door. "I should have listened."

The bell rang. The door shut. Gus was finally gone.

Father held up a finger at Yoshi.

"Never forget when somebody wrongs you," he said.

Yoshi nodded.

Father didn't look away.

"Never forget," he insisted. "Ever."

For the rest of the day, Yoshi couldn't stop imagining Gus and Sarah as a couple. When he swept the store, he pictured them holding hands. When he rode his bike home, he envisioned them kissing. And after supper, as his family sat in the living room, staring anxiously at Mom's radio, his mind drifted to Gus and Sarah's inevitable wedding. Tonight, the president was going to give another one of his so-called "Fireside Chats," where he gave a big long speech to the public. At least, the speeches always seemed really long to Yoshi. Thankfully, they didn't happen too often, but when they did, his family always made him listen. Mom said those Fireside Chats were for stuff that was really important. But compared to the idea of Sarah becoming a Needaburger, did anything really matter?

Nevertheless, as he lay on his belly on the living room floor, he found himself listening to President Roosevelt's smooth, confident voice as it crackled through the radio:

"My fellow Americans, the Navy Department of the United States has reported to me that on the morning of September 4th, the United States destroyer *Greer*, proceeding in full daylight towards Iceland, had reached a point southeast of Greenland. She was carrying American mail to Iceland. She was flying the American flag. Her identity as an American ship was unmistakable. She was then and there attacked by a submarine. Germany admits that it was a German submarine. The submarine deliberately fired a torpedo at the *Greer*, followed later by another torpedo attack. In spite of what Hitler's propaganda bureau has invented..."

Yoshi became anxious. He couldn't figure out why. A strange sensation came over him as soon as President Roosevelt started speaking. His nerves told him that a big, scary realization had just popped into his mind, but he couldn't quite figure out what it was yet. He wondered if anyone else felt as anxious as he did, and he sat up to look. Grandma was asleep in her armchair. Sato was playing with Rutherford in the corner. Across the table from him, Father and Mom leaned against opposite sides of the love seat. They looked, in a way, like mirror images of each other. Both leaned an elbow against their armrests, and they covered their mouths, brows scrunched, deep in thought.

"We have sought no shooting war with Hitler," the president said. "We do not seek it now. But neither do we want peace so much that we are willing to pay for it by permitting him to attack our naval and merchant ships while they are on legitimate business. I assume that the German leaders…"

Did war make Yoshi afraid? Should he be worried about the possibility of America joining the fight? He probably wouldn't be drafted. After all, he wouldn't turn 21 for several more years. But nothing guaranteed the war would be over by then. Shouldn't *that* be the cause of his anxiety?

"The aggression is not ours," the president continued. "Ours is solely defense. But let this warning be clear. There will be no shooting unless Germany continues to seek it."

Unless Germany continues to seek it…

Unless Germany continues to seek it…

Yoshi slipped back into a daydream. Again, he held a burlap sack. Again, the boring thumps of boring potatoes gave him a boredom headache. He imagined himself alone in the grocery store, his weeks flying by, his life *thump thumping* away…until he heard a scream outside the shop. He dropped the sack, somersaulted down the aisle, and looked out the window on the door. It was Sarah Hassenger, being taken away by five…outlaws? No, Nazis! They were leading her into the back of a red, Swastika-covered van. Yoshi shook his head and scoffed. Those no-good Germans were no match against Yoshi Yamaguchi.

"Not today, Nazis," Yoshi said, reaching for the door handle.

It was locked.

This didn't make any sense. How could it be locked from the outside?

Just then, a fighter jet came soaring out of the clouds. The Nazis gasped and pointed at the sky. They tried looking for cover, but one by one, they got shot down.

The jet landed on the street beside the van. The pilot

hopped out and took off his helmet. It was Gus Needaburger.

Gus opened the van and Sarah jumped into his arms.

"My hero!" she exclaimed. "Thank you for saving me.
I'm sure glad we're in love and we're gonna get married."

Gus winked with one of his beady green eyes. "You
sure are lucky to have me. You dig my wiggle?"

She smiled. "That's the swellest expression anyone's
ever come up with. It's sure better than anything Yoshi
Yamaguchi ever said."

"Little Yosh, you mean? That's true. We should laugh
about how lame he is."

"Good idea."

They laughed and laughed and laughed and laughed.

"…with divine help and guidance," President Roosevelt concluded, "stand their ground against this latest
assault upon their democracy, their sovereignty, and their
freedom."

"The Star-Spangled Banner" started playing.

And Yoshi knew. In thinking about Gus and Sarah, in
thinking about the shop…through fears of endless tedi-
ousness and fantasies of heroism…his realization
emerged from the shadows. It promised to redeem his bad
grades, to undo Sarah's laugh at the baseball game. It

gave him a way to outshine his little sister, to make his future exciting. It didn't make him fear the war. It only made him fear his father's rage. All this time, he kept the thought suppressed, knowing that Father would keep the dream from happening. But Yoshi couldn't hide from it any longer: he wanted to join the military.

CHAPTER FOUR

If I WEREN'T A MOPER

Never forget when somebody wrongs you, Father's warning echoed in his mind. *Never forget. Ever.* Yoshi tried
imagining what would happen when he told his father that
he wanted to join the military. "The *military*?" Father
would say. "You know I hate war. You know they
wronged me. How the heck can you go register to fight
when you know about all that stuff? Oh my gosh, I am *so
ashamed* of you!" (Admittedly, Father's phrasing would
be different, but the sentiment seemed about right.)

Yoshi tried telling himself that he didn't have to worry
yet. After all, he couldn't join the military until he turned
eighteen. He still had one more week to go until his birthday on October 10th, and until then, he tried his hardest
not to think about it. Unfortunately, Mom kept asking him

what he wanted to do to celebrate, and even though he appreciated her concern, he didn't like the endless reminders.

"Maybe you can go to the movies with some friends," she suggested.

"I don't really have any friends."

Mom frowned. "What about Freddy? You always got along with him, didn't you?"

Yoshi shrugged.

Every time the topic came up, he was equally dismissive. Mom must have assumed that he was just embarrassed about his lack of friends, because Sato came into his bedroom one night with a list of people who would love to come to a birthday party.

"Julie Miller," she kept rattling off names. "I did student council with her last year. Oh, and Susie Wong! You'd *love* her. She's really into art and animations—she loves Pippy the Pirate, just like you. I think you two would really hit it off."

Yoshi sat on the edge of his bed, and he nervously held up his arms as Rutherford hopped onto his lap. "I don't like getting your friends' pity."

"It's not pity. We've all been wanting to have a party for a while now. We just haven't had a reason. You'd be doing us a favor. I swear it. Besides, you gotta do *something*. Turning 18 is a huge deal."

Yes, it *was* a huge deal. In a way, running into Gus Needaburger turned out to be a blessing. If not for the humiliation of comparing himself to a future air force pilot, Yoshi would never have realized how perfect the military would be for him. He'd show off his patriotism, fight bad guys, and make exciting memories. Not to mention, he'd finally impress Sarah Hassenger. All his problems would be solved.

Once he knew the grocery store wouldn't consume his entire life, he even put in extra effort at his job. He kept the floor immaculate and the shelves perfectly stocked. He smiled at customers, and when his nerves didn't get the better of him, he even managed to talk to them. He wanted to make the most of his job before he left the shop behind.

And, above all, he wanted to please his father. Before too long, the time would come to have that daunting talk about the future, and he wanted Father to be happy when it happened.

So far, the effort seemed to be working. Despite his ever-present scowl, Father had all the signs of being in a good mood. Not only did he give an occasional, satisfied nod; he did his best to carry on a conversation, in the closest thing to talkative he ever got.

"What book do you read?" he asked Yoshi one afternoon.

Yoshi was cleaning the window on the door, and the abruptness took him by surprise. He looked over his shoulder, mouth hanging open.

"I see you read," Father explained, as he unlocked the register and double-checked the cash. "What book is it?"

"It's called *The Disappearing Floor*."

"And what is that?"

"It's Hardy Boys."

"What is the disappearing floor?"

"Oh," Yoshi chuckled. "I don't know yet. I haven't gotten that far." After spending months with the book, he felt a little embarrassed to admit how little progress he'd made with it. "I'll let you know when I find out," he said, wiping the window. He dropped his rag into the bucket and bent down to pick up the towel.

He screamed when he stood up.

On the other side of the glass, a young man had his face pressed against the window. To Yoshi's surprise, the guy who stared back at him was Japanese. At Jackson High, Yoshi was the single Japanese American in his class, and one of only eight in the entire school. In the Yamaguchis' area, most Japanese immigrants lived across the channel on Terminal Island. Father had settled in San Pedro, a town in southwest LA County. He opened his store in a white neighborhood, where he could make more money. Thanks to his time in the military, he had the resources to do this.

When Yoshi opened the door, the young man grinned a mouthful of crooked teeth. He wore a white dress shirt that looked one size too big, which was tucked into a pair of black slacks that looked one size too small. Under a floppy gray cap, little puffs of brown hair jutted in all directions. But somehow, he managed to sport a perfectly knotted black necktie. Unless some fashion miracle had occurred, somebody else must have tied it for him.

"Hi there!" The young man waved at Yoshi. "Are you Mr. Yamaguchi? Oh my gosh, I thought you'd be older. How'd you start a business so young? Golly, there's a lot I could learn from you. Did you buy this place when you were a kid? You must have! How'd you do it?"

Yoshi stared back, lips fumbling for words. "I…Sorry, who are you?"

"Whoops, I forgot that part. Guess I should've started with the introduction. My name is Joey Minami, and I'm with the Japanese American Citizens League. Do you have a minute to learn about our group?"

Father came over and stood beside Yoshi.

Joey looked up at Father. "Wow, you must be a brother. A way, way, way older brother."

"Yoshi is my son," Father said. "I am Mr. Yamaguchi."

"*Oh.*" Joey let out a laugh. "That makes more sense." He peeked between Father and Yoshi. "Nice place you two got. Do you live here?"

Father closed his eyes and let out a long, irritated sigh. He shook his head.

"I know *I'd* live in a grocery store if I owned one," Joey said. "Think about it. You'd never have to leave your home. Wouldn't that be neat?"

"What can I help you with?" Father's question sounded like a statement.

"My name is Joey Minami, and I'm with the Japanese American Citizens League."

"I know," Father said. "What do you want?"

Joey adjusted his stance, as if he needed some movement to jumpstart his brain.

"Well, see, it's like this." Joey kept fidgeting. Remembering what he was supposed to say seemed to be a struggle. "The JACL started in 1929, and it's done some real great stuff. It's the only group for Japanese Americans like it. It's really great. It's all about being Americans, and how we're all great Americans. I think it's really great. We believe that America's a real great country, and…" He looked up at Father and gave a proud smile. This seemed to be all he had to say.

"Do you want money?" Father asked.

"Yeah!"

Father slammed the door. The bell rang.

"Hey, wait!" Joey shouted through the window. "We made some real good laws happen! I mean it!"

The bell rang again. Father stood in the doorway, looking down at Joey.

"Name one," he said.

"Huh?"

"Name one law this group made pass."

Joey turned wide-eyed. In a panic, he patted his pants and dug through his pockets. Finally, he pulled out a handful of notecards and frantically flipped through them. "Shoot, it's called the Nah-Loo…or Noo-Lee…" When he found the right card, he held it in the air like a trophy. "Nye-Lea! Nye-Lea. It's called the Nye-Lea Act. It's what gave World War I veterans citizenship. Passed in…"

He looked at the back of the card. "Passed *on* June 25th, 1935."

To a stranger, the change in Father's demeanor would have been unnoticeable. But to Yoshi, who pretended to organize the vegetables as he watched the scene unfold, the long pause and slight raising of the chin revealed that Father was shocked.

"This group worked on Nye-Lea?" he asked.

"You sure bet." Joey grinned. "Lots and lots of behind-the-scenes work. I mean, I wasn't *there* for it because I was too young to be involved, but Mr. Hamasaki sure was. He's in charge of the local chapter. He's really great. He was new then, and he worked really hard with some of the other leaders. We're a *national organization*, you know." He emphasized "national organization" like he just remembered he was supposed to use the term. "We have over..." He consulted another card. "6,000 members nationwide."

Father raised an eyebrow. "Why do I not know of this?"

"Of the JACL, you mean? Well gosh, it's hard to get credit sometimes. Our work isn't front-page stuff for the big papers. But we're doing outreach to whoever we can. That's why I'm here. Mr. Hamasaki saw the name 'Yamaguchi Grocery' in the yellow pages, and he thought I should give it a shot."

Father scratched his chin. "Nye-Lea is good. I used this."

Joey gasped. "It made you a citizen?" He seemed unusually excited about this fact. "Oh my gosh, that's terrific! I bet I can interest you in getting a membership. It's just a buck a year—after a fifty-cent initiation fee. It's real swell, believe me."

"I dislike begging."

"Not begging. No, sir."

"I will think about this." Father started to walk away.

Deep down, Yoshi wanted to be friends with Joey. The two of them were about the same age, and the guy seemed really nice. Yoshi wondered…would it be weird to invite a stranger to his birthday party?

"That's great!" Joey said. "When should I come back?"

"When I make up my mind."

"Okay! When will that be?"

Father shut the door.

When October 10th came, Yoshi was more conflicted than ever. From one moment to the next, his mood altered completely. He woke up to Mom and Sato singing "Happy Birthday" in his doorway, which brought a smile to his face. But then, right as "thank you" left his lips, he froze in fear. Two different voices shouted in his head:

It's finally your birthday!

Oh jeez, it's your birthday…

You can finally join the military!

Now you have to tell Father…

Yes, he needed to tell Father. But Yoshi was given the day off, and by the time he got out of bed, Father had already left for work. Yoshi would have to wait until the evening to say anything. At breakfast, as his family sat around the kitchen table, he thought he should try testing out the news on Mom, Grandma, and Sato. *I want you all to know that I'm going to join the military. I want you all to know…I want you all to know…*He kept telling himself to blurt it out, but his stubborn tongue refused to form the words. As he scarfed down his waffles, he waited for the topic to come up naturally.

"Oh, Yoshi-kun." Grandma smiled. "How is this that you can be so old now?"

"Seriously," Sato mumbled through a full mouth. "Old man over here." She tore off a chunk of waffle and lowered it for Rutherford, who examined it skeptically.

"You'll need a wheelchair before long."

"No, no." Grandma laughed. "Not yet old enough for this."

Old enough to join the military, Yoshi thought. The sentence stayed in his head.

That afternoon, when Yoshi played catch at the park with Sato and a couple of her friends, he hoped for a chance to open up about his rather unpleasant state of mind. Perhaps he could get some advice on the matter, or if nothing else, at least he could practice saying the words out loud: *I'm going to join the military*. Unfortunately, finding a way to be part of the conversation turned out to be a challenge. Julie Miller and Susie Wong were talking about how the school play was fun, or how science class was hard, or how Susie's parents were Chinese, or something like that. Yoshi was too distracted to listen.

"What kinda stuff do you like?" Susie asked, as she tossed the ball to Yoshi. It took him a moment to realize she was talking to him, and once he looked at her, he cocked his head to the side.

A knot of nerves tightened in his stomach, and he squeezed the ball. *Right now, I really like the idea of joining the military...*

He must have stayed silent for a long time because

Sato eventually answered for him:

"He really likes movies and stuff."

"Anything coming up that you're excited about?" Susie asked.

Yeah! Enlisting! To fight off this voice, Yoshi tried picturing the posters at the movie theater. When one came to mind, he blurted out the title before he could second-guess himself. "I can't wait for *Dumbo*."

Julie raised an eyebrow. "I thought that was a kids' cartoon."

"Oh yeah, I forgot." Yoshi looked down at the grass and gave an embarrassed chuckle. "I guess it looks a little lame."

"You don't like animation?" Susie snapped at Julie. "Don't you realize that *Snow White* is the best film ever made?"

Yoshi tossed the ball to Sato. Now that someone was coming to his defense, he no longer felt the need to squeeze it. He couldn't help but smile. This must have been what it felt like to make a new friend. With any luck, he and Susie Wong could start becoming real buddies. To start, he could tell her about his dream.

Hey Susie, guess what? I'm going to join the military.

But he couldn't say the words out loud. Maybe he

didn't need to practice saying it. He would only say it one time, and he would do it when it mattered.

Dinner would be a good opportunity.

At Ricky's Bistro, the Yamaguchis sat at their usual table and ate their usual dishes. Ricardo came storming out of the back. "Mr. *Yamaguchi*. What are the Nazis *doing*? I tell you, we need to *fight*."

Yes, Yoshi thought. *We need to fight. If we go to war, I want to be there.*

Father looked across the table at Yoshi. He listened with a concentrated frown, his clenched teeth forming bulges in the leathery skin of his jawline. Behind the glare of his thin bronze glasses, his lids drooped. His eyes possessed a heaviness that Yoshi had never seen in him before.

"It can't keep *going*," Ricardo shouted. "I know you read the *papers*. You must hear the *stories*. Nazis round up Jews and send them *away*? What happens to those *people*?"

Father closed his eyes. The sigh through his nostrils sounded like a chalkboard being swept clean.

"Just this *week*," Ricardo added. "Did you see what the *LA Times* had to *say*? Six Jews will be executed for leaving their *ghetto*. The first time it's *happened*. It will only get *worse*."

Father kept his eyes closed. He gave a tiny nod.

"England can fight," he said.

"They can't fight *alone*."

"I want us not to go to war." When Father's eyes opened, he stared right at Yoshi. "The cost is too great."

Yoshi knew his father was talking about him. He felt his ambitions start to sink away. *Stop moping, Yoshi, and say something.* He prodded himself all through dinner, on the drive home, and even as he sat in the living room, waiting to open his presents.

He knelt behind the coffee table, looking down at the three wrapped boxes in front of him. His parents and Sato were crammed onto the love seat, staring across the table at him, eager to watch him open the packages. From her armchair, Grandma smiled back. Yoshi started feeling guilty. Through all the stuff his family was doing to give him a special day, he couldn't even repay them with his best attitude. Despite the smile he tried to maintain, his mind was clearly focused elsewhere. Acting distant and melancholy seemed disrespectful to his family's thoughtfulness.

Sato got him a *Pippy the Pirate* comic book, which did make him smile for a moment. Then Mom leaned forward and nudged the long, rectangular box toward him.

"This one is from me and your father," she said.

Right as Yoshi tore off the first corner of wrapping paper, he could spot the red label over the yellow packaging.

"Oh my gosh!" A burst of excitement managed to calm his anxiety, and he held up the box triumphantly. "A Red Ryder bb gun! No way!"

"You like it?" Mom sounded relieved at Yoshi's joy.

"It's perfect," he exclaimed.

"No shooting here," Father said. "We will practice somewhere. If you like this, I will teach you hunting."

Yoshi tore open the box and ripped away the tissue paper. Jumping to his feet, he squinted through the front sight, put his finger on the trigger, and aimed the empty gun at the door. Fantasies came rushing back to him. He could almost hear the outlaws rattling the handle. He could almost feel Sarah Hassenger's arms wrapped around him. The wooden hand guard felt chilly in his hand, the metal trigger smooth against his fingertip. He couldn't believe it. He was holding a rifle—just like Red Ryder. Just like the Lone Ranger. Just like John Wayne. Just like…an American soldier.

With a gulp, he kneeled back down and placed the gun on the coffee table.

"Boy, it's real swell," he said. "Thank you."

Examining him, Mom forced a smile. She seemed alarmed by his sudden collapse of enthusiasm. Then she nodded toward the little square box. "This last one's from Grandma."

After this, he vowed to himself. *After this, you have to do it. No more excuses. No more waiting. Unwrap the box, thank them, and say it.* The package fit in the palm of his hand. The wrapping paper, cherry red and patterned with snowflakes, was left over from last Christmas. He gently tugged the corners and delicately peeled, knowing that the only thing keeping him from the conversation was the process of unwrapping. One of Mom's trinket boxes came into sight, and when he opened it, he wondered why his family saved this gift for last.

It was a tiny tin Samurai figurine. Its size and base made it look like a missing chess piece. To be honest, the little guy was pretty ugly. His armor looked like a striped dress, with oversized shoulder pads and oven mitts. His hat resembled a turkey. And his face, if being charitable, might have looked more appropriate on an angry turtle. Yoshi liked the thing well enough, he supposed, but it was no Red Ryder bb gun.

"Oh, neat. A real small statue." His appreciative tone

didn't sound convincing. "Thank you."

"It was your grandpa's," Mom said.

Yoshi's eyes widened. He regretted every mean judgment he had made about the figurine.

"His father gave it to him as a good luck charm when he turned eighteen," Mom explained. "He stored it away for years. He was saving it to pass it along to you when you turned eighteen."

Grandma nodded in her chair, fighting back tears. "Oh, Yoshi-kun." Her voice wavered. "How much he would want to see you on this day."

Grandpa's armchair had never seemed so empty.

Yoshi felt a lump in his throat. He stared at the figurine. "Oh jeez, I don't know what to say. Thank you. I really mean it."

A solemn atmosphere filled the room, and disturbing the peaceful moment seemed disrespectful. And so, his anxiety didn't go away. But as he smiled at the comic book, and as he gazed at his Red Ryder bb gun, and as he clutched his grandpa's good luck figurine, he decided he could wait another day to talk about the future.

A day became a week. One week became two. Mental strife and constant mood swings were the new normal for him. Mom asked him several times why he seemed so glum. He never told the truth. He never told her anything. Every time she asked how he was doing, he responded with a shrug. Not too long ago, he suffered from a lack of purpose. Funny how the real trouble came once he had found it.

Two weeks became three. Three became four. Before he knew it, he and his family were sitting around the table for Thanksgiving dinner. With his fork, Yoshi glided the slab of turkey around his plate, knocking it against the green beans and mashed potatoes. He slumped in his seat, and he couldn't help but frown. At some point, he needed to accept that his dream would never happen unless he was willing to upset his father. In theory, mustering up the courage didn't seem so difficult, but imagining Father's disappointed scowl made him feel lousy. Really lousy. The lousiest kind of lousy a person could feel.

In the background, Mom's radio played classical music. Yoshi didn't know the name of the song—or if that old stuff was even called a "song" at all. Whatever it was, one piece flowed into the next. It all sounded the same to him: lots of piano, with harps and violins or something. Mom always played the classic music station on Sundays after church and on holidays like this, because she found those compositions relaxing and classy. To Yoshi, it all sounded serious and depressing, which didn't help his state of mind.

"...but everyone's gonna pick that," Sato said, "and I want to do something different and contemporary, so I was thinking of choosing the last State of the Union."

"That's a nice idea." Mom took a sip of water. "I remember helping Yoshi with that project several years ago."

Yoshi glanced around the table. Everyone was looking at him.

"For Miss Ellison's civics class," Sato explained. "We have to analyze a speech. You did that too?"

Yoshi cocked his head to the side.

"You worked on the Gettysburg Address," Mom prodded. "Remember?"

Sato rolled her eyes. "See? That's what *everyone* picks." Mom glared across the table at her, and Sato quickly added, "But it's still a good choice."

Scrunching his brow, Yoshi gave half a nod.

"I think the music's putting you to sleep." Sato nudged him with her elbow. "Or maybe it's the turkey."

At the end of the table, Father shook his head. A faint scowl returned to his upper lip.

"He does not eat," he said.

After being called out, Yoshi forced himself to sit up straight. He didn't mean to ruin Thanksgiving by looking so glum, but he was too caught up in his own thoughts to put much effort into seeming okay. Unfortunately, Father had a point: Yoshi's plate remained full, while the others had nothing but scraps left. Even Grandma, the slowest eater in the world, had almost finished her mashed potatoes. To keep himself from falling further behind, Yoshi scooped some green beans into his mouth with his fork.

"Don't have an appetite tonight?" Mom asked him. Despite her smile, she sounded concerned. "Maybe you'd like to save it for later?"

"He will eat now," Father grumbled. "I grow tired of this. For weeks, he mopes."

Without thinking, Yoshi swallowed the beans he forgot he was chewing. A knot formed in his stomach.

"May I be excused?" he asked.

"Tell us what upsets you," Father snapped.

Out of instinct, Yoshi just shrugged.

"Then stop this," Father demanded, dropping the chopsticks that he used for every meal. "You have food. You have shelter. You have work. You have family. I have no patience for you today."

"I want to join the military."

Yoshi turned wide-eyed and covered his mouth. The words had spewed from his own lips without his control, like sneezing in the middle of church. Something about his father's condemnation made him break.

If his admission didn't go as expected, neither did the reaction. He waited for someone to faint, or to throw a plate, or to break down crying. None of those things happened. Everyone sat quietly. Sad piano music filled the air. Then, without a change in his expression, Father answered: "No."

Picking his chopsticks back up, Father returned to the final bites of turkey on his plate. He seemed so casual, he could have been eating by himself.

Yoshi lowered his hands, revealing his open mouth. All this time, he braced himself for a giant, emotionally draining argument. He never prepared for a calm and simple rejection.

"I said I want to join the military," Yoshi repeated, as if the words didn't come out right the first time.

Father swallowed his final bite. He patted his mouth with his napkin.

"No," he repeated.

"But—" Yoshi stammered. "But I want to." When he

started the sentence, he hoped a more convincing argument would come out.

Father rose. He left the table and headed upstairs.

Yoshi trembled—in fear, in defeat, and in regret. He wished he could go back in time one minute, before he spoke, when he still believed his dream might be possible.

Footsteps clomped back down the stairs. Father dropped a piece of paper in front of Yoshi and took a seat.

"They said my service would give me citizenship," he said. "After the war, I applied. They sent me this."

Yoshi read the paper, dated June 1919:

Dear Mr. Yamaguchi,

As the matter stands at present, it will be necessary for the government to object to your naturalization on the ground that you are inadmissible to citizenship because of the fact that you are neither a white person nor of African descent.

Sincerely,

Scott Wilson

Chief Examiner of U.S. Naturalization

Reading the letter made Yoshi angry, but he didn't understand why it mattered at this point. Sure, the government broke a promise at first. But even if it took almost two decades to correct, Father became a citizen in the end.

"Serve your country in other ways," Father stated. "I do not trust what they would do with you."

"This was a long time ago," Yoshi pleaded. "Things are different now."

Father pursed his lips. His nostrils flared. "Your mother, your grandmother, they cannot be citizens. The navy refuses you. The Marine Corps refuses you. The air force refuses you. Tell me what has changed."

Yoshi looked around for a defense. He didn't realize that those branches of the military wouldn't take Japanese Americans. This fact made him mad—partly on principle, and largely because it made his case pretty challenging to argue. All he could retort with was this: "I don't want to join those. I want to join the army!"

"No," Father said. "I will hear no more about this."

And that was it. Yoshi looked around the table for someone to help him. Sato and Grandma stared down at their dishes. When Mom made eye contact with him, she gave half a frown and shrugged. If she intended the gesture to look sympathetic, she failed. Instead, she seemed relieved by Father's adamancy.

Yoshi jumped up and stomped to his room. He didn't ask to be excused. With his luck, *that* request would be rejected too. He slammed his door, dove onto his bed, and screamed into his pillow. When a dream dies, he learned, it sounds like a muffled shriek.

Yoshi stopped putting any effort into his work. There was no point. No matter what, the grocery store would consume his entire life, and Gus Needaburger would become a famous air force pilot. A week had passed since Thanksgiving, and he didn't feel even a tiny bit better. As Father checked out customers at the counter, Yoshi held a stupid sack of stupid potatoes, and he *thump thump thumped* them into their stupid basket. His future started playing out in his imagination:

Fifty years in the future, he stood in this exact same spot, leaning against a cane, and holding a potato in his shaky, veiny, decrepit hand. "Ohh," he moaned in pain, as he opened his arthritic fingers. Then really old Gus and really old Sarah came into the shop, holding each other's really old arms.

"We're celebrating our anniversary," Sarah told Yoshi. "I'm sure glad I married an air force pilot because he's really great. It's too bad you've been alone forever. Maybe things could have worked out between you and me if you ever got out of this shop."

Yoshi frowned.

But just then, an outlaw jumped out…

No. He didn't care about his dumb fantasies. He didn't care about anything. He didn't care about the store. He didn't care about decorating for Christmas. He didn't even care when Father offered to take him shooting. When they closed the shop at noon on Saturday, Father suggested going to the park and trying out the Red Ryder bb gun. Yoshi just shrugged and said he wasn't in the mood. And the next day, when they went to church, Pastor Branford's lisp didn't make him laugh at all.

"I would like to revishit the shtory of Moshesh, and why he couldn't enter the Promised Land."

Not even a chuckle.

Yoshi didn't pay much attention to the sermon. He didn't understand why Moses wasn't allowed into the Promised Land, and the whole thing seemed pretty unfair. Wanting something doesn't mean you'll get it—that was the message Yoshi took away. For all he knew, some distant Needaburger ancestor moseyed into the Promised Land without deserving it, because that's how mean the world could be.

As he lay on his bed after church, his head drifted to the left, and his eyes landed on the bookshelf. Grandpa's

Samurai figurine stared back at him. That ugly little turtle-faced tin man looked as angry as ever. Yoshi didn't quite smile—he felt too lousy for that—but the edges of his lips did rise a tiny bit. He supposed he should be grateful that his family cared about him so much. He *was* grateful, but he still resented feeling like their protection would always hold him back. Anyway, all he could do was…

Mom swung open his door. She didn't knock. Tears were in her eyes when she told him:

"America is under attack."

CHAPTER FIVE

THEN THE WAR CAME

The newsman on Mom's radio sounded panicked: *I repeat. This is not a drill. We have witnessed this morning, December 7th, a brief battle in the American territory of Hawaii, with the severe bombing of the U.S. military base at Pearl Harbor by enemy planes, undoubtedly Japanese.*

Even as Yoshi listened to the broadcaster's sharp, aggressive voice, he struggled to accept the news was real. Questions flooded through his mind: What would happen next? Another attack? An invasion? Would Japan kill his family? Would the Nazis? What if America lost the war? What if the bad guys won? What if everything he knew and loved was destroyed, his family killed, his home turned to rubble?

Suddenly, Japan terrified him.

There has been some serious fighting going on in the air and in the sea, the broadcaster said.

Mom covered her mouth. Tears fell from her eyes.

We cannot estimate how much damage has been done…

Sato cried too. Mostly because Mom did.

…but it has been a very serious attack…

Father looked like he had just been told a terrible secret.

…it is no joke. It is a real war.

Yoshi shook.

Nobody came into the grocery store the next day. Yoshi stood behind the counter with Father. They had plenty to discuss, but silence could best express their anxiety. Once in a while, Father cleared his throat. The cough didn't echo, but it roared like it should have. A burst of noise, then silence. It was never followed by any words.

At first, Yoshi assumed people were too scared to leave their homes. The streets *were* emptier than normal. But they weren't empty. Not like the store. Through the window on the door, he could spot an occasional passerby. Sometimes, those strangers looked inside. More often, they scurried past.

As the morning turned to afternoon, more people passed by. Each time it happened, Yoshi felt weirder and weirder. Nothing changed about the shop, but the place seemed wrong somehow. He didn't know why the aisle looked smaller. Or why the air reeked of salt and aluminum. Or why the shelves seemed so delicate, so ready to collapse. And a rhythmic hiss filled his ears for several minutes before he realized it was the huffs from Father's nostrils.

An old woman's face appeared in the window. A black headscarf was wrapped around her white, frizzled hair. She squinted. Her eyelids looked thick, layered with wrinkles. She gazed around the store, shadowing her eyes with a shaking, bony hand. She spotted Yoshi and Father. Those wrinkly eyelids parted. Grey, bulbous eyes stared at them.

She pounded her hand on the window. It was the shrillest noise Yoshi had ever heard.

"SHAME!" she shrieked. "SHAME! SHAME!"

Yoshi's heart raced.

"SHAME! HEY! SHAME ON YOU! SHAME!"

Father closed his eyes. He didn't move.

Yoshi's throat tightened. The words barely squeaked out. He knew the answer, but he asked it anyway: "Is she talking to us?"

Father nodded.

"Why?"

Father said nothing.

The incident wouldn't leave his mind. He didn't understand. Maybe the old woman was confused. Maybe
she'd heard a rumor that the Yamaguchis took part in
Pearl Harbor. It was the only explanation. Nothing else
made sense. At dinner, as Yoshi stared at the pasta on his
plate, he couldn't stop replaying the woman's shrill curse:
shame, shame, shame, shame...

There were two kinds of silence: the *nothing-to-say*
kind, and the *words-just-make-things-worse* kind. This
kind was the latter. Yoshi didn't like this kind. Mom occasionally tried to start a conversation. The pleasantness
in her voice didn't sound genuine, like she would rather
stay quiet too, but she felt obligated to talk.

"Did you get your paper back from Miss Ellison?" she
asked Sato.

Sato nodded. She stared at her food, gliding a chunk of
noodles around the plate with her fork.

"Did she think the State of the Union was a good
choice?" Mom asked.

"I don't think she likes me anymore," Sato said.

A third kind of silence: the *realizing-things-are-as-bad-as-you-feared* kind.

"Oh no, that's not true. I'm sure that's not true at all." Mom pursed her lips and scrunched her brow. She must have realized how insincere she sounded. When she spoke again, her voice was deeper, more serious. "Did you get a bad grade?"

Sato shook her head, but she didn't elaborate.

Mom took another bite and gave a heavy gulp. "I was thinking, for your birthday, Sato, maybe we should have a party at the house. I think it would be safest if—"

"I don't want to talk about my birthday right now," Sato snapped.

Yoshi waited for his father to scold her. Interrupting Mom was disrespectful. He kept waiting, but the scolding never came.

Three days passed, and the store remained vacant. Without any business, his days seemed even longer than they used to. Somehow, he felt bored to death and deathly afraid at the same time. The combination didn't seem possible. He wanted to ask Father about the old lady. He wanted to ask why the shop was empty. He wanted to ask why Sato was having a hard time at school. All he managed to spit out was this: "What's going on?" To which Father replied, "They do not understand."

This response didn't help. In a way, Yoshi could assume the answer to his questions. Japan was the enemy. His family had come from Japan, so people must have thought the Yamaguchis were the enemy too. He had the answer. What he needed was an explanation. Other than the stories his grandpa used to tell, Yoshi knew almost nothing about Japan. He knew about George Washington and Thomas Jefferson and Abe Lincoln. He didn't know the names of any Japanese leaders, except for some guys named Tojo and Hirohito that were all over the news. He didn't even know what kind of government Japan had. Whatever it was, it seemed pretty bad, so he knew it couldn't be a democracy. As a kid, his grandparents exposed him to Japanese artwork and music, so he had a fondness for some things about the culture. But in his mind, he was all American. Why didn't people understand this?

A knock came at the door. For a second, Yoshi panicked, fearing the mean old woman had returned. But when he turned to look, he breathed a sigh of relief. That young Japanese guy from a few months back grinned a mouthful of crooked teeth and gave an enthusiastic wave. He still wore his loose button up shirt, his floppy gray cap, and his perfectly knotted tie. And once again, he stood outside rather than coming in. This behavior seemed a little strange. Perhaps he thought the store was closed, or maybe he really thought this place was the Yamaguchis' home. Whatever the case, Yoshi gave a little smile. Seeing a friendly face was welcome right about now.

Yoshi called to his father. As much as he wanted to let the guy in, he didn't feel like he had permission.

Father peeked out of the office behind the counter. When he saw the young man's face, he closed his eyes and let out a heavy sigh before stomping over to the door.

"Hi! I'm Joey Minami with the Japanese American Citizens League."

"I know who you are," Father said.

"Oh, great, you remember me. That sure is nice!"

"My answer is no."

Joey cocked his head to the side. "Your answer to what?"

"Whatever you want."

Joey's lips hung open like a goldfish. He held up a finger. "One second. Just give me *one* second." His hands dove into his pockets and yanked out some notecards. "I

have a fact I want to tell you, because it's real important."
He frantically flipped through the cards. "And I think
you'll find it real neat…because it's real important…" He
started to panic. "Not Nye-Lea…Not the Cable
Act…Where is it?"

"You could put all this on one card," Father suggested.

Joey froze. After an embarrassed chuckle, he kept flip-
ping. "Well, yeah, sure. But anyways, what I really want
to tell you…what I want to tell you is…our membership
shot through the roof after Pearl Harbor…and if…if
things keep up this way, we'll probably…" He finally
found the right card. "Tripled! Our membership will be
tripled soon, to 20,000 members nationwide."

Father squinted skeptically. "Tell me why."

"Well, see, it's like this." Just like last time, Joey adjusted his stance as he tried finding the right words. "Our
group is all about how we're good Americans, and the
government knows that about us. They like us. They think
we're a pretty swell group, I think. We've been in touch
with them. When people join us—when Japanese Americans join—they're showing the government they're loyal
Americans. That's real important right now. We want as
many members as we can get. Strength in numbers, that's
what Mr. Hamasaki says. He's our local leader."

As this information settled, Father raised his chin. He looked surprised, but he didn't seem disappointed. "This group talks with the government?"

"You bet!"

"And the government likes this group?"

"Yes sir!"

"This is no trick?"

"No way! Not a chance. Mr. Hamasaki's got...he's even got some friends in Washington! They're something in the government, I don't know. But they seem real important."

Yoshi couldn't believe how quickly Father answered: "Show me a contract. If I like this, my whole family signs up."

With a gasp, Joey put his hands against the sides of his head. "Your *whole family*? Oh my gosh! That's amazing!" He started bouncing. "Are they all citizens?"

"I, my son, my daughter are. My wife, her mother are not."

"Well, gee, let's sign the three of you up then!"

Father's nostrils flared. "Three?"

With a timid gulp, Joey slouched. "Well, see, it's like this...It's real important to have a good image for the government. And we, you know, because that's real important…"

Father pursed his lips, daring Joey to say it.

"We only accept citizens," Joey mumbled.

The door slammed so hard the window almost broke. Father stormed away.

And the shop stayed empty. The end of the week arrived without a single customer. Right before lunch on Friday afternoon, Father suggested that Yoshi go home early.

"Take a break," he said. "Today, tomorrow. Next week."

"Next *week*?" Yoshi raised his eyebrows. The offer made him feel strange. As tedious as these days seemed, he didn't want to leave. He wanted things to be normal again. Going home early wasn't normal. Having Saturday off wasn't normal. Taking a week vacation wasn't normal.

Yoshi shrugged. "I'm good to stay."

"Take a break. Go."

"I don't need a break."

Father grunted. "Read your book."

"I finished it," Yoshi lied.

"Get rest."

"I'm not tired."

"Clean your room."

"It's not bad right now."

Father slammed the counter. "I need money to pay you." He had a hint of embarrassment in his voice. He clenched his teeth, cleared his throat, and then slowly straightened his spine. "We have no business. Savings will not last. I cannot pay. Take a break."

Yoshi felt something unfamiliar and strange. He didn't want to call it pity because you can only feel pity for someone you have power over. But he felt something close to it: respectful sympathy, compassionate helpless- ness. Whatever the term was, it inspired his answer. "You don't need to pay me."

Father shook his head.

"I mean it," Yoshi insisted. "I'll volunteer for a while. I don't mind at all."

"I pay for work," Father said. "I cannot—"

The bell rang.

Father gazed at the door like a dog being brought its supper.

"Mrs. Fitzgerald," he said, as if the woman would van- ish if he didn't state her name.

She had been in many times before. Yoshi recognized

her, even though all the female, middle-aged regulars looked the same to him. Mrs. Fitzgerald's short, rolled updo was ginger instead of black—that's what distinguished her—but they all had bony and symmetrical faces, with finely plucked eyebrows, ruby red lipstick, and bright pearl earrings.

"Mr. Yamaguchi," the woman replied. "And junior." She gave Yoshi a close-lipped grin. "How are you two doing this afternoon?"

"Glad for your business." Father didn't quite smile, but his lips parted and turned up slightly at the edges.

Mrs. Fitzgerald avoided eye contact as she headed down the aisle and studied the Campbell's soup cans. Her tone was strange. It was friendly, but distant. Warm, but hesitant. Loud, but unconfident. She acted like she had a splotch on her face and was trying too hard to pretend it wasn't there.

She plopped two Cream of Mushroom cans on the counter. Even though she had a smile on her face, she kept her eyes turned down. In an instant, Father typed in the price on the register. Yoshi started putting the cans in a paper bag.

"Oh no, sweetheart, that won't be necessary. You save that bag for someone else. Less than a handful here."

Father nodded. "Thank you, Mrs. Fitzgerald."

"Oh no, thank *you*." Her smile faded. For the first time, she looked Father in the eye. "Been a slow week, you said?" She started sounding normal, if a bit sad.

Father nodded.

"Well, that is just too bad." She licked her lips. "Some people…They say some silly things sometimes. I didn't want any part of it. I wanted to pride myself on not partic- ipating, but Lordy, if I shouldn't have spoken up sometimes."

Yoshi had no idea what she was talking about, but she had the same mixture of nervousness and relief you might find in a church confessional.

"It's not right, what some of them say," she added. "Not right at all. But that's what the times are doing to people. It's bad times for all of us." She took a handker- chief out of her pocket and dabbed her nose. "I'm still a bit rattled, to tell you the truth. Had to take my son in yes- terday to sign up for the draft. I'd hoped I'd never have to do it, but there it is. That's the times for you."

"Your son, he turned twenty-one?" Father asked.

"No, you didn't hear? They lowered it to eighteen after Pearl Harbor. And Jacob, he couldn't wait a darn minute to register. He wanted to sign right up to fight, actually—

avoid the draft business altogether, being inspired by the attack and whatnot—but I didn't let him. I said, 'Let's put it in God's hands. If you get drafted, it's His will.' To tell you the truth, and he'd hate for me to say it, but I'm hoping he doesn't get called."

They lowered the draft age. Yoshi's dream came rushing back to him. His father would never let him *join* the military, but if he got drafted, maybe he could rival Gus Needaburger after all. He could almost picture the scene: galloping into Japan on a great white steed, American flag waving behind him, saving the world from the bad guys who were doing really mean stuff...

"How old are *you*, sweetheart?" Mrs. Fitzgerald asked Yoshi.

"Eighteen," Father answered for him. "This notice to register, it came in your mail?

The woman nodded. "It's a scary time. I guess we all knew it was coming. But even with all the declarations of war, it's still hard to comprehend. I was even reading about—"

Screams came from outside. People rushed past the window. Yoshi hurried over to the door to see what was going on. Cars kept the normal pace, but all the pedestrians were running for cover. In the distance, someone was shouting. At first, Yoshi couldn't make out what the desperate man was yelling. After the third or fourth exclamation, the words finally became clear:

"They're invading San Francisco! The Japs are invading! We could be next!"

Yoshi's heart pounded.

The woman and Father must have understood too.

Mrs. Fitzgerald dropped the soup cans.

Father pointed at Yoshi. "Lock the door." He hurried around the counter and took the woman by the arm.

Yoshi stared back, in a daze.

"Lock the door!" Father escorted Mrs. Fitzgerald into the office behind the counter.

"Turn on the radio!" she shouted. "Turn on the radio!"

"I have no radio."

"Turn on the radio!"

Yoshi became lightheaded. This was it. The invasion was here. He knew they wouldn't survive. As Father shouted to him, the words barely made sense: "Get in the office, Yoshi. Come here. Get in the office."

Aside from the cars, the street was empty.

"Turn on the radio!"

"The office, Yoshi."

"Turn on the radio!"

"Get in the office."

Just then, another voice: "False alarm! That was a false alarm! The Japs aren't invading!"

Yoshi felt like he had just survived a robbery. He leaned over and trembled in relief.

"It's okay," he tried to yell, but the words came out breathy.

"Get in the office, Yoshi."

"It's okay! It's not happening!"

Father stepped out of the office.

"It's not happening," Yoshi repeated. "It's okay."

But the war was still real. In bed that night, he wondered if his fantasies of fighting were a tad too unrealistic. He did like the idea of wowing Sarah with a uniform, but in the brief moment that he believed Japan was invading, he got a small taste of what complete horror felt like. Maybe the battlefield wouldn't be so great after all. He peeked at the Red Ryder bb gun beside his bed. One of these days, he would get to go shooting, and maybe the practice would energize his dream a bit.

"That's not what I'm saying." Mom's muffled voice carried across the hall.

Silence. Father must have been speaking.

"I understand that," Mom said, "but you need to think about what's best for *him*."

Him. The only person that could be was Yoshi. He peeled away the covers and tiptoed across the floor. With the gentlest turn of his squeaky handle, he cracked open his bedroom door a couple inches.

"Forget about the *principle*, Tanaka." Hearing Father's first name never felt normal, and it always meant something serious was happening. "Always about the *principle* with you. We don't have the luxury of worrying about it."

Father's mumble didn't quite seep through the closed door of the master bedroom. Yoshi could only make out a few words: "…battalion…my experience…not a…"

"There *are* no good choices. *That's* the point. He'll have to fight either way. At least if he signs up he'll have some control—"

"…navy, the air force…refuse…without a…"

"What's to stop them from drafting the Japanese boys for suicide missions, Tanaka? If he shows his loyalty now—"

"…about this…"

"I'm sorry, but you can't pretend it hasn't crossed your mind. He needs to show them he's good. They won't see the good boys as expendable, you know that."

"…another…and useless…"

"We're going in circles, Tanaka. Yoshi *wants* to fight. If he didn't, maybe this would be another conversation. He *wants* to, and it might save his life in the long run."

A long silence.

"…wished…see it."

Another long silence.

Yoshi felt heavy. His dream started seeming melancholy. Tragic, even. Through all his stupid daydreams, he never considered what life would be like away from his family. When he listened to his parents, reality struck him, and an awful, wretched, terrifying realization sank into his gut: soon, he would be separated from them. His eyes gazed past the bb gun, and he stared at his grandpa's Samurai figurine on the bookshelf. *What should I do?* he thought, as if Grandpa would respond.

Footsteps approached.

Yoshi shut his door and leapt into bed, throwing the covers back over himself right as he heard the knock.

"Hm?" He did his best imitation of being woken up.

"Yoshi?" Mom creaked open the door. She crossed her arms and leaned against the doorway. "Sorry to wake you."

With an exaggerated yawn, he pushed himself up and

rubbed his eyes.

"Yoshi, we…Your father got to thinking that maybe it wouldn't be so bad for you to enlist."

He couldn't decide if he should pretend to be excited, scared, surprised, or relieved, so a few seconds passed with him giving her a blank stare. Yellow light from the hallway flooded in behind Mom, making her a silhouette.

"Would you like that?" she asked. "I don't want you to feel any pressure. Just know that if it's something you still want to do, we'll support you with it."

Yoshi nodded. He thought he should say something—he thought he should *feel* something—but everything was numb.

Mom gave a little chuckle and rubbed her forehead. "It could have waited until morning. I don't know why I woke you. We can talk tomorrow. I'm sorry, it's…Goodnight, Yoshi. I love you."

She always said "I love you" when she worried about him.

"Registrar's Report" was typed across the top of the enlistment form. In a room that smelled like sweaty leather and looked as bland as a cardboard box, Yoshi sat on the chair next to his mom, staring at the clipboard on his lap. While trying to complete the "Description of Regis-trant" section, he realized there were some simple things he didn't know about himself. For instance, he needed Mom's help to conclude that his height remained 5'7 and his weight remained 120.

"We haven't checked recently," he said. "It's probably not right."

"It's close enough," Mom said. "See?"

Under "Height" and "Weight," she pointed to the word "Approx."

Yoshi hesitated before writing down the numbers.

Thankfully, he felt confident about some of the details. In the "Race" column, he checked "Japanese." In the "Eyes" column, he checked "Brown." For "Hair," he de-bated between "Brown" and "Black," though his brunette hair was dark enough that he opted for the latter. Mom agreed with his decision.

He reached the "Complexion" column.

"What does 'sallow' mean?" he asked.

"It means almost yellow." Mom looked down at the form. "I think 'Light' would be fine."

He felt like he was taking a test. With a hint of nerv-ousness in his voice, he read the next question aloud: "Other obvious physical characteristics that will aid in identification." He looked up at his mom, hoping she would know what to say.

"Just put 'none,'" she told him.

"I have a couple freckles here." He pointed to his left shoulder. "Should I put that?"

"You can if you want to."

"Do you think I should?"

"I don't think you need to."

When he dropped off his paperwork at the front counter, a man who looked like a butternut squash stamped the form without looking up. The man's tongue peeked out of his panting mouth, and his monotone voice had a shrill raspiness to it as he mindlessly recited: "We'll be in touch about your next steps, so check your mail regularly because you'll hear from us soon. Thank you very much for wanting to serve your country. Have a nice day." He started waddling off with the form before he finished speaking.

As Yoshi watched his application inch away, he sensed he had just made the best and worst decision of his life. Part of him couldn't wait to break the tedious routine of his days. Part of him couldn't bear the thought of losing everything that made him comfortable. When he stepped out of the building, he could almost feel part of himself being left behind. Innocence, naiveté—whatever it was, it was expelled onto his application.

Mom must have felt something get left behind too. On the half-hour drive home, she didn't say much. Her white gloves gripped the steering wheel, and she focused on the road with such intensity, she could have been navigating an obstacle course. Yoshi expected to hear some encouraging words from her about bravery or faith or responsibility. He thought she would tell him that she was proud. When she finally spoke, she didn't mention the military at all.

"Your father and I got to thinking," she said, keeping her eyes on the road. "What if we bought war bonds instead of Christmas presents this year?"

No Christmas presents. Just over a week ago, the agony would have overwhelmed him. With so much else to worry about, he only felt mildly disappointed. He really *had* grown up.

When Yoshi didn't respond, Mom started justifying the idea. "It's important for us to stand with our country right now. We should demonstrate our loyalty."

Yoshi nodded.

She didn't notice. "Would that be okay with you?"

"Yeah."

He thought his short answer conveyed genuine indif-
ference. But Mom started fighting back tears. Her lips
quivered, and she squinted to control her watery eyes.
Yoshi kept waiting for her to explain why she had this
sudden burst of sadness. It remained a mystery. After a
big gulp, she forced a smile. "Why don't you and Sato go
to the movies tomorrow? You would like that, wouldn't
you?"

For the first time, she looked over at him. Yoshi tried
his best to grin, and he gave a little nod.

"Just promise me you'll be safe, okay?" Mom said.
"Come right home if you get a bad feeling about something."

"I won't," Yoshi mumbled.

Mom clenched the wheel. "Yoshi, you *need* to be safe
when—"

"I meant I won't get a bad feeling. Sorry. I'll come
home if I do."

America prepares, the newsman's voice announced.
On the movie screen, a montage showed factory workers
hauling giant pieces of military equipment. *All of America
alters its pattern of life and work to meet the demands of
protection. Industry is in double step to supply...*

For the first time, Yoshi found himself interested in the newsreel. Normally, this part of a movie trip felt like a chore. But when he saw the war unfolding on the screen, he had the feeling of watching a great machine that he would soon become a cog of.

...if democracy is to survive. The muscle of millions of men are working to win for the ways of freedom...

Fewer people than normal were scattered throughout the theater. Yoshi and Sato sat alone in their row. Right behind them, a young couple must have been on a first date, because something seemed phony about their interaction. The guy forced a deep-sounding voice, and the gal exaggerated her interest in what he had to say.

"They should talk about the planes." Covering his mouth to amplify his voice, the guy shouted at the screen, "Hey news jerks, talk about the Jap planes that flew over San Francisco!"

"Those *were* Jap planes?" the gal responded. "Oh *gosh*, I thought it was a false alarm. My brother goes to school up there, and he...he gave us a call, said his roommate was at the Golden Gate bridge when the whole thing happened, said he saw the planes, said they weren't the Japs. Oh *gosh*."

"Don't know what they were, don't know what they

weren't. See what I mean? That's how Japs work. Sneaky-like, it's their style. They wouldn't fly with flags or something, they'd let it be a mystery. You know they're prepping an invasion as we speak. The government just doesn't want us to panic, so they're pretending it was nothing."

"*Gosh*, I sure…I sure *hope* that isn't true."

"I got good instincts on these things. Real good instincts, the best. I get it from my father. He's a cop. He taught me how to fight, too. None of that kung-fu malarkey, I mean real man's fighting. I could kill a guy if I had to."

"Hey, shut up!" someone shouted from the back of the theater.

The guy behind Yoshi jumped to his feet and spun around. "*You* shut up! My dad's a cop, and I know how to wrestle!"

Yoshi and Sato shot each other a nervous look. They each breathed a sigh of relief as the guy behind them sat back down, mumbling something about muscles and girth. Maybe it was the guy's show of aggression, or maybe it was the emptiness of the theater, but something about this trip to the movies felt wrong.

…the nation roars on guard to the end, but Uncle

Sam's manpower and industry shall continue to answer America's call to arm.

Triumphant music played as a couple soldiers carried an American flag past the Statue of Liberty. Then the newsreel ended.

After a few seconds of fuzzy scratching, the theme song for *Pippy the Pirate* filled the theater. Yoshi clapped without thinking. If anything could make him feel better, it was Pippy. The jingle played, and the credits passed. Yoshi leaned forward, gazing at the screen.

The title card appeared on screen: *A Jap's Trap.*

Yoshi gasped.

On the screen, Pippy climbed off his boat and set foot on an island. He was greeted by three Japanese men who looked like monkeys, with squinty eyes and giant teeth. At the same time, the three of them held up a paper to Pippy: *We Want Peace—Sign Here if You Do Too.* Pippy smiled when he saw this. "I want peace too," he said, grabbing the paper. As soon as Pippy had his head turned down, the Japanese trio tossed a stick of dynamite at him.

Yoshi's mouth hung open. A knot formed in his throat. "This one's not so funny."

"Ha-*ha*!" The guy sitting behind him pointed at the screen. "Backstabbing Japs!"

Yoshi felt like he could vomit. His favorite cartoon character would hate him in real life. He slouched in his seat, hoping to turn invisible.

"Maybe we should go," Sato whispered to him.

At that, he fought the urge to run away. "Don't you want to watch the movie?" he spat out, trying his hardest to be a strong big brother.

Sato shook her head.

As soon as they stood up, the guy behind them gasped. "There's *Jap*s here? Sitting in front of us the whole time and I didn't even notice. Sneaky little devils. Out of here, Japs! Plot your invasion somewhere else!"

With tears in their eyes, Yoshi and Sato hurried away from the screen. They ran up the aisle, up the slight incline, to burst out the door in the back. Sunlight swept over them. Until their eyes adjusted, all they could see was white.

Yoshi kept saying to himself, "I didn't like that one at all. I didn't like it at all."

Sato leaned over. She put a hand over her chest. "I thought he'd come after us."

"But it wasn't funny." Yoshi shook his head. "Pippy's always funny. I didn't like it one bit. It wasn't funny at all."

Deep down, Yoshi sensed this would be their final outing for a long time. Until the war ended, neither of them
would want to go outside again. He almost suggested going to get ice cream, so their movie trips wouldn't end on
such a horrible note. But he didn't offer. They needed to
go home because of his promise to Mom: he got a bad
feeling.

Every night before Yoshi went to sleep, he remembered the terror of running away from the screen, of
running away from the shout. In a way, he felt like he was
still running. He would never be free from that incident as
long as it stuck in his mind, and he knew he would never
forget it. It stuck with him through Christmas, which
passed like any other day. It stuck with him through New
Year's Eve and the first few weeks of 1942. It stuck with
him, until he realized how badly he wanted to escape.

Then all he could think about was the army.

His letter of acceptance still hadn't arrived. He didn't
know if he should be worried. When he first brought up
his concern, Mom told him to wait until the first of the
year. Once the first came, she told him to wait a full
month. Then a month passed since he dropped off his
form, and he still hadn't heard anything.

"Maybe we should go back," Yoshi insisted one night. "Maybe they lost my form or something."

"Let's give it until the end of this week." With her pastry bag, Mom was squeezing *Happy Birthday Sato* in pink frosting across the top of the cake.

"But if they lost it, they'll need a new one."

"We've been over this a hundred times, Yoshi. I'm sure they haven't lost it. Processing paperwork can take a long time."

He couldn't tell if Mom was just preoccupied, or if she started having second thoughts about Yoshi's enlistment. Either way, he didn't appreciate the coldness. He dragged his feet out of the kitchen and into the dining room, where Sato stood on one of the chairs, hanging up a birthday banner for tomorrow's party. Grandma sat at the table, her shaky fingers folding another origami swan. Already, a half-circle of paper birds adorned the middle of the table.

As Yoshi watched his family decorate, he wanted to say something. He didn't know what, exactly. Just something. They each reacted so differently to their circumstances that none of them seemed to connect anymore. Father kept to himself, silent and angry. Grandma acted like nothing had changed. Mom landed somewhere in the middle, fluctuating between forced cheeriness and ill-concealed despair. Sato's changes were inconsistent too. Sometimes, she seemed to have aged ten years. She would walk around with her chin up and her eyes turned down, confident in her melancholy wisdom. Other times, she acted like a little kid again, pouting and rambling and laughing obnoxiously.

He wanted to exclaim, "Everything is terrible, and I don't know how it will ever get better." But the air felt fragile, and telling the truth would be tossing a stone. He decided not to say anything. He would quietly yearn for escape, waiting and waiting for the army to get back to him. Yes, that would be his means of coping: keeping to himself.

So the next day, he didn't talk to customers. And he dreaded going to Sato's birthday party. If a miracle happened, the store would have a rush of business, and demand would force Yoshi to stay.

That didn't happen. Father told him to go.

Yoshi shook his head.

"I tire of your moping," Father said. "Go."

Hanging his head, Yoshi dragged his feet to the door of the shop. Then he looked back at Father.

"What if they lost my form?" he asked with a frown.

Father threw his arms up in the air. "Enough of this.

Go."

"I'm sick of waiting around," Yoshi mumbled. "I just want to know."

After a grunt, Father escorted Yoshi to the back office. He pointed at the phone on top of the desk.

The receiver shook in Yoshi's sweaty palm as he picked it up. His index finger shook as it spun a zero on the rotary.

A deep female voice: "Operator."

"Hi there, Mrs. Operator." Yoshi nervously scratched his neck. "How are you?"

"Who do you need to contact?"

"Oh yes, please, if you don't mind, could you please get me the recruiting station near San Pedro, please? The one on Washington Street, please. Thank you very much, Mrs. Operator."

Ring...

Ring...

Ring...

Ring...

Yoshi wanted to hang up. He looked up at his father. "Maybe I should just—"

Finally, a nasally voice answered: "Office of Registration."

"Hi, yeah. Hi. My name is, uh…My name is Yoshi. Yoshi Yamaguchi, and I…I applied to join the army last month, and I haven't heard anything so—"

"Repeat the name."

"Yoshi Yamaguchi."

"Is that Chinese?"

"It's Japanese." Yoshi gulped.

There was a long pause.

"At this time, I can tell you that you would be classified 4C."

"Oh, okay. Thank you." Yoshi started to shake. "What does that mean?"

"Registration denied, based on your status as an enemy alien."

The receiver fell from Yoshi's hand, dangling by the cord off the side of the desk. His eyes widened. His mouth hung open.

"I'm a citizen," he whispered to himself. "I'm a Nisei. I'm a citizen."

Father raised an eyebrow.

Yoshi didn't have the strength to explain. He grabbed his bike and ran out of the store. He pedaled, pedaled, pedaled, pedaled, never riding so fast in his life. He wanted his mom. He wanted home. He didn't want the party, but he wanted a safe place.

Leaving his bike on the grass, he burst open the front door of his house, too distraught to be self-conscious. He awaited the stares of Sato's friends as he stormed inside. He saw no one, but he heard a sob. He followed it to the dining room.

Sato had her arms on the table, her head buried in them. "I knew they wouldn't come," she sobbed. "I knew it."

Mom kneeled beside her, rubbing her back. "I'm sorry, Sato. I'm so sorry."

Yoshi gasped. He didn't realize he had tears on his cheeks until Mom looked up at him and covered her mouth.

"Nobody cares about me anymore," Sato sputtered through her sniffles.

"They're supposed to be here for you." Yoshi shook his head. "They're supposed to be here!" Without thinking, he rushed back out the door. He hopped on his bike and rode through the cross streets—left, right, right, left—until he reached Jackson High. He needed to find Sato's friends. He needed to convince them to go to her party. She made *his* party special. Now he needed to be a good big brother.

Somehow, his feet had left the pedals. They were stomping through the school's hallways. This place still looked like a gray asylum. It still smelled like a rubbery garage. An hour after school got out, only a few people were passing by the lockers. They all stared at him.

"Do you know Sato Yamaguchi?" he pleaded to anyone he saw.

Eyes turned down.

"Do you know Sato?"

Nothing.

"She's having a party right now! You should come! You all should come!"

A familiar face rounded the corner: Susie Wong.

"Susie!" Yoshi exclaimed. "Susie!"

She froze, became wide-eyed, and turned the other way.

"Wait! Susie! Wait! It's me, Yoshi. Sato's brother. From the park. We played catch."

Nervously biting her lip, she turned around to face him. Just then, Yoshi noticed a big red button she had pinned to her blouse. In capital white letters, it said: *I AM CHINESE*.

"What are you doing here, Yoshi?" she whispered.

"Sato's birthday! You need to go!"

"Do you know how hard things are for me right now? You know my parents would kill me if they saw me talking to you? Do you realize *this* is saving my life?" She pointed to her button.

"But she's all alone…She's all alone…"

A teacher spotted the two of them and came scurrying over.

"What's this?" the woman said to Yoshi. "Get out, before I call the police."

"But she's all alone!" Yoshi cried. "She's all alone!"

"Out!" The woman pointed.

Then he was no longer at Jackson. He was running through alleys, down streets he didn't recognize. He panted. His heart raced. His feet were moving. He passed unfamiliar stores and unfamiliar churches. He reached a park he'd never been to before. It had a grassy little amphitheater. Two hundred people filled the concrete benches. They cheered as a middle-aged man and a middle-aged woman took the stage. Both their hair looked fake. Both their skin looked plastic.

"My name is Mortimer Needaburger—"

"And my name is Sharol Needaburger—"

"President of the local chapter of the Native Sons of the Golden West—"

"President of the local chapter of the Native *Daughters* of the Golden West—" A big, phony grin.

"And we're calling on President Roosevelt to please…"

They both spoke together, sticking their thumbs out in a choreographed movement: "Get those Japs *out* of here!"

Cheers from the crowd.

"It is a known fact that *all* Japs—"

"Every single one of them—"

"Has innate, natural loyalty to Emperor Hirohito—"

"Being un-American is in their very *blood*—"

"And the president needs to understand that this is a war—"

"We can't afford to be nice right now—"

"Our national security *demands* that we take action—"

"Which is why we think the president needs to revoke all citizenship—"

"From *every* Jap, then send them back to where they came from."

"It's the only way we can all be safe. Our son Gus joined the air force—"

Cheers.

"He joined the air force to keep us safe from dangers abroad. Not taking drastic action on the home front would be a slap in the face to *all* our sons in uniform."

"Remember Pearl Harbor!" the two of them shouted together.

The audience roared.

Yoshi turned around. If anyone spotted him, he would be in danger. He had to find his way home. He had to backtrack. Back through alleys. Back through streets. Strangers stared. He could hear the clicks of doors being locked. *Remember Pearl Harbor* echoed in his mind. Remember Pearl Harbor. Remember the attack. Remember when everything started to collapse. Remember the old woman, her awful voice: *SHAME!* The way it stuck with him, the way he never spoke of it. *SHAME! SHAME!* He couldn't run from it all, but he tried. He sensed he was being chased. Chased by the words. Chased by it all.

SHAME!

"4C..."

SHAME!

"...enemy alien."

SHAME!

"Remember Pearl Harbor!"

SHAME!

"Plot your invasion elsewhere!"

SHAME!

"I'm not good with that foreign stuff…"

SHAME!

"…if they saw me talking to you?"

SHAME!

"Nobody cares about me anymore!"

SHAME!

"It wasn't funny at all!"

SHAME!

"This place is for Americans!"

SHAME!

"Out!"

"Out!"

"Out!"

"Out!"

Yoshi stumbled. He felt his knees crash onto cement, but he didn't know where he was. He sobbed into his arms, making sure no one could see his face. He had no

idea that Gus's parents were involved in a racist group. If the Needaburgers hated him, then Sarah probably hated him too. Somehow, that hurt more than anything else.

A deep voice: "Problem, son?"

Yoshi jumped. A cop was staring down at him.

In a panic, Yoshi started scooting back. "I'm sorry. I'm sorry."

"Woah there, son. Hold your horses." The man scratched his big black mustache, then stuck his thumbs into his belt. "We got reports of a crazed Japanese boy running around here. A lot of people were awful worried. Thought they might be in danger."

Yoshi said nothing.

The cop took a knee and raised an eyebrow. "You wouldn't happen to know anything about it, would you?"

After thinking for a while, Yoshi gave a little shrug.

"People are spooked," the cop said. "War's got everyone on edge. Hearts get racing at the leap of a grasshopper. I sure hope everyone's careful. I wouldn't want anyone getting hurt." He leaned down his chin like he wanted a particular response, but Yoshi didn't know what to say. "Where do you live, son?" The cop finally asked. "Hop on in. Let me take you home."

❖

Yoshi would never forget the terror and outrage and sadness that greeted him when he returned. Mom embraced him like he might blow away in the wind, and one month after that incident with the cop, she still wouldn't let the issue go. From time to time, she repeated what she told him that day: "You were *lucky* he was a nice policeman. You were *lucky*. Do you have any idea what could have happened to you? *Never* do that again."

After Yoshi's breakdown and Sato's disastrous birthday party, the Yamaguchis started talking more about what was happening to them. They had to. The topic couldn't be avoided. They spoke of staying strong, of sticking together, of persevering. They told each other that life would return to normal soon enough.

Then February 19th came.

President Roosevelt issued Executive Order 9066. By presidential decree, he authorized the military to establish zones where "any or all persons may be excluded." This executive order didn't mention Japanese Americans, nor did it establish where these "areas of exclusion" would be, so the Yamaguchis didn't know what to think. All they could do was wonder if their lives would be affected.

And so, after February 19th, 1942, their conversation shifted from "we can make it through" to "what happens next?" Father felt confident that EO 9066 was the start of something bad. He mostly kept quiet, but if politics ever came up, he would grumble, "It will get worse. You will see."

The weeks passed. Yoshi waited for something to happen. He tried figuring out what the worst-case scenario would be. If his home ended up being in an "exclusion area," would he have to move to another neighborhood? Another state? Would everybody move? What if the Needaburgers got what they wanted? What if he lost his citizenship and was shipped off to Japan? He never wanted *that* to happen. But in all honesty, he knew something needed to change. Life couldn't keep going this way forever. If all the racist fears persisted, the Yamaguchis' business wouldn't last. Neither would their sanity.

In desperation, Father hung a sign outside the grocery store. *I Am American*, it said. It didn't make much of a difference. Some of the regulars had already started coming back. Others never showed up again. An occasional stranger would buy an item or two, but it wasn't enough. Wartime rationing was recently put in place, meaning people couldn't buy much even if they wanted to.

Father stopped making any effort to hide his worry. He stomped around with clenched fists and pursed lips. He shushed every attempt to start a conversation.

And when he heard the knuckles tap against the pane, he stormed over to the door. There was only one person who knocked on the window instead of coming into the shop.

Joey's voice didn't have its normal enthusiasm. He sounded on the verge of tears. "Hi, I'm Joey Minami with—"

"Leave," Father said.

For the first time, Joey wasn't wearing his perfect tie. He kept his eyes turned toward the ground.

"I just want—"

"No. Your group refuses us."

"Not *all* of you."

"When you refuse some, you refuse all. Go."

Father started to shut the door.

"Please, just listen!" Joey exclaimed. "Things have been real bad for me too. Things have been *real* bad. You can't even know how bad. Just listen to me."

Father took a deep inhale. "How does this group fight 9066? Tell me how they fight it. Tell me what they will do if all goes bad."

Joey fell silent. He bit his lip, like a little kid getting caught in a lie. "We'll do whatever the president asks of

us." He held up his arms defensively and hurried to justi-
fy. "It's *so* important to show loyalty right now—"

Slam!

As Father walked away, he spat out a single word:
"Cowards."

In the end, wartime rationing turned out to be a blessing. Business started picking up. Attitudes didn't change,
but people needed goods. Specifically, they needed wheat
and sugar. Shipments to stores were extremely limited,
and after weeks of little business, the Yamaguchis had
plenty of each stocked. By the end of March, Yoshi started feeling hopeful. Customers were ruder than they used
to be, and dealing with ration books could be quite the
headache, but at least his family could pay the bills. Maybe things would start getting better. Maybe the mean
people would start to get kinder. Maybe everything would
turn out fine…

Father was handing two women change when the noise
came. A dull shriek: the sound of masking tape being un-
wound. Yoshi's heart raced at what he saw. Two
uniformed men stood outside the door, taping a poster
onto the window. The paper was filled with text, and Yoshi couldn't read most of it backwards. But he could make

144 · ANDREW HAYES WILLIAMS

out the giant, bold words across the top: *INSTRUCTIONS TO ALL PERSONS OF JAPANESE ANCESTRY.*

As soon as the uniformed men left, Father hurried outside to see what the poster had to say. He put a hand against his forehead. His face turned gray. His eyes gaped, as if he were watching future news footage of his own death.

The bell rang as he came back inside. It had never sounded so shrill before. Ignoring the two women, he looked Yoshi in the eye. Then he said it:

"We have to leave."

CHAPTER SIX

JUST SOUTH OF INDEPENDENCE

They had three days. Monday night, all they could do was panic. The poster didn't specify what would happen to them. It only said this: *All Japanese persons, both alien and non-alien, will be evacuated from the above designated area by 8 a.m. Friday, March 27th, 1942.* What struck Yoshi was the terminology: "alien and non-alien." A "non-alien" would be a citizen. That meant *him*. Why couldn't they say that? Why couldn't they call him a citizen?

The poster instructed the head of each family to go get more information between 8 a.m. and 5 p.m. on either Tuesday or Wednesday. Father raced out as early as possible. None of them could prepare until they knew what

was in store for them, so on Tuesday morning, they waited. Mom, Grandma, Yoshi, and Sato sat in the living
room. They said nothing. Nervous breathing filled the air,
along with the *tick tick tick* of the kitchen clock. Rutherford fidgeted as Sato squeezed him in the corner.
Grandma nodded her head to stay awake in her armchair.
Mom covered her mouth and leaned forward on the love
seat. Any moment, Father would return. He had to go to
some place called a "Civil Control Station." Whatever
that was, it sounded really serious. Was Father at some
sort of prison? What were they telling him? What if he
didn't come back?

Hugging his knees, Yoshi felt the edge of the coffee
table jab into his back, the knots of the maroon rug press
into his tailbone. He stared at the brick fireplace across
from him, at the mounds of charcoal lying under the wood
grate. He examined the light blue vase on the hearth, at
the framed family portrait on the mantelshelf. His two
front teeth were missing in that photo, and he sat on
Grandpa's lap. That seemed so long ago. It *was* so long
ago. And this room, it hadn't changed much since then.
The square end table beside the fireplace now held Mom's
radio instead of a bonsai tree, and a decade ago, Mom
painted over the old white walls with a dull, greenish yel-

low. But this was the same living room, the one he grew up in, the one where he spent every Christmas morning, the one where Grandpa used to make Yoshi and Sato laugh.

All the stuff in the room was just stuff. But Yoshi started to realize that every little thing had a story behind it. Painting the walls was a story. Buying the vase was a story. Replacing the bonsai tree with the radio was a story. Most of these stories, Yoshi didn't remember well. Some of them, like how the fray appeared on the window curtains, he never knew at all. But he could feel them. Everything looked this way for a reason. He didn't know where his family would be sent, but he knew those stories would soon vanish for good.

The door swung open. They all sat up as Father dragged his feet through the doorway.

"They call it a 'relocation center,'" he said. His eyes squinted, in a combination of sadness and concentration.

Evacuation, relocation center—these words sounded so innocent, so harmless. What did it all mean?

Sato squeezed Rutherford tighter. "Where is it?"

"Just north of a town called Lone Pine," Father said. "Just south of a town called Independence. We take only what we can carry. I know little else."

"But what about—?" Sato began.

"I know little else." Father's lips pursed in anger, and he stared at Yoshi. "That place, that Civil Control Station. It was made from a JACL office."

Yoshi cocked his head to the side.

"It used to be JACL," Father explained. "The army turned it into what it is now. That man, Mr. Hamasaki. He was there. Helping the government. Smiling and sucking up." Father scowled like he wanted to spit. With so much else going on, it seemed strange that he would waste any energy complaining about the Japanese American Citizens League. His hatred of the group must have been intense.

Mom scrunched her brow, looking for an explanation of what the JACL was, but Father dismissively waved his hand.

"We must sell what we can," he said. "Now pack."

He couldn't. Or he didn't. Whatever the case, Yoshi found himself on his back on the love seat. Around him, everyone packed. He lay there, listening. Not even watching. Just letting the world fall apart around him. Hours might have passed for all he knew. He had experience with depression. He had experience with anxiety. He had experience with self-consciousness and terror and outrage. But he had no experience with complete powerlessness, with feeling so helpless that he couldn't even care. If he acknowledged how terrible his situation was, he would break. Forced numbness was his only self-defense.

Whap.

Yoshi's eyes shot open. After striking the back of the couch, Father stared down at Yoshi and pointed at the stairs. Even though he wanted to respond, Yoshi couldn't think of anything to say. After a moment, his eyelids slid back down.

"Pack," Father demanded. "Yard sale items go in boxes. Toss what we cannot sell. Do it."

With a groan, Yoshi pushed himself off the love seat and climbed up the steps, every foot seeming as heavy as an anvil. On top of his unmade bed, there sat three cardboard boxes and a couple of suitcases. As he stepped inside, he tripped over the pile of dirty clothes in front of his bed. He had a strange sense that the laundry was precious. He stared at the *Hopalong Cassidy* poster and the framed *Life Magazine* cover on either side of the door. He scanned the old clothes hanging in his open closet, the unread books lingering on his shelf. He hadn't finished *The Disappearing Floor*, and at this point, he never would. Somehow, that seemed tragic.

Then he realized…his Red Ryder bb gun wasn't beside his bed. And Grandpa's good luck figurine wasn't on the shelf. Yoshi looked in the empty boxes and suitcases. He searched the closet. He dug through the pile of dirty clothes. No luck—they were gone.

Footsteps rumbled down the hall. Yoshi stepped out of his bedroom right as his father passed by.

"Where are they?" he asked.

Father stared back.

"My bb gun and the figurine," Yoshi said. "Grandpa's figurine. I can't find them."

"The dumpster," Father answered.

Yoshi's jaw dropped. "The *dumpster*? What do you mean they're in the *dumpster*?"

"I tossed them."

A knot formed in Yoshi's throat.

"But those were my birthday presents!"

"We cannot have these things," Father said.

"I wanted those!" Yoshi knew he sounded like a little kid. He was too upset to be embarrassed by that. "It was Grandpa's! I wanted those!"

"They warned me today. They call it contraband. We must have no weapons, no things from Japan. They see it as loyalty to the emperor."

"And you'll just do whatever they say? You'll just *do* it?"

"I do what I must. Stop being a fool." Father pointed to Yoshi's door. "Now pack." He disappeared into the master bedroom.

"Those were my birthday presents!" Yoshi shouted again, as much to himself as to his father. It didn't change anything. He would never hold his Red Ryder bb gun again, and he didn't even get to shoot it once. Not even once.

Wednesday was sunny. Yoshi resented that. It was a lousy day, and lousy days didn't deserve to be sunny. He had been up since six, helping his father carry the heavy things out onto the lawn. By ten o'clock, the front yard was filled with people and furniture and boxes and signs that said *Everything Must Go*. Only the most basic necessities remained inside, like a telephone and a handful of dishes to tide them over.

Right outside the front door, Yoshi sat behind the dining room table. Father had brought the cash register home from the grocery store, and Yoshi was tasked with checking out customers. Behind the makeshift counter, he watched as strangers dug through boxes of his family's belongings and looked at the furniture. They examined the love seat, and the pair of recliners that used to be for Grandma and Grandpa. They scrutinized the bed frame that Yoshi had slept on the previous night. Mom and Father wandered through the crowd, answering questions and making offers.

A middle-aged woman approached the table. "How much for these?" she asked, holding up a pair of Sato's old roller skates.

Yoshi shrugged.

"They're pretty worn," the woman said. "How about ten cents?"

With half a nod, Yoshi opened his hand.

Dropping a dime into Yoshi's palm, the woman laughed in disbelief. "Ten cents for skates. Can't beat that. Say, you don't happen to have a car for sell, do you?"

Yoshi nodded towards his father, who was in the middle of another negotiation.

She ran off with an eager grin. "Let's see if we can get you a car before you ship out," she told a young man. The guy made eye contact with Yoshi for half a second, then quickly turned his head down. It took Yoshi a few seconds to recognize him: it was his old teammate Freddy from high school.

When Yoshi didn't look away, Freddy gave half a smile and a timid wave, then slowly approached in what seemed like obligation. Yoshi told himself to say something—even a simple hello. The words didn't come. Freddy stood in front of the table, gave an uncomfortable laugh, and shrugged. Then he walked away.

Freddy was the only person who was ever nice to Yoshi at school. They weren't best friends. Not even great ones. But Freddy's kindness used to mean so much to him, and in this awkward tension, Yoshi could feel the old friendship die.

He closed his eyes and sighed. His muscles throbbed from squeezing furniture through the doorway. His eyelids drooped from lack of sleep. This had to be the loneliest he'd ever felt. Freddy was the closest thing he had to an old friend; Susie Wong was the closest thing he had to a new one. Neither of them cared about him anymore. He slouched in his seat, and his mind drifted to Joey. If Yoshi ever saw that JACL guy again, maybe the two of them could become friends. Hopefully Father's outburst hadn't ruined the possibility.

A familiar voice reached Yoshi's ear. "Mr. *Yamagu-*

chi. How can this *be*? This is simply *terrible.*" Ricardo's bald spot glistened in the sun. His frown caused his big red mustache to droop.

Father gave a solemn nod.

"Oh, Ricardo." Mom put a hand over her heart and hurried over the moment she saw him. "You didn't have to come out this way."

"I *called.* As soon as I heard the *news.* Mr. Yamaguchi said you had to sell *everything.* I had to stop *by.* I had to see you *off.*" He shook his head. "This is *unbelievable.* Completely *unbelievable.* You know what happened to *me*? The FBI asked me some questions—a few *questions.* That's *it.* Nothing like *this.*"

Yoshi almost forgot that America was at war with Italy, too. German Americans and Italian Americans weren't all being sent away to mysterious places. Why was Japan any different? Then he remembered the Japanese characters in the *Pippy the Pirate* cartoon and the racist rally he'd stumbled upon. He thought about the stuff his father had told him, about the immigration ban and the denied citizenship after World War I. Yoshi was starting to feel the effect of those old ideas.

"But *please*," Ricardo added. "That doesn't *matter.* That doesn't matter *at all.* Tell me how I can *help.*"

"I want no charity," Father said.

"No *charity*, but…" Ricardo took a quick glance into the nearest box. With one hand, he took his billfold out of his pocket, and with the other, he pulled a spatula out of the box. "I came prepared to *buy*." He handed Father twenty dollars.

Mom covered her mouth. "We couldn't possibly, Ricardo."

"I need a *spatula*. I need it for my *restaurant*."

"It's worth thirty cents at the most," Mom said. "It would be a miracle to get this much for the sofa."

"I need a *spatula*," Ricardo insisted. "It's not for *you*. It's for *me*. My restaurant is *without*. How can I get by with no *spatula*?"

Mom spun around and covered her eyes. She lowered her head, and Yoshi could tell that she was crying. Ricardo patted her on the back, and she turned in to give him a hug.

Sato rushed out the front door. She scanned the yard, then stood next to Yoshi. "Have you seen Rutherford?"

Yoshi shook his head.

"I can't find him anywhere. Dad!"

Father approached, leaving Mom behind as she cried into Ricardo's chest.

"Dad," Sato said. "What happened to Rutherford?"

Without a pause, Father answered, "I sold him."

Sato gasped. Tears rushed to her eyes before the word came out in a breathy whisper: "*What?*"

"I sold him," Father repeated. "We can take no pets."

"You *sold* him? You *sold* him?"

Father nodded.

"You didn't even *tell* me? You didn't even let me say *goodbye*?"

"It is a cat. It does not care."

"I can't *believe* you! I can't *believe* you! What if he's in a bad home? What if it's a bad home?!"

"I got good money," Father said. "You are too young to understand."

Sato stormed back into the house, screaming, "I can't believe you! I can't believe you!" If there was one thing she hated more than anything else, it was being told she was too young to understand something. All the shoppers froze as they stared at the front door. Then they went back to rummaging.

Even though Yoshi never liked that cat, he knew how much his sister loved it, and he felt a gaping void on her behalf. He kept his head turned, staring at the front door, hoping his sister would come back out. He wanted to tell her he was sorry. He wanted to give her a hug and be a good big brother. But there was nothing to say, and there was nothing to do, and…

"We-heh-hell. Little Yosh."

The most horrible, wretched, disgusting nasally voice came from behind him. He recognized it in an instant, and he felt like he could vomit in rage. Yoshi slowly turned his head back around to see Gus Needaburger standing in front of the table.

Yoshi couldn't hide his scowl. His hands clenched into fists at his side. "I thought you were in the air force."

"Back home from training for a few days. I gotta tell ya, Little Yosh, it's everything I hoped it'd be and more. I just can't wait to get out and start blasting Japs for real. Ka-pow!" He pantomimed shooting a gun, then looked around and smiled. "Nice sale you're havin', Little Yosh. I guess you could call it explosive. Explosive like…*Pearl Harbor*." He laughed and shook his head. "Looks like the eagles are coming home to roost."

Yoshi stared back, speechless.

"It's like that thing people say, 'the chickens are coming home to roost,' about getting what you deserve. But my version is more patriotic. I just came up with it. I got a talent for expressions, you dig my wiggle?"

Yoshi heaved through his nostrils. He wanted to pick up the cash register and hurl it at Gus's smug, stupid face. Then a blonde-haired, blue-eyed girl approached, and Yoshi thought his heart might stop.

It was Sarah.

In each hand, she held a white, ceramic trinket box with pink roses painted on the lid. Years ago, Grandpa bought these as an anniversary gift: one for himself and one for Grandma.

"We should get these, baby," she said. She didn't even give Yoshi a wave.

"Why? What's it for?"

"They're trinket boxes. I was thinking—"

"*Obviously* they're trinket boxes." Gus rolled his eyes. "What's the point?"

"It's small enough that you could keep it with you to remember me when—"

Gus's hideous cackle cut her off. "Gosh, you're cute when you're dumb. I told you. I can't carry…" He tapped her nose with his index finger on each word: "Any. Extra. Weight."

Yoshi could feel a volcano rumble in his belly.

"It's nothing, Gus." Sarah weighed the boxes in her hands. "You won't even feel it."

"Come on, you need to dig my wiggle on this, okay? There's things you just don't understand. How much are these things, anyway?"

He took them from Sarah's hands and examined them.

"Seventy-five cents apiece," she answered.

"*Seventy-five cents*? Gosh, are they Japs or Jews?"

Yoshi felt like the rope in a tug-of-war: the rage inside pulled him towards a violent outburst, but his exhaustion and humiliation refused to let him move.

"This one's got a little smudge on it," Gus said, holding up the box in his right hand. "I think I should get a discount. Whuddya say, Little Yosh? Buy one, get one half off or something?"

Yoshi refused to cry in front of Sarah. He *refused*. But he feared his voice would quiver if he spoke.

"Gone deaf, Little Yosh? I asked if I can get a discount. Maybe buy one, get one *free*?"

Closing his eyes, Yoshi gave a tiny nod. All he wanted was for Gus to go away.

"Weh-he-hell." With a wink, Gus elbowed Sarah's arm. "I guess you could say I'm a pretty good negotiator, you dig my wiggle?" He smiled at Yoshi. "Alrighty, Little Yosh—buy one, get one free it is. Seventy-five cents for the two of 'em. This is one great…" As his words trailed off, Gus's jaw dropped. His eyes widened, and he let out his shrill, breathy cackle. Not until this moment did Yoshi realize that a tear had broken through his levee of shame. He wiped it away as quickly as he could.

"Oh my gosh!" Gus shook his head. "Are you *crying*, Little Yosh? What, are these flower boxes *yours*? For your *makeup*, maybe? So you can powder your nose? Gosh, if all the Jap guys are as wimpy as you, the war will be over in a *week*. This'll be easier than I thought!"

Yoshi didn't know how it happened. But somehow, he had leapt over the table, tackled Gus to the ground, and started punching. *Bam, bam, bam, bam*—on those beady green eyes, on that stupid button nose, on those ugly little lips—as Yoshi wailed, "I hate you! I hate you! I hate you! I hate you!"

Screams came from all over. Arms wrapped around Yoshi's stomach. He kicked in the air as he was pulled off the ground. When he was tossed to the side, he saw that his father was the one who had picked him up.

"*Inside*, Yoshi. *Get inside.*" Father extended a hand to help up Gus.

Gus smacked it away. "You're crazy. You're all crazy."

Yoshi shouted, "I hope your plane gets shot down and

you die in a ball of fire!"

Gus gasped. "Traitor! Traitor! Did you all hear that? He's a traitor!"

"Inside, Yoshi. *Now*." Father pointed at the front door, then tried again to help up Gus.

Yoshi couldn't believe it. How could Father take Gus's side? Why was he complying so much? Everything felt wrong. Father wasn't acting normal. Home didn't feel like home. Sarah would never like him after what had just happened—and stranger still, he didn't even care. Sarah didn't matter. The military didn't matter. Nothing mattered.

He ran inside, sobbing.

As soon as the front door slammed, Grandma came out of the kitchen.

"It's stupid," Yoshi cried. "It's all stupid!"

"What is this, Yoshi-kun?" She approached him as quickly as she could.

"All of it! It's all stupid!" He collapsed onto the stairs. He covered his face with his hands.

Grandma sat down next to him. "Tell me, Yoshi-kun. What is this now?"

"She saw me like this. She saw me crying, and…" He leaned onto Grandma's shoulder as she hugged him. "He

threw out the figurine, Grandma. He just threw out
Grandpa's figurine like it's nothing. And then she saw me
like this!"

"Oh, Yoshi-kun, how much these things can hurt."
Grandma couldn't have understood what he was talking
about, but she didn't ask for an explanation. Yoshi appreciated that.

"I can't believe I cried in front of her. I can't believe I
cried. I just wanted…" He wiped his nose. "I don't
know."

"What is this you wanted, Yoshi-kun?"

He shrugged.

"What is this you wanted?" Grandma repeated.

"I didn't want her to think I'm a coward," he said. "I
wanted her to think I'm brave."

Grandma squeezed him a little tighter. She shook her
head. "Oh, Yoshi-kun, what good would this be?"

He didn't answer. The question made no sense to him.

"You think a person is good because of being brave?"
Grandma added. "To run into battle…This is brave, yes,
and yet the Nazis do this too. You cannot say a Nazi is not
brave. Does this make him good? To bomb like they did
at Pearl Harbor, could a coward do this? No, it must be a
brave man to fly into enemy's land. Were these men

good? I do not think so. And to invade a place like Mr. Hitler has done, this needs courage too. All of these things, they are brave, but are they right? No, Yoshi-kun. Brave means to stand by beliefs, but what if beliefs are very bad? Then this is no good. What matters is not courage, but empathy."

Yoshi frowned. "I don't think Sarah wants empathy."

"Who is this girl? What is this she wants?"

"Gus Needaburger. That's what she wants. The most awful person to ever live. And he's horrible to her. He's *horrible*."

Grandma's brow scrunched, and her lips wavered. "Sometimes, Yoshi-kun, we do not feel whole. We become afraid of being loved or being left. Some fear both. This is no good."

Once again, Yoshi didn't know what she was talking about. The words sounded pretty, but he wasn't sure they meant anything. Her calmness frustrated him, and he had a strange urge to disprove her.

"You don't seem scared at all," he said.

Grandma let out a little laugh. Her typical, gentle smile remained on her face. If Yoshi didn't know any better, he would think these times were just like any other. This irritated him even more. For the first time ever, Grandma made him angry.

"How can you be so calm right now?" he snapped. "Don't you realize what's happening? Don't you see it?" He pointed at the door.

"Yoshi-kun—"

"Don't you *see* it? If being brave is such a bad thing, why aren't you panicking right now?"

"Yoshi-kun," Grandma repeated. "Being brave and being at peace, these do not have to mean the same. Brave can be good. Brave can be bad. But brave means to fight. I do not fight what I cannot. *Shikata ga nai*. It cannot be helped."

Yoshi wasn't in the mood to listen, and he really wasn't in the mood to understand.

"It's not fair what's happening to us," he said. "Forget all that. It isn't fair."

Then Grandma said something that Yoshi would never forget, something that seemed both overly simple and overly complicated:

"Our country wants this of us," she said. "And so, we do it."

The night before the evacuation date, the Yamaguchis visited Grandpa's grave, knowing they might never visit it again. When they got home from the graveyard, a message in graffiti waited for them on the door. It stared at them in big, red letters: *NO JAPS WANTED*. Yoshi should have felt humiliated or afraid. He felt nothing. Curses like these fit into the new order of things.

"Should we clean it off?" Mom asked.

Father shook his head. There was no point.

The whole house was dark because they had sold most of their lamps. With careful steps, Yoshi went straight to his room. His mattress and blankets stood in the middle of the floor, surrounded by only a couple of suitcases. He could hear Sato crying, and he leaned his head toward her room, as if he could stare through his closet at her. He couldn't, of course. Once his eyes adjusted to the dark, all he could see was a bunch of empty hangers and a couple old shirts that weren't worth selling or packing.

Then his eyes drifted down to the shadowy hardwood floor. His high school graduation cap rotted in front of his closet. The tassel was splayed out like a dead man's broken hand. When he earned that cap, he thought it would remind him how bad times always come to an end. The thing he didn't realize when he graduated was this: it's not just bad times that come to an end; it's *everything*. He no longer liked the reminder. At this point, he almost missed Jackson High. If he could undo these past few months, he would gladly choose to be a student there forever.

Then his parents started talking, and he tiptoed to the doorway so he could eavesdrop.

When Father spoke, Yoshi could only make out a few words: "…way…like that."

"It can't be, Tanaka," Mom said.

"…more concerned…they would…if we do *not* go."

"No, Tanaka. You know they would never do that here."

"…Jews…never expect…in Germany they…"

Yoshi's eyes widened. He didn't know exactly what the Nazis were doing to the Jews, but he knew a lot of people were being sent away to ghettos. And several months ago, Ricardo mentioned that some Jews who had escaped would be executed.

"It can't happen in America," Mom said.

"Pearl Harbor…want revenge…kill us all."

Yoshi's heart pounded.

"You know they won't do that, Tanaka. You know—"

"I know *nothing*," Father exclaimed. "I am afraid."

Hearing this, Yoshi gasped. Father wasn't afraid of *anything*. All at once, his compliance started making sense. He was scared about what would happen to his family if he disobeyed. Stubbornness was a luxury unfit for dangerous times.

In shock, Yoshi fell back onto his mattress. He lay there, staring into the distant, shadowy ceiling. If he slept at all that night, he didn't realize it. From what he could tell, his thoughts never stopped for an instant. What if Father's fears came true? What if his whole family was killed? If not, what then? What would a "relocation center" be? How long would his family stay there? A year? Ten years? Until the war ended? How long would that take? What if America lost? He asked himself these questions until the birds started chirping outside. The time of departure was creeping forward like a monster, and as much as he hated admitting it, he knew he couldn't escape this situation. He had no power. He had no hope. All he had were two suitcases full of necessities and exactly $7.94 in cash.

He rolled off his mattress and peeked out the window. In the distance, golden light heralded the imminent sunrise. Before long, he would have to go downstairs and share one last morning at home with his family. After that, his life would change forever.

Part Two:

INFAMOUS DAYS

CHAPTER SEVEN

THE STING OF RED NUMBERS

What was the difference between departing and disappearing? As Yoshi stood with his family in the empty living room, suitcases in hand, about to step outside, this was the question that ran through his mind. There would be no more dinners at Ricky's. No more trips to the movies with Sato. No more shifts at the grocery store. Everything he knew would soon be gone.

Father checked his watch again. He crossed his arms, tapped his bicep, and stared back out the window. Ten minutes ago, he called the cab that would take them to their meeting place. Any second, it would arrive.

Yoshi listened to the faucet's running water in the kitchen, along with the clinks and scrapes of dishes being cleaned.

"Why is Mom doing the dishes?" he asked.

Father let out an angry sigh.

"They have taken all other power from her," he answered.

Yoshi didn't understand what this meant. He decided not to ask.

The ticking of Father's watch filled the room. Every second sounded like a taunt.

"Do you really think they'll kill us?" Sato blurted out.

Father glanced down at her. His ever-present scowl became a little more exaggerated. Then, with his eyes glued to the street, he replied:

"I never said this to you."

Sato gulped. "But you said—"

"I never said this to *you*."

"I overheard you last night," Sato admitted. She seemed too scared about the prospect of dying to worry about starting an argument.

"Do you think…" Sato prodded. "Do you think we should not go?"

With a grunt, Father answered, "I do what my country asks of me."

"Sato-chan," Grandma said with a smile. "We all are

together. This is all we need."

"You're not scared at all, are you?" Sato asked her.

Yoshi remembered his recent conversation with Grandma. He could practically hear her answer: *Shikata ga nai*—it cannot be helped.

"Scared?" Grandma said. "No, no. Why would I feel this?"

"Because we don't know where we're going," Sato said. "And we don't know when we'll be back. Or *if* we'll be back."

Grandma smiled. "Sato-chan, is my memory no good, or did you say to me that you no longer are liking school?"

Sato nodded.

"And how come this is?" Grandma said.

Sato hung her head. "Because of the way they look at me," she mumbled.

"Wherever we are going, everyone will understand," Grandma said. "Everyone around you will know of these feelings. Did you not tell me you wish for people who understand these things? Is this not what you had a wish for?"

Sato's lips tightened, forming something between a grin and a frown.

"In some way," Grandma continued, "you get this wish now. Remember, Sato-chan, you cannot always choose what place life will send you, but you can always choose what to see when you get there."

A cupboard in the kitchen creaked open, and the dishes clanked as Mom stacked them. Right as she stepped out of the kitchen, the cab pulled up to the curb. The Yamaguchis looked at the living room one final time. With all the furniture gone, it seemed hauntingly empty: a brick fireplace, blank walls, a few spare boxes, and nothing else. Yoshi didn't want to be the person who opened the door. Everyone else seemed to be waiting too.

Then Father stepped out first. Everyone else followed, and in a few seconds, home was gone.

They were instructed to meet at a Catholic church fifteen miles south of their house. When the Yamaguchis' cab arrived at the spot, thirty people were already lined up on a lawn of dying grass, waiting to get on one of the three Greyhound buses parked along the front curb.

"I thought we were getting here early," Sato said.

Mom stared at the line. "Looks like others had the same idea."

When Yoshi learned they would be meeting at a

church, he imagined a cathedral overrun by guards, like a gothic castle preparing for battle. An event so consequential to his life and his country seemed like it should be accompanied by some sort of wartime spectacle. But no sign of a major military operation could be found. This building was not some sprawling, isolated sanctuary, but a converted one-story house, painted solid white and adorned with a handful of crosses.

That said, there *were* a couple bayoneted guards standing near the stained-glass double doors. And on the front of their white helmets, there were two letters: MP.

"What does 'MP' mean?" Yoshi whispered, sensing it stood for something very serious. He was right. He shivered when his father answered:

"Military Police."

Seeing those guys made Yoshi's heart race, and he almost screamed when another uniformed man scurried towards them. This MP wore the same thick, olive green, double-breasted pea coat as the guards by the church doors, but he carried a clipboard instead of a rifle, and he was at least four inches shorter than his armed companions.

"Last name?" the MP asked Yoshi's family.

"Yamaguchi," Father answered.

"Is that spelled Y-A or Y-O?" His eyes scanned the top sheet. "Oh, Yamaguchi, I see. Wait right here."

As soon as the short MP left, Yoshi glanced back at the guards by the door. Thankfully, they didn't appear to be studying his every move. If anything, they looked a little bored. Behind their blank expressions, they didn't seem to be paying much attention, and once in a while, they fidgeted to keep themselves from slouching. One of them even nibbled on a bagel.

A little relieved, Yoshi took a deep breath, and his eyes started scanning the crowd. He realized he was searching for Joey. Oddly, that JACL guy was nowhere to be found. Yoshi sighed. Even if Father wouldn't let the two of them be friends, Yoshi yearned to spot a familiar face. At least, he wanted to find someone who understood his pain. In thinking about it, he didn't want anybody else to see him lined up like a prisoner, and he prayed that Sarah or Freddy or even Susie Wong wouldn't stumble past this place.

The short MP came back with a handful of light brown tags. "Every family has been given a number," he said, looking through the five-inch slivers of paper. "This will be your means of identification once you get to camp."

"Means of identification," Father grumbled under his

breath. "They even take my name."

With his eyes focused on the tags, the MP didn't seem to notice Father's comment.

"Sato?" the MP asked, reading from the first tag in his hand.

Sato nodded. The guard placed a light brown tag on each of her bags, then strung an identical tag around her neck.

"Yoshi?"

After the little piece of paper was hung around his collar, Yoshi examined it. Below the handwritten name, a vertical line divided the badge in two. On the right side, the date was scribbled in cursive. On the left side, "3845" glowed in big red numbers, with the words "Family No." typed in black ink beside it. Yoshi felt a knot in his gut. Why did the tag bother him so much? It was just a piece of paper—weightless, worthless, and easy to ignore. But the stupid thing made him feel unwanted and powerless, like a stained jacket hanging from a clearance rack.

"If anyone needs to use the facilities, make sure to do so now," the MP said, once the whole family had tags tied around their luggage and their necks. "The trip will take six or seven hours, and there will be no stops. Understood?"

As the MP started walking away, Father called off to him:

"I am a veteran of the United States army. This is how you treat me."

The MP glanced back over his shoulder, but he didn't respond. He just kept on walking.

Sato played with the tag around her neck.

"It's like an ugly necklace," she laughed.

Father jerked his head down. The corners of his jaw bulged as he clenched his teeth. Sato's laugh retreated into an uncomfortable smile, but Father didn't stop staring.

"They put collars on us like dogs, and you make a joke of it," he said.

"Sorry."

"I do not want you to be sorry. I want you to be angry."

Sato's mouth hung open. Yoshi nervously bit his lip. They all stayed silent until, at last, the line started to move.

Gasoline fumes filled Yoshi's nostrils as he neared the vehicle, but when he climbed the steep steps into the bus, that smell of exhaust became replaced with a vague hint of urine in the musty air. Father held Grandma's arm and eased her into her seat. Yoshi helped Mom load their luggage into the overhead compartment, but after cramming everyone else's stuff onto the shelf, there was no room left for his own bags. He headed down the aisle in search of an opening. Every inch of space was taken.

About three quarters of the way back, he slouched in defeat, dropping his suitcases down on the aisle. Nothing ever worked out. Even finding a place for the few things he had left was a big, lousy headache.

"Here, you can take my spot," someone said.

Yoshi's eyes widened. A girl was talking to him. A real girl, about his age. Her face was round, with a tiny dimple on the left side of her mouth. She was a couple inches shorter than him, and she had straight black hair hanging down to her shoulders, with a few stray strands frizzing off to the side. What stood out more than anything, though, was her confidence. Her voice didn't waver the way Yoshi's did. She kept her chin up, and she looked him in the eye when she spoke. And yes, those dark brown eyes…there was a melancholy calmness in them. Why wasn't she terrified like him?

Yoshi's muscled tensed. As the girl tugged her duffel bags out of the overhead compartment, Yoshi felt his mouth twitch, fumbling for words:

"Oh gosh, thank you. Just…thank you a whole bunch, but no, there's no way I could take—"

"It's fine. I've got room." She nodded toward a couple of empty seats a few rows down. "There's no one sitting next to me."

Puzzled, Yoshi stared at the vacancy as he tossed his suitcases onto the shelf. "You're here all by yourself?"

She nodded, and Yoshi could tell there was a story behind her answer. He wanted to know all about her, why she travelled alone, and how she could stay so composed in the midst of this terrifying uncertainty. For a shameful second, he considered asking if he could sit next to her, even though he knew he should go back to his family.

"See you around," she said, when Yoshi didn't leave.

He gave her a thumbs up. As soon as he realized it, he dropped his hand and blushed. With a roar of the engine, the bus began to move, and he wobbled as he hurried back to his family. He slouched into the cracked leather seat, wondering if he would ever again run into that amazing girl. At first, he didn't understand his captivation. He wanted to learn her story, but his interest was more than simple curiosity. In a way, she was his opposite, seeming independent and confident while he felt vulnerable and shy. But aside from their differences, something about her connected with him. Without knowing anything about her, he struggled to pinpoint what he had in common with this mysterious girl who traveled by herself. Then he realized: she looked as lonely as he felt.

Lost in thought, he forgot to catch one last glimpse of his neighborhood from the highway. When he remembered to look, it was too late. Only the outskirts of town passed by him, and other than some street lamps and a Texaco sign, the urban landscape faded into desert farmland. Trying not to knee the seat in front of him, he stretched out as much as he could and hoped to make up for last night's lack of sleep. He didn't have much luck. Questions flooded through his head about Joey, the war, the girl, and above all, what awaited him at the end of the day. He still had no sense of what a "relocation center" would look like, and he couldn't decide what unnerved him more: not knowing at all, or knowing he would soon have an answer.

CHAPTER EIGHT

THE DUST STORM

Nowhere.

When Yoshi stepped off the bus, standing at the base of a giant square of barbed wire fence, that's where he felt like he was. He was nowhere. Outside the fence, there were miles of tan, flat earth, speckled with prickly desert shrubs. In front of him, this place looked more like the sorry remains of an ancient desert city than a project in development by the world's most powerful military. There were *tons* of wooden buildings—many of them only halfway built. Around these unfinished structures, patches of buffelgrass appeared to be one spark away from erupting into flames. Yoshi searched for something positive about this place. Miles in the distance, he saw a range of purple, snow-capped mountains, which he sup-

posed was a pretty sight. And he wouldn't run into Gus
Needaburger here, which was certainly worth something.

And the girl on the bus… *she* was here. Somewhere.
Yoshi couldn't find her. He had fallen asleep in the last
hour of the trip, and when he woke up to the sight of everyone disembarking, she was already gone. She must have
stepped off the bus the second it arrived. And she must
have known where she was going, because she wasn't in
the crowd of families who stood with their luggage, looking around, waiting for some sort of instruction.

Yoshi glanced up at his father. If anyone could figure
out where they were supposed to go, it was him. But Father wasn't paying attention to the barracks in front of
him. His eyes were focused on a tall wooden structure on
the other side of the barbed wire fence—a little windowed
box held up by crisscrossed support beams.

It was a guard tower.

"It's nice they want to keep us safe," Yoshi said.

Father glared at him.

"Their guns face *us*."

It was true: the armed guard inside the tower was examining the arrivals. Yoshi's eyes widened. His heart
pounded.

"Do you think they'll…?" He couldn't say "kill us,"

but his silence finished the question. Before Father could answer, two MPs approached, squabbling with each other:

"Because they're *early*, Gary!" one of them said. "The others won't be here for another two hours!"

The other guy shrugged. "What do you want me to do about it?"

"Is admin even *ready* for them yet? We barely have dinner under control!"

"What do you want me to do about it?" the other guy kept repeating. "What do you want me to do about it?"

The two MPs stormed off to a security booth that was made of rocks.

Finally, Father answered Yoshi's question:

"They will not kill us. This would need competence."

His voice conveyed an anger that was bitter—even profound—but it no longer had that tinge of terror. He seemed to be having a realization: this "relocation center" wasn't a grand scheme to murder everyone, but a last minute, ill-prepared, under-funded mess.

The breeze picked up a bit, and the dusty air caused a tickle in Yoshi's nostrils. The tag around his collar fluttered in the breeze. The American flag started flapping from the pole ten feet in front of him, its snap hooks clanking against the aluminum. Outside the barbed wire fence, an automobile chugged along the highway. Aside from the jangling flag and the engine's fading rumble, only the wind's high-pitched howl filled the air.

Grandma started coughing.

Mom put a hand on her back. "We need to get you inside, Mama."

"No, no." Grandma smiled and cleared her throat. "The dust won't blow me over."

"Attention everyone!" The flustered MP finally returned. "Administration is ready to process you. You will be checking in at the Block 8 recreation hall. That's Block 8, Building 15. Take the South Firebreak to get there. Block 8 will be the second block you pass, and Building 15 will be at the far end of it."

All around, people mumbled in confusion. Rolling his eyes, the MP led the group parallel to the highway until they reached a dirt pathway—a *massive* one. Yoshi's mouth hung open. Over two hundred feet wide, this route appeared impossibly long, and dust blew up from it like rising steam from an endless vat of burning coals.

With a little hesitance, everybody followed the MP down the firebreak. Along the right side of the path, frames of buildings still in development jutted into the distance like a skeletal forest. Along the left side, rows of completed barracks lined the way as far as Yoshi could see. Those finished ones also looked pretty meager. Each building was one hundred feet long, and tall tin tubes jutted from the tops of the long gable roofs. Each of the barracks was propped a couple feet off the ground by wooden supports that were stuck in cement cubes—what must have been the cheapest and quickest foundation available. Up close, the buildings' tarpaper walls looked rough like an elephant's skin, because the dirty wind had already left some permanent damage on the measly structures.

The MP stopped. He pointed at one of the buildings, and everyone formed a line outside the door. The Yamaguchis were close to the front, and Yoshi caught a glimpse inside. There was a white man in a suit sitting behind a cluttered table, looking down at a clipboard. He must have been some sort of administrator. When the Yamaguchis reached the front of the line, they stepped inside and approached the man.

"Number?" the guy said.

"Yamagu—," Father began. Once the question registered, he scowled and held up his tag.

The administrator leaned forward and squinted at it. He scanned the sheet, mumbling to himself, "3845,

3845." His head popped back up. "Yamaguchi?"

Closing his eyes, Father nodded.

"Okay, looks like you'll be in 9-8-1," he said, handing Father a key. "That's Block 9, Building 8, Apartment 1." He pointed to the spot on a map.

Seeing an aerial drawing of this place was strange. Yoshi's new world could be reduced to *this*, an elaborate pencil sketch on a grid. Each block had fourteen barracks, a latrine, a mess hall, and one of these "recreation centers." There were four firebreaks, the North, South, East, and West, intersecting in a way that resembled a number sign. These giant paths connected the thirty-six blocks, most of which were clumped together in groups of four.

"In an hour or so, we should have some blankets here for you to pick up, courtesy of the army surplus," the man continued. "You'll find some bales of hay outside the barracks for you to fill your mattresses with. Please mop at least once a day, as the barracks don't fare well in this climate. For that reason, we also ask that you keep your belongings at least six inches off the floor. We don't have the mess halls finished yet, but we'll have a table outside this building serving dinner at 5:30 p.m. In the meantime, proceed to Block 1 for your immunizations. Next!"

"I hate shots," Sato grumbled as they headed back

outside. "Do you think we have to get them?"

"Yes," Mom insisted. "Just think how quickly a disease could spread here. But we should drop our bags off first."

They were given a corner barrack, right on the intersection between the South and East Firebreaks. A wooden sign on the right side of the barrack's face told them this was the spot: BLK 9. BLDG. 8, with a little addition below that said APT 1. Yoshi took a deep breath before stepping inside. Maybe for a month, maybe for a year, or maybe for the rest of his life, this place would be his home.

All along, that concept had been hard to grasp, but when he entered the apartment, it became ever harder. This room didn't look like a home at all. There was no furniture except for eight springy cots, four on each side of the room, spaced about three feet apart from one another. Without any blankets, the rusty bed frames were exposed, and the only thing that covered each cot was the lump of an empty mattress sack. Above him, there was no ceiling, so he could see the cluster of diagonal beams holding up the gable roof. Below him, a thin layer of dirt had blown up through the holes in the floorboards and spread across the entire room. The walls were made with planks of oaken brown, all exactly the same color, aside from the blotches of dark knots in the wood. And twenty feet in front of him, a huge white cloth hung from the ceiling. From the secure ties on the top and bottom, this hanging was clearly permanent—the four apartments within each barrack were separated by cloth partitions instead of real walls.

"Where do we set our bags?" Sato asked, mouth agape. "If we're not supposed to keep our stuff six inches off the floor—"

Father dropped his suitcases on the dirty floorboards and stomped outside.

With a little reluctance, the rest of the family followed Father's example. They set down their bags and followed him to the second building of Block 1, where people stood in line, waiting to get immunized. One by one, with surprising quickness, the Yamaguchis inched closer to the doorway.

Sato scowled. "I hope these people are good at giving shots."

Yoshi would never, ever admit this to anyone, but he was nervous too. He hated needles as much as his sister, but he didn't want to seem weak. While he tried his very best to be expressionless, an anxious tingle in his belly grew worse with every step forward.

"I'm going first," Sato said. "I want to get this over with."

She stepped into the room, approaching three Japanese nurses. One of them checked off names on a clipboard. The second nurse, with an alcohol cloth in hand, pulled up Sato's sleeve and wiped her arm. The third nurse held up the needle.

"What are we getting these for?" Sato griped. "Ow!"

"Typhoid," one of the nurses answered, removing the needle. "Come back in a week for your second one."

"There's *two*?"

"There's three. Next!"

Three?! Yoshi gulped. He stepped inside. This so-called "clinic" looked just like his family's apartment—it didn't seem like a medical facility at all.

The nurse rolled up his sleeve.

"You're tense," she said.

Heart racing, Yoshi looked around to make sure the girl on the bus wasn't around. The last thing he wanted was for her to think he was a baby. Come to think of it, he didn't want *anyone* to think he was a baby.

"Loosen up," the nurse instructed, gently shaking his arm.

Yoshi cleared his throat and said as deeply as he could, "I'm tense from doing lots of paperwork." This seemed like a pretty adult thing to say.

The nurse jabbed the needle in. Yoshi let out a tiny squeal, which he tried to conceal behind a fake cough. Clenching his teeth, he climbed down the steps and stood next to Sato, who frowned and rubbed her arm.

Inside the facility, Mom and Father had to hold Grandma up. With all this walking and standing, she was clearly getting exhausted.

After their shots, Father helped her sit down on the steps. "They put out no chairs," he grumbled. "She needs rest. She cannot make it back."

Grandma's mouth hung open, and her lips wavered like she wanted to say something. Only a groan came out.

As the Yamaguchis waited for Grandma to regain her strength, the wind kept growing stronger. The air kept getting colder. Before too long, the sun started setting, and dust lingered in the sky. What started as low-hanging dust clouds turned into an all-encompassing fog of dirt. Soon, everything around him was filtered through an amber hue, as if he were an ant at the bottom of an empty root beer bottle.

"We need to get back," Mom shouted over the wind.

She put a hand on Grandma's arm. "Will you be okay, Mama?"

"Oh," Grandma groaned. "The dust won't blow me over."

She tried to laugh, but Yoshi could tell she was getting worn out. The dirt blew against their faces as they walked back, and Grandma didn't have the strength to hold up a hand to cover her eyes.

When they finally reached the intersection of the great paths, they stared across the two-hundred-foot width of the East Firebreak. Through the dusty haze, Yoshi could see the faint outline of his family's barrack. He groaned as he stepped forward. The distance might as well have been ten miles. Not only was he worried about Grandma, but he realized he felt pretty awful himself. He had a churn in his belly, like there was a toxic bubble growing and growing and trying to break out of him. Fighting against the wind took most of his strength, but the little energy he had left was spent holding down his vomit.

"I don't feel good," he said.

Sato scrunched her face like she smelled something horrible. "Me neither. I think it was the shots."

Father's eyes widened, and he put a hand over his belly.

"I think you might be right," Mom said to Sato, before looking over at Grandma. "How's *your* stomach, Mama?"

Grandma slouched a little more. She looked like she was falling asleep, and she nearly tumbled over. She said nothing, and the answer was clear: she was not okay.

CHAPTER NINE

CARRY ON

The mess hall bells rang for supper. After a month of living here, Yoshi had engrained the camp's schedule into his mind: breakfast at 7, lunch at noon, dinner at 5:30, and a block-wide headcount every night at 9. He had already grown so accustomed to this routine that he couldn't imagine his life being any different. He almost wondered if he had dreamed all that stuff about Sarah Hassenger and Gus Needaburger and Pippy the Pirate and Ricky's Bistro. Then one day, as proof of their old life, the Yamaguchis received a letter from Ricardo:

Dear Yamaguchis,

How truly terrible it is that this has happened. It is my hope that you are okay at this place. You deserve a place that is okay. I miss you at my restaurant. I think of you

*every time I use my spatula. All my best to Mr. and Mrs.,
to Grandma, to Yoshi and Sato.*

Sincerely,

Ricardo

Yoshi liked knowing that *somebody* was thinking about him. But in a way, he was thankful that he didn't have a bunch of friends back home, because there weren't too many people he was missing. Sato, on the other hand, must have felt really lousy. She had stopped referring to her endless list of friends, as if she didn't want to think of all the people she had lost.

And that wasn't all. On one of the many nights that Yoshi couldn't get to sleep, he heard his sister quietly crying to herself. He climbed out of his cot and tiptoed over to her.

"Sato?" he whispered. "Are you okay?"

She wiped her nose and looked up at him.

"I miss Rutherford," she sobbed.

Yoshi wanted to be a good big brother, but he couldn't think of anything to say. He just climbed back into bed, resenting all the things he didn't like about this place. He didn't like that the apartment had no closets. He didn't like walking all the way to the block's latrine whenever he had to go to the bathroom. He didn't like the lack of privacy. He didn't like the guard towers or the barbed wire fence or the icky food at the mess hall.

He especially didn't like the tedious boredom. Between meals, his days consisted of ambling along the firebreaks and napping in the afternoons. And he had daydreams, lots of daydreams, mostly about the girl on the bus. He still hadn't run into her again, and at this rate, he never would. Over the last few days, almost 4,000 new people had arrived, more than doubling the camp's population. If he couldn't find her with only a few thousand people living here, then he *really* wouldn't be able to find her now.

Maybe he would run into her if he got a job. Because of all the new arrivals, businesses and services started popping up around camp, and the girl on the bus would surely visit one of them at some point. Unfortunately, Yoshi didn't feel like he had the skills to work at the camp's barbershop or beauty parlor, let alone the bank, the post office, the library, or the camp newspaper. He definitely wasn't fit to be a doctor or a nurse. And if he was a mess hall cook, he'd probably be too busy sweating in the kitchen to go out and meet anybody—which, after all, was the whole point. His experience at the grocery store might have qualified him for a job at the canteen, but working at

a shop for someone other than his father seemed, somehow, like a betrayal.

And Father wasn't about to get a job. The pay was
measly, and working wasn't necessary. Many people took
jobs for a sense of pride, or to contribute to the war effort
in some small way, or just to have something to do, but
these reasons didn't make sense to Father. In his view, a
man should only work for one reason: to support himself
and his family. The Yamaguchis had money in the bank
from selling their belongings, and they didn't have big
expenses like rent or food. Why, then, would he work for
a fraction of what he was worth? Not to mention, those
businesses were collaborations between the internees and
the camp's administration, and Father wanted nothing to
do with the guys who oversaw this whole ordeal.

Instead, Father spent a good amount of his time sprucing up the apartment. He nailed soup can lids over the
holes in the floor to keep the dirt from blowing into the
room, and he built little nightstands for each of the cots
with some scrap lumber he had found lying around. But
most of Father's time was spent at the hospital. Every
day, he and Mom walked Grandma there, hoping to finally get her the help she needed. Despite its recent move
and expansion, the hospital remained under-equipped and

understaffed. Only three doctors, four registered nurses, and six student nurses were available for the entire camp, and the beds lacked life support, oxygen, or any form of hydration system. Yoshi tried his hardest not to worry, but Grandma's eyes looked pink and grimy, her stomach was queasy, her bones ached, and her head throbbed. Many people felt unsettled by the immunizations, but a week had passed since their final injections, and Grandma still showed no signs of improvement. Yoshi knew the shots couldn't be the problem. Something else was going on with her—something bad.

And so, when the mess hall bells rang for supper on April 28th, 1942, Grandma was in the middle of a doctor's visit. Yoshi wanted to stay behind with his family, but at Father's insistence, he and Sato headed back to their block. They breathed in the crisp spring air and kicked up the dirt as they dragged their feet.

When they reached the Block 9 mess hall, Yoshi groaned at how long the line was. Typically, they showed up early and got a spot up front. At this distance, he couldn't smell the food, so he felt like he was standing in line for someone's apartment. After all, the mess halls looked like all the other barracks, with those tin tubes sticking out of the gable roof, those ten square windows lining each of the long walls, and those cement-based support planks elevating the building a couple of feet off the ground. The only noticeable difference was the width, since the mess halls were about twice as wide as the residential barracks.

Yoshi's belly rumbled.

"It better not be mutton again tonight," he said to Sato.

"It's hot dogs," the guy in front of them said. A gray cap sat on his head, and when he turned around, he smiled a mouthful of crooked teeth. "Oh, hey there!"

It was Joey from the Japanese American Citizens League.

Yoshi gasped. He gave a little smile and a timid wave.

Sato cocked her head to the side. "You guys know each other?"

"I used to come into Yamaguchi Grocery!" Joey shook his head and laughed. "Boy, that always ended lousy."

The girl beside Joey looked back to see who he was talking to.

As soon as Yoshi saw her face, he froze. He lost his breath. He clenched his teeth. This was her. The girl from the bus. And she was with *Joey*. Yoshi almost fainted. He hoped the two of them weren't dating, because he liked Joey, and he didn't want his own jealousy to get in the way of a potential friendship.

"Golly, hi!" Yoshi blurted out before he could think about what to say. "It's me, Yoshi! Remember? From the bus?"

She nodded, but Joey replied instead:

"Nice to finally meet ya! Every time I went to the store, you were being real quiet all by yourself."

Yoshi tensed up. He faked a laugh and rubbed the back of his neck. "Yeah, because lots of security and doing business and focusing and things."

Words had left his mouth. He just wasn't quite sure what they were.

It didn't seem to matter. Joey grinned and nodded.

Up front, the line started moving forward.

Yoshi rushed to change the subject. "Did you guys just move to this block?"

Living near the two of them would be both exciting and terrifying.

"Nah." Joey laughed. "We're only here for the food. When I heard this block was serving hot dogs tonight, I said, 'Well gosh, I know where *I'm* having dinner.' It's slop suey night in our block. That's what we call that pasta stuff, those noodles in that runny sauce. It's real bad. But hey, at least things have gotten better since all the people got here. Before everyone showed up, I was living in a tent and eating beans from a can."

Yoshi cocked his head to the side.

"Oh, you must think I'm crazy." Joey chuckled before he started to explain, "Me and some of the guys from the JACL showed up early to help the military build this place. We figured it would be smart to get on the camp's good side. And hey, it seems to be working. How do you think we found out about the hot dogs? We were meeting with some of the camp's staff and this guy from admin let us know."

So *that's* why Joey wasn't at the church on the day of the evacuation. Some guys from the JACL had arrived early to help the government build the camp. If Father ever learned this fact, he would probably punch a hole in a wall.

Yoshi forced a smile. "I didn't know the JACL helped out."

"Yep!" Joey gave a proud smile. "Well, it wasn't exactly a JACL thing, but a lot of the guys that came out early are with the group. We're all over in Block 2 now, so it's kind of a boy's club over there. Just the guys and Emi! Right, sis?" He nudged the girl's arm.

Yoshi turned wide-eyed. *She's Joey's sister?!*

"I had to save her a bed since she met me here later," Joey explained. "She was lucky. As soon as the bus got here, I showed her all around—helped her skip the lines and stuff!"

"Are you with the JACL too?" Yoshi asked Emi, hoping she would talk to him.

"An ally," she said, giving half a shrug.

Once they reached the steps of the mess hall, they climbed up, stepped inside, and washed their hands in the sink by the door. Behind a table, three Japanese men, all wearing little chef's caps and white, button-up shirts, dished a hot dog onto every passing plate. Yoshi scanned the wooden picnic tables, hoping to find enough room for Joey and Emi to sit with them.

"I found a spot!" Sato hurried to a table in the back.

When Yoshi turned around, Emi was already gone. With a big, disappointed sigh, he slouched.

Joey tossed his plate onto the counter, holding up the hot dog in his hand and taking a big bite.

"Delicious," he said through a full mouth, before looking around for his sister. His head shot back and forth, and then he stared at the door. With his free hand, he patted Yoshi on the shoulder. "I guess we're heading back. But hey, if you're ever interested in joining us at the JACL,

I'm sure there's plenty of jobs you'd be great for. We're always looking for some new friends, and we get some pretty nice perks and stuff. Just stop by Mr. Hamasaki's office in Block 2. It's Building One, Apartment One. See ya!"

Yoshi smiled and nodded. Before he could say anything, Joey ran off. With a little smile on his face, Yoshi met Sato in the back of the mess hall. He sat down across from her, and they spread out as much as they could to save seats for their family.

Sato raised an eyebrow and suppressed a little grin.

"What?" Yoshi blushed.

"Nothing."

"No, what?"

"*Nothing*. You just seemed really happy to meet her." She sat up straight, waving at the front of the building, and Yoshi turned to look. Mom and Father approached, each carrying a plate.

"Grandma's not up for dinner?" Sato asked.

Father set a plate with two hot dogs on the table, and then he squeezed in beside Yoshi.

"Grandma needs rest," Mom said. "We'll bring dinner back to her."

"At the hospital?" Yoshi asked.

Mom shook her head. "They still don't have room to keep her. She has to stay with us in the apartment for now."

Father scowled and poked at one of the hot dogs with his chopsticks.

"Garbage," he muttered.

Mom took a bite and slowly chewed, keeping her eyes down on the table. Even during the evacuation, she had never seemed so melancholy.

"Is Grandma...?" Sato started to ask.

"They think she has pneumonia," Mom said.

"Isn't that just like the flu?" Yoshi asked.

"It can be deadly." Mom pursed her lips and took a deep sigh.

Deadly. The word echoed in Yoshi's mind.

For the rest of the dinner hour, everyone stayed quiet.

Back at their apartment, Grandma only ate a couple of bites. She thanked them for bringing back the meal, and she pretended like this fatty, unfamiliar food settled in her stomach without a problem. It didn't, of course. The food never agreed with her.

Later that night, Yoshi woke up to the sound of her groaning. Mom and Sato got out of bed so they could escort her, through the freezing wind, to the women's latrine in the center of the block. As they left the apartment, the floorboards creaked beneath their feet, and Grandma whispered an apology for being such an inconvenience. Every night, this same thing happened, and every night, Yoshi just stared into the blackness above him, focusing on the itchy straw mattress to distract from his anxiety.

At least he knew what to expect. Grandma would return, thank Mom and Sato, and try to silence her whimpers of pain. Then, in the morning, the mess hall bells would ring again for breakfast.

CHAPTER TEN

A PLACE THEY CALL
MANZANAR

Again, she groaned. Grandma needed help walking to the women's latrine—at this point, she didn't even need to say anything. Yoshi and Sato rushed to help her up. Their ears had been against the double doors, trying to overhear Mom and Father's argument outside. They didn't make out much, but they knew what the fight was about: Mom wanted to keep trying the hospital, and Father thought those trips were pointless.

As Yoshi opened the doors, the sunlight stung his eyes. But he could tell that Mom and Father were staring up at Grandma.

"The wind is a bit strong right now," Mom said to her. "Do you need to go this moment, or should you wait a few minutes?"

"Right now, I think, is needed." Grandma put a hand over her stomach. "The dust won't blow me over."

"You keep saying that," Sato said through a forced chuckle. In their usual way, Mom supported one of Grandma's arms and Sato held the other as they helped her hobble down the steps and toward the center of the block.

Yoshi couldn't imagine how Grandma must be feeling. Not only did she ache from constant sickness, but she suffered the indignities of camp as an elder. After she lived a life of compassion and kindness, the world repaid her with humiliation. Needing help from her daughter and granddaughter to relieve herself...sitting in a latrine without any stalls, exposed for everyone to see...how could her life end like *that*?

When Yoshi finally gathered the strength, he stepped outside and approached his father. He couldn't believe he was asking this question, but somehow, the words left his mouth:

"Is Grandma going to die?"

The wind softly rumbled. Father took a long, deep inhale.

"You can tell me the truth," Yoshi added. "I'm not a

kid anymore."

"Your country does not care for you." Father didn't look down at Yoshi. "Here is your truth."

"Maybe…if we take her to the doctor again…"

Father shook his head. "They cannot keep her there. The long walks make her worse."

Yoshi needed to find a reason to be hopeful. He *needed* to. He heard that just a couple days ago, on June 1st, a new government agency called the War Relocation Authority took control of all ten internment camps. Before then, they were run by a temporary agency under the War Department called the Wartime Civil Control Administration. Maybe this new agency would improve things. They must have been serious about making changes, because they even renamed this place. It was no longer called the Owens Valley Relocation Center. Now it was called Manzanar.

"Those new people, that agency thing," Yoshi said. "The WRA. Maybe they'll make some real good changes to the hospital."

"You are a fool," Father said.

"Maybe the doctors don't understand how bad she is," Yoshi said. "If she keeps going, then they'll see that—"

"Ten thousand people locked here. Many sick. An

outbreak of measles and dysentery. They have no reason to care most for her." Shaking his head, Father headed back into the apartment.

Yoshi hated this feeling of helplessness. He wished he could do something to get on the camp's good side, to make the administration care, to make everyone realize how special Grandma was, how horrible the world would be without her...

We're always looking for some new friends, Joey had told him, *and we get some pretty nice perks and stuff.*

Of course. He could join the Japanese American Citizens League! If he got on the camp's good side, then maybe *somebody* could do *something*.

He rushed back inside. "What if we gave them a reason to care?"

Father took a seat on his cot and raised his chin.

"I know what you're going to say," Yoshi said. "But...I think I might have a real swell idea. A real swell idea. I think it could be really good."

Father raised an eyebrow.

Knowing his idea was about to be rejected, Yoshi tried finding the courage to blurt it out. "I met this guy..." He didn't want to mention Joey's name, because Father would stop listening. "He's a real swell guy, I think. Real swell. And he told me about this work he does, and maybe I could do that work too, and maybe it would make this place help her."

Yoshi waited for a response.

"Does this involve the black market?" Father asked.

"Nothing like that." Yoshi nervously laughed. "It's not illegal. It's…the JACL."

The moment Father heard the name of the group, he shot up. His nostrils flared.

"Just think about it!" Yoshi pleaded.

"No."

"Why not?!"

"They are backstabbers."

"Not *all* of them!"

"They are backstabbers," Father repeated.

Yoshi felt an eruption inside himself. "You don't know anything about it!"

"They do not take Issei. They do not like—"

"I won't sit around and watch Grandma die!"

"Better to be dead than a *traitor's* ancestor."

The doors creaked open. Mom, Grandma, and Sato stood at the top of the steps. Their mouths hung open.

Father charged at the open doorway. With every thundering stomp, the leftover dirt on the floorboards leapt into the air. Sato stepped behind Grandma to give him passage down the stairs, and they all watched him turn onto the road.

When he was out of sight, Mom rushed inside. "Yoshi, what happened?"

"He called me a traitor! Did you hear that? He called me a traitor!"

"Yoshi," Mom said, putting a hand on his shoulder. "Just tell us what happened."

"I wanted to help! That's it! I just wanted to help, and he called me a traitor!" Yoshi wiped his eyes with the back of his hand.

Mom squeezed Yoshi's shoulder. "You know he didn't mean it. That was just his temper talking."

"What did you say to make him so mad?" Sato asked.

"Nothing! I just told him I wanted to work for the JACL."

Sato rolled her eyes. "Is this about that girl?"

"Hey!"

"Sato, please," Mom said.

"*What?*" Sato snapped.

"They get benefits," Yoshi explained. "The camp likes them. But now he thinks I'm a traitor, and Sato's making fun of me!" He blushed at how immature he sounded.

"No I'm not!" Sato exclaimed.

"Apologize to Yoshi, Sato," Mom said.

"For what?!"

"You hurt his feelings."

"I was just being honest."

"No, you're being rude."

Sato rolled her eyes. "That doesn't make it any less true."

"Please apologize," Mom said.

"No. I didn't do anything wrong."

"Please, just apologize."

"No!"

"Fine!" Mom shouted. "Fine, you two! Do whatever you like! You think this is easy on me? I hate this as much as the rest of you, but at least I'm trying!" She closed her eyes and took a deep breath. "Forget it." Her words lingered in the air as she left the apartment.

"Mom, wait," Sato said, following her out. "Mom, I'm sorry."

With solemn eyes, Grandma watched them leave. Concerned whispers from the neighbors pierced through the silence, and a cold feeling of guilt rotted in Yoshi's stomach. He shouldn't have said anything. Even though joining the JACL seemed like a good idea, he should have known that suggesting it would only cause trouble.

"I'm sorry, Grandma," Yoshi said, helping her sit down on her cot. "I wanted to help. I really did. But I've just made everything worse."

"Yoshi-kun." Grandma patted the mattress. Obeying, Yoshi took a seat next to her. "Your grandfather," she continued. "When younger, he had a dream. Do you know of this?"

Yoshi felt a little sad thinking about Grandpa. "You guys came to America so he could farm," he said.

"No, no. This, he did. I ask you if you know of his dream."

Yoshi shook his head.

"Soon after we came to America," Grandma said, "we went to a play. He could not quite afford this, but oh…He did these things. *Sauce for the Goose*, I am thinking, this was the name. I cannot remember any of what was the story. But I will never forget how much it was funny. Oh my, it was funny. I can see it still in my memories…little things of it…some actors on stage, digging through clothes to stop a ringing clock…and an old man, jumping up and down to get attention." She laughed, gazing off at the other side of the room, as if the performance replayed itself in front of her. "Once all this ended, your grandpa stood up…and he pointed at the stage and said, 'I want to do this. Someday, I will make people laugh.'"

As she grinned, the wrinkles deepened around her eyes, like every crease revealed an old smile lost to time.

"He never did get onto a stage," she said, seemingly to herself. "After some years on the farm, he no longer spoke of this."

Grandma's trance subsided. That stage she envisioned in front of herself once again became a collection of wall-boards, support beams, and dirty square windows. Then she looked at Yoshi and started to laugh.

"I had a reason for this story for you…Now, I think, this reason cannot come to me."

Yoshi frowned. "So Grandpa didn't get to do what he wanted."

"Oh, he *did*. His dream was to make people happy, and oh, how he could make you and Sato-chan smile. Can you remember these things? He balanced the sofa pillow on his head…He said, 'I cannot find it.' Can you remember this? No, I think you were too young."

"I remember," Yoshi mumbled.

"He practiced this every morning. He put his pillow on his head after he was waking up. He wanted to get better at all of this joking with you. He asks you where it is, and you point to his head, and he looks up—where is this?—and the pillow falls to the floor. You and Sato-chan, how much you laugh at this…" Her grin slowly faded from her face. "Oh, I miss him."

"I miss him too." Yoshi leaned his head down. "I guess it's a good thing he didn't have to go through all of this."

"All of what, Yoshi-kun?"

"You know." He gestured to his surroundings.

"We are not all together? We have no roof? We have no food for eating? All is fine, I think."

"Grandpa would want us to be better off than this."

"Grandpa would want us to be happy, to be as one. Yoshi-kun…your father…I do not know what things he spoke of…I want you not to feel you must change what cannot change. These things will only hurt you."

"But what about you? I know you're not okay."

"When my family is fine, then I am fine."

In her own way, she was telling him not to join the JACL. Father remained the head of the household, and betrayal would tear their family apart. Yoshi hung his head.

"I feel like I don't have the freedom to do anything," he said.

"Yoshi-kun, do not feel powerless. Even if all becomes gone...Even if all you can decide is whether you will still breathe...you always have a choice. Remember this."

Yoshi nodded. He knew he had to obey his father, but still, he found himself asking his grandma, "What if you don't make it?"

At this, she put a hand on his knee.

"*Shikata ga nai*, Yoshi-kun."

CHAPTER ELEVEN

THE DUST WON'T BLOW ME OVER

Each morning, Yoshi woke up to the song of a house wren. The bird chirped a familiar tune—one he used to hear every morning at home. Knowing that birds sang the same melody all over the world was strangely comforting. And as he listened to the house wren's song on the morning of June 26th, 1942, he felt rested. Typically, Grandma's midnight trips to the latrine made everyone exhausted. But this morning, for the first time since arriving at Manzanar, he awoke from a full night of undisturbed rest. Sato, Father, and Mom did as well.

Grandma did not.

With a "time to wake up," Mom bent over to give her a gentle nudge. "Mama, wake up." By the second time she said it, she already knew. Mom stood up and covered her eyes. Her cry was quiet, like she had been preparing for this day since the attack on Pearl Harbor.

And it didn't seem real. Yoshi couldn't accept it. At first, he tried to look away from Grandma's body. Once he glanced at it, he couldn't help but stare. She didn't seem any different. Her thin white hair was messy from sleep. Her mouth hung slightly open, as if she were still breathing. Death didn't give her a new face. She still had those wrinkles around her eyes from a life filled with joy, but he knew those lines would never furrow again. He resented that the answer seemed so simple. All she had to do was open her eyes. All she had to do was smile one more time. A laugh, a grin, and nothing else would matter. He could accept a life of imprisonment. He could dismiss his unfulfilled dreams. Everything would turn out fine, if only his family survived it all together.

Then, in the distance, the mess hall bells heralded the first meal of the day. The neighboring families made small talk beyond the cloth partition, and a mother on the firebreak shouted at her child to slow down. Yoshi used to assume that these moments possessed a certain melancholy peace. If fate were kind, everything would have been silent. Grandma deserved a calm world for her passing. She didn't get one. As he listened to the clamor sweeping over Grandma, he wished he could cling to her forever, but the only thing that felt eternal was his memory of her.

The Yamaguchis notified the medical center of her death, and the administration made arrangements for her body to be cremated at the nearby town of Lone Pine. A few days later, the ashes were delivered in a little clay jar. Mom placed the urn on top of a stumpy nightstand that Father had built out of scrap lumber.

Then everyone was silent. Mom rubbed her head, and Father sat beside her. Sato stared down at the floorboards, spreading some leftover dirt around with her foot. This whole time, Yoshi just slouched in the corner and listened. He couldn't take his eye off the urn or the empty bed in front of it.

The wind pressed against the double doors, causing the hinges to creak. Yoshi could usually ignore the sound, but now the shrillness stung him. *You had a chance*, he scolded himself. *You could have tried to save her, but you did nothing.* And the room looked smaller. And the air smelled stuffier. And all at once, he had to vomit.

With his right hand covering his mouth, he used his

left hand to push open the doors. He started running toward the latrine, but he couldn't bear the thought of
putting his face near one of those awful toilet bowls. Instead, he ran along the East Firebreak, one foot over the
next, passing strangers to his left and right. Self-
consciousness told him not to draw attention to himself,
but another voice drowned out his shyness:

You did nothing.

You did nothing.

Grandma's dead, and you did nothing.

He curled over and coughed. Only a few spits came
out. He wiped his mouth, raised his head back up, and
peeked around to see how big of an audience had formed.
Thankfully, he didn't see anybody. The heat of early
summer must have kept most people out of the sun.

Panting helped suppress the churning in his stomach,
and as he took a seat on the dusty ground, he tried to figure out where he was. Way out in front of him, he saw the
barbed wire fence. To his left and right, blocks of barracks lined the massive dirt pathway. This must have been
the intersection between the North and East Firebreaks,
and he was at the very center of it.

He slowed his breaths. His belly grumbled. The hot
breeze blew against the back of his neck. If his mind

wasn't plagued with guilt and despair, he could have drifted off to sleep.

"Are you okay?"

Yoshi looked over his shoulder. A Japanese woman stood behind him. She wore a rose-patterned apron over a white, short-sleeved shirt, and a sleeping three-year-old rested his head on her shoulder.

Yoshi closed his eyes and nodded.

The woman looked down at the tiny pile of spittle by Yoshi's shoes.

"The wait for the medical center isn't too bad right now," she said. "I just took this little guy there."

Her phrasing struck him—why did she refer to the child in such an impersonal way?

"That's not your son?" As soon as the rude question left his mouth, Yoshi covered his mouth and blushed.

"No, we're just heading back to the Children's Village." She nodded toward three barracks standing in the North Firebreak, way down the road. From here, the buildings looked tiny.

Yoshi cocked his head to the side.

"It's where they put the kids who were sent over from orphanages," the woman explained. "I worked with little Danny here back at the Maryknoll Home in LA, so at

least he's got one familiar face still taking care of him."
The little boy started crying, and the woman patted his
back. "We better head back," she said, walking away. "I
hope your day gets better."

Yoshi nodded goodbye, but his mouth hung open.
They sent *orphans* here? Could anybody really think that
orphans posed a danger to this country? What would happen to those kids when the camp finally closed? Would
they just be sent away to any shelter that was open?
Would they stay in the barracks until some foster parents
came along?

In that moment, Yoshi didn't understand why he had
left his family in the apartment. He couldn't imagine what
his childhood would have been like without the dinners at
Ricky's, without the Christmas mornings, without Grandpa's games of find-the-pillow. He was blessed to have a
family that loved him, and he stood up and hurried back,
as if they would disappear if he didn't return immediately.

As he scurried along the East Firebreak, he saw his
parents and Sato walking his direction.

"There he is," Sato said, her voice hushed by the distance. "I told you he ran off this way."

They met in the middle of the path. Grandma's urn
was wrapped in Mom's arms.

Yoshi scrunched his brow—where were they taking Grandma's ashes?

Sato was the one to explain:

"We're going to set her free."

The cemetery sat in the back of camp, just outside the fence. A hundred-foot opening in the barbed wire allowed the Yamaguchis through. A crisscross wood fence and the nearby guard tower told them not to go out any farther.

Mounds of dirt, decorated with stones, indicated a handful of graves. Only a few people were buried here, because nobody wanted a loved one to stay interned forever. Some families sent bodies home. Many chose cremation. Not everyone had a family, though; some of these graves were for the lonely.

The Yamaguchis approached the back of the cemetery and faced the outside world. Shrubs of green and brown filled the land on the other side of the wooden fence, and the purple mountains had never looked so close. Yoshi almost believed he and his family could hop the fence, reach the summit, and find a new home together. But from the nearby perch, an MP aimed his submachine gun at them, and the hope of starting over felt as fleeting as a spark.

They all took a few steps back. They didn't want to look suspicious. Mom placed the urn on the ground and tipped it forward. A pile of ashes spilled onto the dirt. Just a few inches farther, and the ashes would have reached the other side of the fence. Yoshi prayed that the breeze wouldn't send her back into camp.

In the setting sun, the shadow of the mountains approached them. Yoshi put his hand to his forehead, partly to shade the blinding orange light and partly to hide his tears. He hung down his head and kept his eyes to the ground. His guilt refused to go away. Above the sounds of tears and sniffles, he could still hear an echo in his head: *you did nothing, you did nothing*. It was accompanied by a warm evening breeze—unfittingly pleasant, mockingly pleasant—against the question he scornfully asked himself: *Why didn't I even try to save her?*

What started as a gentle breeze became a stronger gust. Grandma's ashes danced around for a second, warning the Yamaguchis that this would be their final moment with her. They whispered "goodbye" as the warm air swept her up.

The wind was on her side; she blew away from Manzanar.

Part Three:
A PRISONER OF MIND

CHAPTER TWELVE

OUT

The double doors squeaked open as Mom, Father, and Sato came back from lunch. Yoshi didn't bother looking at them. He just stared at the roof's support beams. His long, greasy hair itched the back of his neck. His ungroomed facial hair felt prickly. Once in a while, he would use a pair of clippers to cut down his beard, but he didn't even bother using a mirror to do it. Looking decent no longer seemed important to him.

"I brought back lunch for you," Mom said, setting a plate on the nightstand next to him.

Yoshi didn't respond.

"Eat." Father stepped up to Yoshi's bed.

If I didn't listen to you, I wouldn't be in this situation, Yoshi thought. *I could have joined the JACL. They could have made the administration give her the treatment she needed. They could have saved her. But you ordered me to do nothing, and I listened.*

"Maybe you should get some fresh air," Mom suggested, when Yoshi didn't even look at the food.

Yoshi shook his head.

"Get up. Go," Father said. "For three months, you mope."

"There's nowhere to go," Yoshi mumbled.

"You could have gone to church with us this morning," Mom said. "You could have gone to breakfast or lunch."

Yoshi just groaned.

"Take a walk," Father said. "Shower. Clean yourself."

Yoshi closed his eyes.

He heard footsteps on the floorboards. The doors creaked open and shut. Yoshi thought he was alone again, but his mattress sank as Sato sat down on the edge of his cot.

"Dad has a point," she said. "You could stand to take a shower."

He turned onto his side, his back towards her, but Sato didn't get off his bed.

"Don't you have homework to do?" he said over his

shoulder.

Sato nodded. "There's a really important paper due tomorrow."

She still didn't get up.

"It's not your fault, you know," she said. "About Grandma."

"I know," Yoshi spat out, startled by her abruptness.

"I don't think you do. Most people don't want to be alone when they're grieving."

"Maybe I'm just different."

"Or maybe you're just beating yourself up. Things haven't been normal since you and Dad had that fight all those months ago."

Yoshi opened his mouth to respond, but no words came out.

"I think you just need a fresh start," Sato added. "Remember Emi? She sits next to me in one of my classes."

Yoshi sat up. "You go to *school* together? How are you in the same grade?"

"The same class, not the same grade. She's a senior. But we're in U.S. history together because I already took civics. And we've actually gotten pretty close. Her brother stops by at the end of the day, and we all chat for a little while. Maybe the four of us can go do something together."

Not too long ago, Yoshi would have jumped at the offer. But now he felt so gross, so ugly and guilty, that he didn't dare to show his face in front of Emi or Joey. He shrugged.

"Come on," Sato prodded.

Yoshi laid his head back down and tried to fall asleep.

"What's this?!" Mom said the next morning. Yoshi peeked an eye open to look. She was leaning over Sato's bed. "Yoshi, get up!"

"What is it?" He shot out of bed, dizzied from standing up too fast.

"Look at this," Mom said. She held up Sato's notebook, which was open to a page with this note written on it:

I'll only turn this paper in if Yoshi delivers it. It's for my last class of the day, so he can drop it off after school. Don't mess this up for me.

Love,

Sato

Yoshi's heart raced. What was Sato thinking? There's no way Emi or Joey could see him looking like this.

Glaring at Yoshi, Father pointed outside. "Go."

With a gulp, Yoshi shook his head.

"She has perfect scores," Father said. "You will go, or I will drag you."

"I can't."

Mom pursed her lips and sighed through her nose, like she had to suppress a scream.

"Yoshi," she said, "we have been sympathetic with you. *Endlessly* sympathetic. We know you're upset about Grandma. We all are. But Sato needs you right now. She did this because she cares about you. Can you not show her the least bit of care in return? Just think how disappointed Grandma would be if she could see you like this."

Tears filled Yoshi's eyes, which surprised him. He thought he was too numb to cry.

"Look at me," he said, gesturing to his disheveled face.

Father reached into his pocket and shoved a quarter into Yoshi's hand.

"For the barber," he said, placing a hand on Yoshi's back and pushing him toward the double doors. Then, just like that, Yoshi was outside—for the first time in months, not to use the latrine. The early autumn sun was warm, but not hot. The air smelled fresh. As he dragged his feet to the men's showers in his block, he kept his head hung low, fearing Emi or Joey might pop out at any moment and laugh at his uneven beard and shoulder-length hair. And when he reached the barbershop in Block 21, he hesitated to step inside. He had been here a couple times before, but never looking like *this*.

The barber sat alone in the shop's chair, reading the latest issue of the camp's newspaper, the *Manzanar Free Press*. As soon as Yoshi entered, the middle-aged Japanese man set down his paper, adjusted his glasses, and stood up.

"What can I do for you, young man?" he asked.

"I'm here to fix…" Yoshi gestured to his head. "All this," he muttered, as if he were confessing an embarrassing secret.

The barber laughed. "No need to be shy. You should have seen this place when I first opened. There was a line out the door with men who hadn't gotten a trim since before the roundup." He twisted the chair towards Yoshi. "Take a seat, my boy. Are you looking for something special, or just getting cleaned up?"

"I want to look…" Yoshi slumped his shoulders and looked down at his lap. "Really good. My best."

"I know just the thing," the barber said. He spun the chair towards the mirror.

Yoshi hadn't seen himself in months. Never before

had he grown his hair this long, and he used to shave every other morning. He almost didn't recognize his own face.

"This is what all the stylish young men request." The barber rubbed some shaving cream in his hands and spread it on Yoshi's cheeks and neck. "I'll give you a pachuco cut."

The warm breeze of late September tickled his clean-shaven face. With his hair slicked back, Yoshi carried Sato's notebook in his hand. His head felt light from all the lost hair. Feeling a little better about himself, he improved his posture. As he approached Block 3's recreation hall where Sato's class was being held, he tried swallowing his anxiety. Soon, he would meet Emi and Joey again.

Just as Yoshi thought it, he spotted Joey sitting on the steps.

"Hey there!" Joey's crooked teeth showed off as he grinned. "How ya doing, buddy?"

Yoshi smiled nervously. Before he could respond, he heard the class start to sing through the doors of the building.

"The alma mater," Joey explained, pointing at the door behind him.

Despite the flat and muffled group of voices, Yoshi still made out the lyrics of the school's song: *We are building for tomorrow for a strong and active life. Not for fame or gold to borrow, nor to wage a war of strife. Forward, forward, forward for America.*

Joey hopped off the steps. The doors opened, and about eighty students left the building. Yoshi's heart pounded. Ideas raced through his mind about how he should greet Emi:

Hey there!—too excited.

Hello.—too boring.

How do you do, Miss Emi?—too formal.

Do you by chance remember me?—too embarrassing.

He ran a hand through his slicked-back hair to push down any loose strands. Then, behind the rest of the group, Sato and Emi came out.

"Look at you!" Sato said, pointing to Yoshi's hair. "Got my homework?"

Nodding, he handed the notebook to her, and she ran back inside.

Yoshi and Emi made eye contact. *Say something*, he told himself. *Anything. Just do it.*

As Emi came down the steps, she spoke first. "Good to see you, Yoshi."

She remembered his name! For half a second, he lost his breath.

"I'm sorry about your grandma," she added.

Then he realized: his sister might have explained everything—the months of moping, the lack of showers. He could almost hear the story: "My brother sleeps all the time because he's real lousy, and you're sure lucky not to know him." Emi's tone *was* pretty sympathetic. In an instant, Yoshi's excitement turned into humiliation.

Sato came back out. "Do you guys want to do something, or do you need to get to your meeting?"

"Mr. H. is waiting for us," Joey said. "But another time, you bet! We'll do something real soon."

As Emi and Joey walked away, Yoshi felt strange.

"How much do they know about me?" he asked Sato.

She raised an eyebrow. "What do you mean?"

"All that's happened…the fight, the sleeping a lot, or whatever. How much do they know?"

"They just know that Grandma died," Sato said. "That's it."

"But they don't know…about me being real lousy?"

"Real lousy?" Sato scoffed. "They know your name, and they know you're my brother. That's about it."

Yoshi smiled. Emi and Joey would become his friends,

just like he wanted. Overwhelmed by gratitude, he looked at his sister. He wanted to say something, but all he could do was nod.

"You're welcome," she said.

It suddenly seemed so obvious: Grandma wanted her family to be happy. Denying that wish would forsake her legacy, and nothing could be more disrespectful than that. He was allowed to be happy. He was allowed to make friends. And despite his father's hatred of the JACL, he was allowed to spend time with Emi and Joey without joining their group. Heck, if the two of them got Yoshi out of bed, then Father would be thrilled.

Yoshi's heart raced. He would actually get to spend time with them. He would actually get to spend time with *her*. He felt excited. Yes, of course he felt excited, but…whenever that day came, what would he say to her?

CHAPTER THIRTEEN

10/10/42

"Ready?" Mom said to Father and Sato. Once she started singing "Happy Birthday," the other two followed along. They stood around Yoshi's cot, all wearing cone-shaped birthday hats made from torn-out pages of the *Manzanar Free Press*. Mom's hat was the sports page, while Father's announced the times and places of the morning's religious services. The only thing Yoshi could read on Sato's hat was an advertisement for 39-cent Fleisher's Yarn.

Father mumbled the lyrics to the familiar tune while Mom mostly talked her way through the verse. Only Sato stayed on pitch, thanks to years of old piano lessons. Yoshi sat on his bed and smiled. He clapped when his family finished the song.

"We couldn't get a cake for you," Mom said. "But we got you a little something instead."

Father reached under his bed and pulled out a root beer. He twisted off the cap and handed the bottle to Yoshi.

"Root beer!" Yoshi gasped and took a sip. "I haven't had one since Ricky's!"

"They sell them at the canteen," Mom said. "I hope it's not too warm. We wanted to surprise you."

"Pretend this has 19 candles," Father said.

Yoshi blew on the top of the bottle, causing a hollow whistle. Father pulled out another three bottles, and pretty soon, everyone had a soda in hand.

"And now for the real gift," Mom said. She pulled a package out from under her bed.

"What?!" Yoshi grinned as he set his root beer down on the floor. "You guys didn't have to get me anything!"

"Of course we did." Mom handed Yoshi the rectangular box. He set the package on his lap and ripped off the cream-colored wrapping paper. Once he tore open the box, he looked at what was inside: a folded, light brown leather jacket. The leather was thick, and the inside was lined with khaki. At the bottom, a hand warmer pocket sat on each side of the copper zipper. The top was collared like a dress shirt.

Yoshi's jaw dropped as he held it up. "This looks way too expensive."

"No returns." Sato waved a finger.

"We sold everything from home," Father said. "And now, no expenses. We have much in the bank. We do not feel the cost of this."

"We thought it would fit your new style," Mom said.

"Oh gosh, I love it!" Yoshi exclaimed. "How did you get it?"

"There's a J.C. Penny not too far from here, and we noticed an ad in the paper for mail orders," Mom said. "All we had to do was send in a check, and they delivered it a few days later while you were out."

"Remember last week, when I wanted you to go to the library with me after school?" Sato said. "That was just killing time."

"Oh gosh. Thank you so much. Thank you *so much*." Yoshi got up to try on the jacket. One arm at a time, he squeezed a hand through the cuffed sleeves. He held out his arms, awaiting a response.

Mom examined the shoulders, then smiled. "It fits perfectly."

"You look like a gangster," Father muttered.

"No, it looks great," Sato said. "You should wear it to-night."

Tonight. Thinking about the evening's plans caused a nervous flutter in his belly. He was going to go to a movie with Emi and Joey—their first real outing together. When he first heard about the event, he thought it was too good to be true. How could there actually be something fun to do at an internment camp? But Joey assured him the event was real. Apparently, the internees who had set up the camp commissary also owned a film projector, and with a little help from the WRA, they got access to old movie reels.

After dinner, Yoshi's nerves got even worse. He sat next to Sato, staring at the new fish pond in Block 15, knowing that Emi and Joey would arrive any minute.

Yoshi shrugged and ran a hand over his hair.

"You look nervous," Sato told him. "You've got nothing to worry about."

She was right—he didn't need to worry. He and Emi had seen each other several times, and the interactions always went well. Still, spending a few minutes together in passing wasn't the same as making actual plans, and, truthfully, he always got nervous right before seeing her. Each time they met, she became a little less reserved, but there was still so much he didn't know about her. He wanted to be somebody she felt comfortable opening up to.

No matter what, he wanted to feel confident when she showed up. No mumbling, no blushing—none of it. His hair looked nice, his jacket fit great, and as he stared out at the fish pond, he decided that transformation could start on the surface. Not too long ago, this whole camp was just a big pile of dirt. Now there were fish ponds and gardens all over the place because the internees wanted something pretty to look at. That must have taken a ton of effort. Not only would the ambitious internees need to get fish and water from the nearby river; they also needed to order vegetables and water lilies through the mail. Golly, if families could make this place feel like home, then Yoshi could make himself seem like a pretty swell guy. Between the two, his task was easier.

And he didn't have to be perfect—not the handsomest, or the cleverest, or the smartest, or the most talented. He just needed to be confident. This fish pond, for instance, was the closest one to Yoshi's block, but it wasn't the best one in camp. It was the *third* best. That was even the name of it, "Third Place Garden," based on the competition that the *Manzanar Free Press* recently ran. The first-place fish pond was all the way back in Block 34. But even if this one wasn't the best, it was still great, looking a bit like a sunflower with its squiggly outline and small island in the center. And as Yoshi stared at the pink chrysanthemums growing on that little island, he decided that this fish pond was *his* favorite, which was all that really mattered.

Anyway, the point was this: he shouldn't try to be better or worse than anyone else. All he could do was be the very best *him*.

"We're here!" Joey called.

Yoshi and Sato stood up and turned around.

"Happy birthday!" Joey approached with an arm behind his back. With one quick gesture, he stuck out his hand to reveal what he had been hiding.

"Behold..." He deepened his voice to sound dramatic. "A real dessert."

He held out a little dish of brownie pudding—one of the treats still possible to make despite the war rationing.

Yoshi gasped. "Oh gosh, thank you! They make those here?"

"No, my friend got it from a little diner in Lone Pine. His dad is part of the WRA staff. All that's missing is a candle." He started to extend the dish to Yoshi, but then he froze like he just had a realization. "Hold this." He handed the dessert to Emi and pulled a matchbook out of his pocket. He struck a match and stuck it in the brownie. "Blow it out quick." He tore the dish from Emi's hands and gave it to Yoshi.

Without thinking, Yoshi puffed as hard as he could.

"Hope you made a wish," Sato said through a laugh, as a slender stream of smoke rose into the air.

Yoshi pulled out the match and ran the back of it through his mouth, cleaning off the chocolate. He looked around for a place to toss it out.

"Keep it," Joey said. "It's good luck."

With a nod and a smile, Yoshi stuck the matchstick in his pocket. He took a whiff of the brownie, and he insisted that the four of them should share it, but no matter how hard he pushed, they all refused.

The four of them sat by the pond, squinting as the sunset reflected off the water. In the distance, shouts of kids playing baseball in the firebreak echoed through the blocks. All the while, Sato and Joey competed for the better joke.

"A teacher asks her student where the Declaration of Independence was signed," Sato began. "And the student says, 'Probably at the bottom.'"

"Good one," Joey laughed. "Why did the cookie go to the doctor? Because he felt crummy."

"Not bad," Sato giggled.

"Your turn!" Joey nudged Yoshi.

"No, I'm bad at jokes." He smiled awkwardly, but they all prodded him to try. "Broken pencils are pointless," he finally said.

Once the joke settled, everybody laughed.

A baseball rolled their direction, and a little boy chased it. Sato and Joey both rushed up to grab the ball, but Sato beat him to it. She tossed the ball back to the kid. "Three and a half years of softball," she said, smirking at Joey.

"I bet I've got the better arm," Joey retorted. "Hey champ, mind giving me a shot?"

For a second, the boy just stared back with his mouth open. Joey held up his hands, indicating he was ready to catch, and the kid tossed the ball at him. It bounced off Joey's hands as he tried to clasp it.

"Get a load of that!" Sato laughed. "Better arm, you said?"

"Throwing, not catching! That's what 'better arm' means!"

"I bet you think you're faster, too."

"I *am* faster—"

"First one to Block 9 wins." She darted off.

"Wait!" Joey shouted, running behind her. "We need to set up boundaries first!"

As Yoshi tossed the ball to the boy, he had a flashback to high school. He hadn't touched a baseball since those awful days at Jackson, and he couldn't help but wonder what Sarah Hassenger and Gus Needaburger were up to. He wondered if they remembered him. To be honest, he hoped they didn't.

But none of that mattered now. What mattered was this moment, being here with Emi. She kept quiet, and Yoshi knew he needed to find something to talk about. Thinking about Gus inspired the question: "Have you ever met anyone that's real lousy?"

Her eyebrows scrunched. "What do you mean?"

"Some people, they can be real lousy sometimes. But there's different kinds of lousy. There's some guys who are real jerks, and that's lousy. And there's some guys who are just no good, but maybe that's lousy too."

Emi stared back blankly. "What are you asking, exactly?"

He had no idea. Despite his efforts not to blush, his cheeks turned red, and he shrugged.

A few seconds passed before Emi spoke. "What about you?"

"Huh?"

"Do you know someone you consider lousy?"

"Oh." He chuckled as he pictured Gus Needaburger's stupid face. "Well sure, I guess. Some people are real mean sometimes, and I don't like that at all. But that's just the way stuff is, I think. There's lots of real mean people in the world, but I guess you can't change it, so you can't get too down about it."

Emi nodded. "*Shikata ga nai.*"

Shikata ga nai. Those words felt like a punch in the gut. A scarring wound ripped back open. His throat tightened, and he tried his hardest not to cry.

When Emi noticed Yoshi's watery eyes, she leaned toward him. "Are you okay?"

Dabbing his eyes, he nodded. "That's just something my grandma used to say." He gulped down his tears, and he was warmed by the genuine concern he heard in Emi's voice. In an instant, something changed. As much as he hated appearing vulnerable in front of her, he no longer felt like he was performing. He broke down an emotional wall, and for the first time, he felt a genuine connection with her. "It's still a little hard sometimes."

She looked down at the water. It seemed to Yoshi like she was debating what to say. After a silent moment, she confessed, "It always will be.

Yoshi opened his mouth to respond, but only an unclear syllable came out. He just stared back, concerned and curious, eyebrows scrunched and lips frozen mid-word.

"My mom," she explained. "She passed away when I was a kid. Tuberculosis."

Yoshi gazed at the water, as if some words of wisdom were floating towards him.

"Golly." He shook his head. "That's…That's just awful. Real awful. I don't even know what to say."

"No, it's fine. Really. It's all in the past now." She stared across the pond. "You just never forget, that's all."

Joey and Sato came running back, panting and laughing as they slowed to a stop.

"It was a tie," Joey announced.

"No it wasn't! I beat you."

"Only by a…" He leaned over, putting all his weight onto his knees. "…second."

Sato looked down at her watch. "Movie time!"

"Already?" Joey took a deep breath.

Emi stood up and reached a hand out to Yoshi.

"Come on," she said, pulling him up. "Let's go."

They headed toward the screening venue, which was set up in the intersection of the North and East Firebreaks. As they laughed and joked with each other, Sato and Joey walked at a faster pace. Emi and Yoshi, strolling a bit behind them, were caught in the middle of a conversation.

"No, it's embarrassing," Emi protested.

"Golly, what could be embarrassing about having goals?" Yoshi replied.

She bit her lip and shrugged. "I'll only tell you if you promise not to laugh."

"Oh my gosh, I could *never*. I *swear* it."

She took a long inhale and looked Yoshi in the eye. "I want to be the first Japanese woman elected to the Senate."

Yoshi almost jumped in the air. "No way! Sato wants to do politics stuff too! It could be the two of you—how swell would *that* be?"

Emi gave a timid smile.

"Well gee, how is that embarrassing?" Yoshi said. "That sounds like a real swell goal to me."

"It's ambitious."

"So what?"

Emi raised an eyebrow at him. "Like you said, some people are lousy."

Yoshi frowned. "People don't support you?"

"Joey does. My dad does."

Her dad? Ever since Yoshi saw Emi by herself on the bus, he wondered what had happened to her parents. After learning about her mother, he assumed her father must have died at some point too. Now, she made it sound like the man was still alive.

"Your dad," he struggled to say. "He's…?"

"Not here."

Yoshi nodded. He didn't want to pry, and for a few seconds, neither spoke.

"You want to know what happened," Emi stated.

Yoshi stammered a bit before landing on a sentence. "Oh jeez, that would be nosy."

"That would be honest," she laughed. "It's okay. No need to be phony." As they neared the intersection, they practically slowed to a stop. Sato and Joey looked back to make sure they hadn't left their siblings behind. As Yoshi waved at them to indicate they were on their way, Emi gazed off, like the right way to tell her father's story was hidden somewhere in the distance.

"He was the vice principal of a grade school," she began. "Compton Elementary—it's just a little school back home. I'd never heard of an Issei getting a job like that, but he did it somehow. It was a huge immigrant community. Most of the students were Japanese, so I'm sure that had something to do with it." She spoke at a slow pace, crafting each sentence before speaking. "The kids looked up to him. Everyone did. He stayed after school most days to give extra help to the students who had a hard time speaking English. Nobody paid him for it. He just did it because he wanted to." She stopped moving her feet. "After everything he's been through," she said. "After losing Mom...he's still kind. And he's still humble. He talked all the time about how he showed up from Japan with pennies in his pocket and worked his way up to a dream job. He said only in America was it possible to do that." She paused for a moment, lost in thought and memory. "He loves this country more than I can describe. He made me and Joey love it too."

Yoshi's mouth hung open. In a way he had never experienced before, he hurt on her behalf.

"Well gosh," he said. "Did he...? Is he okay?"

Emi looked down at the dirt. "Right after Pearl Harbor, the FBI raided our home and took him away. They were afraid he would use his influence to brainwash kids into supporting Japan. If they'd bothered to learn anything about him, they would know how stupid it was to even consider that." She started rushing through her words, and Yoshi could hear the resentment in her voice. "I almost couldn't believe it when it happened. How could they take *him*? The kindest, the gentlest, the funniest...I guess the FBI was reading *Pacific Citizen*. That's the JACL's

252 · ANDREW HAYES WILLIAMS

newspaper. It likes to highlight good people in the community, and it ran a little article on him. That must have
been what put him on their radar. It must have been what
made them come knocking, what made them take him off
in handcuffs…" Her eyelids drooped. She looked defeated. "That was ten months ago. I haven't seen him since."
She took a deep breath and gave a little smile. "It's okay,
though. We've stayed in touch by mail. He's being kept at
a detention center in North Dakota, and he thinks he'll be
sent here soon."

Yoshi pursed his lips. He couldn't figure out what to
say.

"Gee," he said. "I can't imagine how tough that must
be."

"I'm holding up fine. It's Joey I'm worried about. He
acts like such a knucklehead, but I know he's hurting
more than he lets on. I don't hide from my feelings. He
does, and I know it can't be healthy." Emi sighed. "Anyway," she said, taking on a more cheerful tone. "Enough
about this. What about you?"

"Me?"

"You must have goals too."

At first, nothing came to mind. Yoshi had to think for
a few seconds before he answered. "I want to join the ar-

my." As he said it, he felt like a younger, more innocent version of himself resurfaced from the past. "Gosh," he continued. "Not too long ago, I wanted to fight more than anything. I can't believe I almost forgot about that dream."

Yoshi wanted to hear Emi's reaction. He hoped she would say, "Wow, you must be real brave and strong if you want to do that." She didn't. She just nodded.

After a moment, she nudged his shoulder. "Movie's about to start."

They reached the crowd of moviegoers. A couple hundred people, who were looking for a free distraction, faced a propped-up bed sheet. Yoshi, Emi, Sato, and Joey took a seat at the back of the crowd.

A white teenage boy sat next to Joey.

"The brownie was a success," Joey whispered to him. "Thanks again."

The night was a comfortable 58 degrees, and the air smelled crisp and fresh. Under the glowing stars and a nearly full moon, a film projector filled the screen with the quirky antics of Abbott and Costello. *Hold That Ghost*, the film was called, and the comedy duo cracked up the entire audience. With a burned match in his pocket, and a new leather jacket keeping him warm, Yoshi glanced over at Emi. The light of the projector's beam cast a silver glow on her smiling face. When he turned his head back towards the screen, he had a hard time focusing. All he could think about was this unusual feeling: for the first time since Pearl Harbor, he was happy.

CHAPTER FOURTEEN

TRY NOT TO MISPLACE IT

Less than a week after Yoshi's birthday, the WRA finished upgrading the camp's schools. Manzanar High
found a permanent home in the repurposed buildings of
Block 7, and the students finally had desks, textbooks,
and plenty of non-volunteer teachers. Some chatter even
started about making a yearbook and electing a homecom-
ing queen, though neither were feasible during the first
academic year. By early December, Sato and Emi had
shared plenty of stories with Yoshi about their experiences at school. From what he could tell, the routine at
Manzanar High sounded similar to his own experience at
Jackson: reciting the Pledge of Allegiance in the morning
and trying not to fall asleep in those tedious hours after
lunch. Hearing about all that stuff reminded him how

much he hated high school.

Winter had yet to fully arrive, and while the mornings were brisk and foggy, the afternoons could climb upwards of 60 degrees. Snow had already gathered on the distant mountaintops, but it had yet to reach the flat earth below. Taking advantage of the last few weeks of decent weather, Yoshi and Joey played a game of H-O-R-S-E on Block 2's miniature basketball court. Joey fumbled his way to the deciding shot. He took Yoshi's place eight feet from the hoop, aimed his arms, and threw the ball.

"Aw, horsefeathers!" Joey shouted as the ball bounced off the rim. "Give me one more shot. That was a practice throw."

"You can only use the practice excuse on your first throw, not your last," Yoshi laughed.

"I break the rules. I do things my own way." Joey turned his back to the hoop and held the ball out in front of him. "Check this out." He threw the ball behind his head. It bounced off the cement court and rolled onto the dirt. "I swear that worked once!" Joey tossed the ball back at Yoshi. "How'd you get so good at this, anyway? You said you were rotten at sports."

Yoshi shrugged. "Maybe this helped." Holding the basketball in one arm, he reached into his pocket and pulled out the burned match from his birthday brownie.

"No way," Joey exclaimed. "You kept that?"

"You said it was good luck." He tucked the match away again.

Out of nowhere, Joey gasped. He put a hand over his own pocket. "I almost forgot! I have to go deliver something. Come on, let's go!"

Without thinking, Yoshi started running behind Joey. "Where are we going?"

"Mr. Hamasaki's!"

As soon as Yoshi heard the name, he froze. Mr. Hamasaki was the president of the local chapter of the JACL back home, and he remained a leader of the group in camp. Father hated the guy. *Hated* him. Yoshi would never forget when Father came back from the Civil Control Station to get information about the evacuation. "That man, Mr. Hamasaki," Father had grumbled. "He was there. Helping the government. Smiling and sucking up." The only reason Father didn't complain about Emi and Joey was because they brightened Yoshi's life after months of crippling depression. But seeing Mr. Hamasaki would be too much. If Father found out about a visit with the JACL leader, then Yoshi's friends might get ripped away.

"I can't," Yoshi said.

"It'll just be a minute," Joey prodded. "Your pop doesn't have to find out."

Yoshi looked around, trying to find some inspiration for an excuse. As he brushed his hair out of his face, he felt a little perspiration on his scalp. "I should go shower."

Joey dismissively waved his hand through the air. "He's not some crumb, don't worry. You'll like him."

That's what I'm afraid of, Yoshi thought. "At least hold onto your basketball." He tossed the ball over, and then hesitantly followed Joey over to the first apartment of Building 1—the Block Leader's office.

"Joey!" Clad in a perfectly pressed suit, Mr. Hamasaki rose from behind a desk. The man was slender, and though his tiny bald spot and his perfect posture gave him the distinguished air of an elder, his lack of wrinkles indicated he was just in his mid-thirties. His hair was combed to the side, looking thick and shiny from a heavy coat of hairspray. In spite of all this, the first thing that caught Yoshi's eye was a striped red, white, and blue tie tucked behind the man's double-breasted jacket. Beside it, the left lapel was adorned with a little flag pin.

"I was starting to think you had forgotten," he said to Joey through a big white smile.

"I almost did," Joey confessed. "We got caught up in a game. Mr. H., this is Yoshi. Yoshi, Mr. H."

"So *this* is Yoshi. Nice to finally meet you." Mr. Hamasaki extended his arm for a strong handshake. Smiling awkwardly, Yoshi shook his hand, subtly glancing around to see if anyone was watching.

This office looked just like the Yamaguchis' apartment, with three windows on each side of the room and soup can lids nailed over the holes in the floorboards. However, this room only had one bed, nestled in the back corner. A desk stood in front of the cloth partition, with a pile of paperwork stacked on top. A little shelf was attached to the right wall, with four books sitting on top: the Bible, the Book of Mormon, the *Complete Works of William Shakespeare*, and an English-Japanese translation dictionary.

"Who won the game?" the man asked with a grin.

"Yoshi won the last round," Joey admitted. "That was my warm-up game."

"I was more of a baseball guy myself." Mr. Hamasaki sat down on his cot. He bent over to put on his dress shoes. "Though I would never imply that I was very talented at it." The man laughed as he tied his laces. He patted his knees as he sat back up. "Tell me, how is camp treating you, Yoshi? Not too badly, I hope?"

"It's okay," Yoshi answered.

"Good, good. Admittedly, it's a work in progress, but we're doing what we can to see that things improve. Are you familiar with the Japanese American Citizens League?"

A pang of nervousness struck Yoshi's gut, as if mentioning the group's name out loud would cause his father to appear in the room. Yoshi tried too hard not to appear judgmental; he smiled, raised his eyebrows, and nodded frantically.

"Mr. Hamasaki helped lead the fight to give Japanese vets citizenship," Joey said with a grin. "He was only 24 at the time! And tonight, he's going to Salt Lake City!"

"That's right," the man replied. "I'll be flying out in just a few hours, actually. There's a national JACL meeting in the morning for a secret project we're all very excited about. I'll be representing Manzanar."

Some internees, like fishermen and cooks, were occasionally given permission to go past the fence. But they couldn't go great distances, and they couldn't stay out long. Flying to another state would be unthinkable for anyone but this one man.

"The camp is letting you leave?" Yoshi asked.

"Just for a few days," Mr. Hamasaki said. "This is a special circumstance. It's our annual meeting. The camp respects that."

Yoshi didn't hate the group the way his father did. On a certain level, he even admired their work from afar. Still, something seemed wrong about giving this man perks that others only dreamed of. Suddenly, Father's resentment made a bit more sense.

"Which reminds me," Mr. Hamasaki looked at Joey. "You remembered to bring a picture for the presentation?"

"Right here." Joey reached into his pocket.

"We decided it would be nice to share the stories of some of our members," Mr. Hamasaki explained to Yoshi. "There's so much negative media coverage going around, we're trying to spread the word about how many good, loyal Americans there are here."

"Here you go!" Joey handed his picture to Mr. Hamasaki.

When the man saw the photograph, his lips tightened into a sympathetic frown. He looked down, gave a little nod, and patted Joey on the shoulder. "You're sure you don't want to hold onto this one? I would hate for it to get misplaced before I can get it back to you."

In the picture, Joey looked about 15. His ears were just as floppy then, but his face was slightly rounder. Grinning with pride, he held up a large trout. A bald man stood beside him, gazing a little to the right of the camera. His thick hand rested on Joey's shoulder, and he smiled with only the left side of his mouth, like he wanted to hide his teeth despite his genuine happiness. The moment Yoshi caught a glimpse of the photo, he knew the man must be Joey's dad.

"I'm sure," Joey answered. "That's the one I want people to know me by."

Mr. Hamasaki carefully dropped the picture in a big yellow envelope, and then stuck the package in one of his suitcases. "Mr. Minami isn't in camp yet," he explained to Yoshi. "There was a bit of a complication."

Yoshi couldn't decide whether or not to admit he knew the story. Even though Emi had already filled him in, she had told him in private, and he sensed it was a bit of a secret. Joey rarely mentioned his dad—and he never spoke about what had happened to him. Yoshi just nodded.

"I've got good news, though!" Joey blurted out. "He's getting here on January 20th!"

"That's great, Joey," Mr. Hamasaki said. "Really

swell!"

"Yeah! Pretty soon, I won't even need that picture."

Mr. Hamasaki squeezed Joey's shoulder. Nobody spoke, and Yoshi almost felt like an invisible observer. He sensed there were many conversations concealed within their quiet exchange, and he was happy that Joey had the support of a mentor.

"We should let you get to packing," Joey finally said.

"You know where to find me if you need anything," Mr. Hamasaki said. "Thanks for dropping off that photo." He turned to Yoshi and smiled. "It was a pleasure meeting you, Yoshi. And hey, I know we're not popular with everyone in camp, but just remember there are two sides to every story." He winked. "See you guys around."

"Have a good trip!" Joey said as he hopped down the steps.

Yoshi couldn't decide how he felt about this man. At first, there seemed to be something phony about his extreme niceness. Maybe there was, but at least his concern for Joey felt real. And even if the pleasantness came across as somewhat fake, Yoshi couldn't deny the man was likable.

"He's great, isn't he?" Joey said.

"He seems real nice." A question popped into Yoshi's

mind. "Is he here all by himself?"

Joey nodded. "He moved his parents to the east coast so they could avoid all this. He *chose* to come here. He could have moved too, but he didn't.

Yoshi wished his family could have moved east too, but they didn't have the time or money to make it work. Mr. Hamasaki seemed to be doing well here. Yoshi tried his hardest not to resent that, and he tried not to wonder if the man could have saved Grandma somehow. Yoshi didn't want to feel guilty all over again.

"I think you'd really like him if you got to know him," Joey added. "He sure is great. He's been…" As Joey trailed off, the smile faded from his face. Yoshi knew how the sentence was going to end: *he's been my temporary father.* "But I can't wait for you to meet my dad!" Joey added. "He's the nicest guy you'll ever meet, I swear. And he tells the best jokes. When you see him, ask him about the one with the grasshopper." Joey started laughing.

Yes, Yoshi wanted to meet their real dad, the guy Emi and Joey loved so much. And on January 20th, he would get a chance.

CHAPTER FIFTEEN

SOMEONE ELSE ENTIRELY

They stood in the snow, staring at the front gate, shivering as they waited for his arrival. Their breaths blew out in front of them like four runaway ghosts, vanishing long before reaching the fence. Emi had a gray blanket draped over her shoulders, and she held a bouquet of flowers that she had ordered from a mail order catalogue. Yoshi squeezed his arms against his chest, trapping in the body heat that escaped from his leather jacket. Sato held a plywood board with "WELCOME!" written in red paint. Joey clasped the fishing photo of himself and his dad that Mr. Hamasaki had recently brought back from the JACL conference in Salt Lake City. With a bit of scrap lumber, Joey had pieced together a little wooden frame for it as a welcome gift.

Yoshi hadn't been to the camp's entrance since the day he left home. Everything looked exactly as he remembered. The flag waved behind him. That little rock sentry house for the MPs stood to his south. Guard towers loomed far off in each direction. Seeing the camp from this perspective took Yoshi back to his first day at Manzanar. Before his transformation, before the hardest months of his life, and before Grandma's silent goodbye, his family wore tags around their collars and prepared for a scary new life. Back then, he only knew Emi as the girl on the bus. Now, he stood beside that same girl—and only because she wanted him here.

"I'm nervous," Emi stammered through her chattering teeth.

Almost two hours had passed, and so far, only a semi-truck had trudged along the highway.

"He'll get here," Yoshi promised. "I know it."

"Maybe we have the wrong date," Sato said.

"No," Joey mumbled. "Today's the day."

"The wrong time?" Sato suggested.

Joey shook his head.

"Maybe there was a delay and he wasn't able to contact you," Yoshi said.

"Maybe," Emi sighed. "You don't have to stay if you don't want to."

"I want to," Yoshi answered. "I'm sure he'll get here any minute."

Emi stared out at the cloudy, marble-looking sky. Her brow scrunched, and she hung her head. She appeared to be having some kind of sad revelation. Then she dropped the bouquet on the snow, turned around, and walked away. Yoshi glanced at Sato and Joey. In unspoken agreement, they decided to give up too.

Then, as soon as their backs were turned toward the highway, they heard a faint grumble coming from the distance. They stopped. The gruff roar amplified as it neared. Fearful of disappointment, Joey and Emi hesitated to look. When they turned around, they saw what they'd been waiting for: a Greyhound bus chugging through the gate. The bus pulled left, the engine shut off, and the crisp air stunk of burnt rubber and gasoline. Through the tinted glass, they spotted his profile in one of the windows. Sato held up the sign. After tossing her blanket to Yoshi, Emi rushed to pick up the bouquet of flowers.

The silhouette rose and moved to the front of the bus.

The door swung open.

"There he is!" Emi shouted. She sounded a little surprised, like she half expected to see a stranger in his place. Yoshi understood the feeling. When you wait for something long enough, sometimes you feel like the day will never come. But it was here. Their dad stood at the top of the bus's steps, holding a cane. "Dad!" She ran towards him. Joey sprinted forward too. Once the man hobbled to the ground, he embraced his children.

Sato and Yoshi stood back, letting the Minamis share their moment together. They smiled as they watched the exchange.

"I was starting to get a little worried," Sato said.

From the tone of her voice, Yoshi sensed she wanted to say something else. For a few moments, she just quietly watched as Joey and Emi wrapped their arms around their dad. Mr. Minami put a hand on the back of each of their heads, pulling them close.

"He's not what I pictured," Sato finally said. "I don't know what I was expecting."

Yoshi gazed at Mr. Minami's face. Without a doubt, this was the same man from Joey's old photograph. Yoshi recognized the bald head, the big hands, and the half smile on the left side of his mouth. He had big floppy ears like Joey. He had a round face like Emi. But Sato was right. Something seemed strange. Joey's photograph was only four or five years old, but Mr. Minami seemed to have aged twenty years. His frame was thin and gangly. Some graying stubble peppered his face and neck. And that hobble of his...

"Do you know if he used a cane before?" Yoshi asked.

Sato shrugged. "They never said. But they did say he used to go on walks by the water. I can't imagine he would have done that with a cane."

Emi and Joey held onto their dad's arms as he walked, apparently too excited to consider that they never had to support him this way before. Yoshi tried hiding his concern as the three of them approached.

"Dad," Emi said. "This is Yoshi and Sato."

"They're our best friends," Joey added. "They couldn't wait to meet you!"

With an expressionless face, Mr. Minami gave a cordial nod. "Where are we staying?" he asked Joey.

Joey's mouth hung open, and his gaze bounced back and forth between his father and Yoshi.

"We're over in Block 2," Emi answered. "It's this way." She mouthed "thank you" to Yoshi and Sato before turning to help the man stagger away. The engine of the Greyhound bus revved up again, and the vehicle drove back out the gate. A couple MPs closed the fence. With Emi's blanket in his hands, Yoshi looked at Sato and opened his mouth to speak. Nothing came out but foggy breath.

Over the next two and a half weeks, Yoshi saw much less of Joey and Emi, and the little time they spent together didn't feel the same. Joey stopped goofing around as much, and Emi always looked like she was on the verge of falling asleep. According to Sato, Emi stopped turning in most of her homework and started leaving class early. And whenever she was asked how her father was doing, she simply answered "fine."

Yoshi and Sato sat on the steps of their apartment, waiting for Emi and Joey to meet them for their first outing since their dad's arrival. It was the first Saturday in

February, and the following weekend, Block 9 would hold a Valentine's Day dance in the mess hall. Ever since Yoshi heard about the event, he debated whether or not he should ask Emi to be his date. With all the pressure she was under, he didn't want to give her any extra stress. If he weren't still so shy about sharing his feelings, he would have asked Sato for her advice. Gulping down his embarrassment, he almost managed to talk to her about it when Emi and Joey came walking towards them.

"How's he doing?" Yoshi asked.

Joey faked a smile. "He's doing okay."

Father had given Yoshi some money to buy bread and peanut butter so the four of them could eat something other than a mess hall meal. On their way to the canteen, Joey mentioned his excitement about eating a peanut butter sandwich, and he tried convincing Sato that nuts were technically considered vegetables. As the two of them argued over the matter, Yoshi turned to Emi and quietly asked again about her dad's condition.

She thought for a moment before whispering, "He doesn't really talk about what happened. All he says is they showed him the real America. He swears they didn't hurt him or anything, but..." Leaning her head forward, she checked to make sure Joey wasn't listening. "I think something broke."

They passed a bulletin board advertising next weekend's event.

"That's right," Sato said. "Our block's having a dance next Sunday. You guys want to go?"

Joey looked over at Emi, who responded with a shrug.

"Come on!" Sato prodded. "You guys deserve to have a little fun."

Emi stared at the flyer. *Public Notice: Valentine's Night Dance in Block 9*, it said.

"You want to?" she asked Joey. With a close-mouthed smile, her brother nodded enthusiastically.

Deep down, Yoshi felt both thrilled and disappointed. In a way, he got what he wanted without having to ask for it. At the same time, he wondered if the four of them were just going as friends or as some kind of double date. Sato and Joey didn't have feelings for one another, but a Valentine's dance had to be at least a *little* romantic. Anyway, there was no reason to worry until the night of the dance came. And even though he couldn't pinpoint exactly what it was, he had the strangest sense that something big was coming.

Part Four:

FEAR ITSELF

CHAPTER SIXTEEN

DON'T LOCK ME UP

They handed it out to everybody aged 17 and older on Wednesday, February 10th, 1943. Yoshi reread his copy every day since then. At night, he stayed up for hours, playing the questions over and over in his head. As the deadline neared, the pressure grew.

Statement of United States Citizen of Japanese Ancestry, it said across the top. The forms given to Mom and Father had another title: *Application for Leave Clearance*. Both versions looked almost identical, with four tan pages of personal questions asking about one's religion, membership to any clubs or organizations, the names and addresses of relatives living in Japan, the location and reason for any prior international travel, and knowledge of the Japanese language.

Of all the questions, the last two gave everyone the most concern. Yoshi's looked like this:

27. Are you willing to serve in the armed forces of the United States on combat duty, wherever ordered?

28. Will you swear unqualified allegiance to the United States of America and faithfully defend the United States from any and all attack by foreign or domestic forces, and forswear any form of allegiance or obedience to the Japanese emperor, or any other foreign government, power or organization?

For Mom and Father, question 27 asked about their willingness to serve in the Army Nurse Corps or the Women's Army Auxiliary Corps. They didn't understand. Why would Father be asked about joining these female units of the military? Did "Application for Leave Clearance" mean they were about to be sent away? Where to? Would they be separated? And as for Yoshi, would he be drafted to fight? What did the government have in mind for those they deemed "disloyal"?

None of the administrators provided any clarification. All they said was that everyone under the age of 17 would stay with their parents, and everyone over 16 was required to answer. Nobody explained the purpose of these loyalty questionnaires, and nobody made clear what would happen next.

Still, the choice seemed simple on the surface. The government wanted Yoshi's vow of allegiance, and all he had to do was answer yes. He thought he knew what he would do, but his confidence didn't last once his family made him think harder about it. For days, their arguments played over and over in his head:

"It's trick question," Sato warned when she studied the papers. "Look! It says, 'Will you *forswear* allegiance to the emperor?' *Forswear*. You can't give up something you don't already have. If we say yes, that means we were loyal to Japan before!" If Sato turned out to be right, then they should answer no.

Mom's main concern was about Yoshi. One night, when he was pretending to sleep, Yoshi overheard a whispered argument between his parents. "They'll send the Japanese boys on the most dangerous missions," Mom insisted. "The government won't value their lives as much as the white ones. You know it's true." If Mom's fears were legitimate, then Yoshi would have to consider the dangers he would face by answering yes.

Father took the most frightening view. "Think if Japan wins, what they would do if they saw this." As much as they all hated the thought, Japan might win the war. If the

Yamaguchis denounced the emperor on paper, then the Japanese army might kill them all. In Father's view, a "no" could end up being fatal.

On a balmy Valentine's afternoon, Yoshi sat on his cot and stared at that fourth page. By now, he had filled out everything except for numbers 27 and 28. He needed to turn in his questionnaire before 9 o'clock the next morning, and he still had no idea how he would answer those two questions. His legs shook. Even before receiving the loyalty questionnaire, he was nervous for tonight. Emi and Joey would arrive for the dance at any minute, and Yoshi hadn't figured out if this was a date or not. Emi clearly cared about him on some level, because she opened up to him when she didn't seem to open up to anybody. But Yoshi wasn't sure if their bond was romantic, and with tomorrow's deadline looming, his feelings became more urgent. Pretty soon, Emi might be sent off to a different place than him, and Yoshi wanted to understand their relationship before they parted ways.

"You both look wonderful," Mom told Yoshi and Sato. "I wish I had my camera with me."

Sato wore a beige, puffy-sleeved, button-up blouse and a knee-length, belted navy skirt. Yoshi wore his white dress shirt, which Mom ironed for him at the laundry room, and Father helped him perfect his bow tie. He re-visited the barber shop earlier that day, so his slicked-back pachuco cut looked shiny and fresh. Sprucing himself up was a nice distraction. But once he looked the very best he could, his attention went back to the questions in his hands.

Mom put a hand on his shoulder. "Don't worry about any of this right now." She took the questionnaire from him and placed it back on one of the nightstands. "There's nothing else we can possibly say about it. The best thing you can do is clear your mind. Just try and have some fun tonight. We can make our final decision tomorrow morning."

"This dance is not free," Father said. At first, Yoshi didn't realize that this was his father's way of offering to pay.

"Five cents per couple," Sato answered.

Father reached into the tin can by his bed and pulled out a couple of nickels, then tossed the change at Yoshi.

"I still have seven dollars left," Yoshi mumbled. "I can afford it."

Father shook his head. He picked up the can of change and rattled it around. "Soon, I will dump this." When nobody reacted to his comment, Father stormed over to the pile of questionnaires and held them up. "After *this*, we will have *nothing*. I say this now, and you will see."

Everyone stared at Father, but nobody responded, causing an awkward tension to fill the room.

Then a knock came at the door.

"Thank you," Sato whispered in relief as she stood up. Yoshi gave a quick sweep over his hair as Mom opened the door and smiled at Joey and Emi. "Come on in, you two. You both look terrific." The Minamis stepped inside the apartment. Emi wore her hair in curls. Her tight black dress cut off at the knees, and a white beaded necklace matched her pearl earrings. Whatever courage Yoshi had mustered to ask Emi about their relationship disappeared the moment he saw her. He felt a tingle in his belly—a combination of nerves and awe. At some point in the night, he vowed to himself, he would call her beautiful.

"My goodness, Joey," Mom said. "Don't you look sharp?"

With his hair slicked to the side, Joey looked completely different. He gave a shy smile and stuck his arms out to show off his suit.

"Mr. Hamasaki got this for me a few months ago." His voice trailed off a bit when he realized he shouldn't have brought up the JACL. "Hi, Mr. Yamaguchi."

Father gave a quiet sigh before approaching the door. He shook Joey's hand and nodded at Emi.

"How are you two doing?" Mom asked. "Yoshi tells me your father made it here safely. I'm so happy to hear that." Yoshi hoped he wasn't blushing, but Mom talked to his friends like he wasn't standing right beside her.

Joey nodded. "He's okay."

"Good." Mom's voice was warm and sympathetic. "And Emi, how's school? I hear Mrs. Fletcher gave you an extension?"

Sato rolled her eyes. "Don't even mention that dumb electoral college project right now."

Emi chuckled. "We're getting a couple extra weeks because of the…with everything that's going on."

The loyalty questionnaire hovered over the room like a ghost that nobody wanted to speak of.

"I'm sure that helps," Mom said with a smile. "Listen," she added. "Have some fun tonight. You all need it."

Everybody smiled and waved goodnight, and Sato led the way down the steps. She balanced carefully when she touched the ground, trying not to dirty her saddle shoes as she landed. Emi followed closely behind, and Yoshi hurried after her. They walked around the Yamaguchis' barrack, then started following the narrow path between

Buildings 8 and 9 toward the heart of the block.

Emi turned to Yoshi and smiled. "You look nice!"

Tell her she's beautiful, Yoshi hounded himself. *This is your chance.* He opened his mouth, took a deep inhale, and forced out a reply. "Thanks. So do you." As soon as the words left his mouth, he cursed himself for failing to say it. *Come on! Just do it!* But by now, Emi had turned to talk to Sato, and it was too late. An ugly mixture of disappointment and timidity churned in Yoshi's gut. Shyness around girls was nothing new to him, but this was worse than usual. Never before had he grown so close to someone he had feelings for, so he couldn't ignore his nervousness about screwing up. In the past, he would make himself feel better by daydreaming about being a hero. That old trick no longer worked. He had outgrown his cowboy phase, and with the loyalty questionnaire always on his mind, he didn't take any comfort in the image of himself as a soldier.

Trapped in a whirlwind of thought, Yoshi dragged his feet along the shadow of the barrack, falling behind the pace of the girls. If he wasn't so distracted, he would have noticed sooner that Joey hadn't made any jokes or silly faces so far. Both the boys just slugged along beside each other, their backs slouched and their expressions looking equally as glum.

"You okay?" Yoshi asked.

Joey said nothing for a moment. With his hands in his pockets and his head hung low, he kicked a pebble along the path in front of him.

"It's this loyalty thing," he eventually answered, in a tone more serious than Yoshi had ever heard from him before. "I just don't know."

Yoshi searched for advice, or at least some comforting words, but nothing came to mind. Deep down, they both felt the same apprehension.

"Let's try and forget about it for now," he said, taking his mom's advice.

Joey forced a smile, and for the first time, it didn't appear genuine. If his normal enthusiasm was a mask, then the edges were peeling off.

Sato and Emi waited for their brothers to catch up, and muffled music started filling the block as the four of them approached the mess hall. Two members of the Social Activities Department stood by the door, exchanging nickels for reentry tickets. Yoshi and Joey both took out 10 cents as the building swallowed up the line. Nearing the door, they had to shout over the music.

"I'm happy to cover it!" Yoshi said.

"It's no big!" Joey answered. "You should save your dough!"

"Really, I don't mind!"

"Don't worry!" Sato chimed in. "Our dad gave it to us!"

I knew she would say that. Yoshi clenched his teeth. He wished he could at least pretend he was taking out a girl on a real date.

"I'd hate to take his money!" Joey protested. "Really, I got it!"

"Let's just split it!" Emi suggested.

Yoshi almost jumped—this was his chance. "Good idea!"

"Sure, why not?" Joey said. "I'll cover me and Emi!"

"Yeah, and I'll get me and..." Yoshi realized what Joey had just said. "...me and Sato," he muttered to himself.

When they reached the entrance, one of the women handed out reentry tickets, while the other woman tallied the four of them off on a clipboard. She counted out loud as her pencil ticked: "144, 145, 146, 147." As Yoshi climbed the steps of the mess hall, the woman's voice drowned out beneath the blare of trumpets and saxophones.

All the overhead lights were off. Moonlight illuminated the building through the dust-stained windows, casting a gravelly glow across the couples. Tables were pushed up against the walls, and a lonely young man sat on one of the benches, peeking down at his watch. The air smelled of wood and cheap perfume, though a leftover hint of beefy onion still lasted from supper's stew.

Sato bopped her head as she led her friends toward the middle of the floor. They squeezed between the jiving couples, who shook their hips, kicked their legs, and twirled beneath their partners' arms, always careful not to knock into their peers but letting their jitters flutter away. A swing band played in the back, made up of eleven young Japanese musicians who refused to abandon their instruments at home. Their corner was lit up by an orange-filtered construction light. Four saxophonists sat on a bench, reading sheet music from cardboard stands, while six trumpeters wailed behind, and a lone drummer pounded on his single paradiddle drum.

With such a vibrant atmosphere, Yoshi couldn't conceive how this same room had hosted all those meals. Seeing this familiar place in such a different way made him feel like he was dreaming. Exhaustion from the draining week added to the sensation. He had a minor headache between his eyebrows, the kind he sometimes got after rolling out of bed. His eyes felt dry and prickly, causing his lids to droop. Between the blaring music, the sleepy dark blue hue, and the energy all around him, Yoshi didn't feel completely conscious. He was in one of those states of mind where stupid things seemed hilarious and petty problems felt tragic. Usually, he only reached this point when he stayed up really late.

In the middle of the dance floor, Joey halfheartedly rocked his head. Sato took his hand and tried getting him to dance, but his limp arm just flopped around. She clasped his other wrist and lifted both his arms into the air like a marionette. This time, he smiled for real. For a few seconds, he leaned back and forth. Then his knees caught on, his shoulders followed, and he finally succumbed to the music. The duo twisted their knees, slowly bending over, slowly getting up, joining the frenzied motion of the couples all around them.

Yoshi looked at Emi. They shrugged at each other, and he grabbed her hand. He felt a warm shiver in the small of his back, then it moved up his spine and turned into a sway of the shoulders. Moved by both the feeling and the groove, he shimmied away his reservations. He couldn't believe it, but he was dancing. He twisted his knees, grinned without even thinking about it, took her other hand, flapped his elbows up and down, shook his head around, jutted out his back side, stood up straight, pulled her close to him, and stepped back away. The whole crowd moved without any unity or coordination. Couples and singles both danced their own way. Some kicked out their legs. Some just rocked and snapped. Some had perfect rhythm. Some couldn't keep the beat. It didn't matter. Nobody cared. If only for a night, they felt like no one was watching them.

Everybody cheered as the band transitioned into "Sing! Sing! Sing!" The burst of trumpets sounded like a pack of angry elephants. Yoshi swung his shoulders—left one forward, right one forward—and kicked out the opposite foot, forgetting about his fear of looking silly. Shadowed faces surrounded him. The music swept over him. Emi smiled in front of him, her face nearing his as the dance pulled them together, her body falling away as the moves yanked them apart. Her curls jiggled with every twist. Her smile glowed in the speckled moonlight, nearing him then falling away. High heels clicked on the ground against the *wah-wah-wah* of the saxophone wail. The air grew stuffier with every heavy exhale. Her face neared his then seemed so far away—nearer, farther, nearer, farther, nearer, almost right in front of him...

The music stopped and everybody clapped. "Thank you!" one of the saxophonists stood up and shouted. He wore a red flannel shirt under a dark green sweater vest and a pair of navy jeans folded up at the ankles. "We are the Barbed Wire Brothers, and we'll be back in ten for another set!"

Yoshi's ears rang as the room filled with chatter. He panted, feeling like he had just woken up from being hypnotized. A few seconds ago, he and Emi were almost cheek-to-cheek. Now that it was just a memory, the moment seemed impossible. The music's spell was broken, and they stood a couple feet apart.

"Let's go say hi to Ken," Joey said. His hair was shiny with sweat, and he smiled like his old, energized self. This sudden enthusiasm relieved Yoshi. Before tonight, he had seen Joey look disappointed and nervous, but never depressed. Thankfully, the outing seemed to perk him up.

"Who's Ken?" Sato asked.

"My friend, the bandleader. Come on!" He grabbed Sato's hand and ran to the back corner. Yoshi and Emi followed behind.

The bandleader was wiping his mouthpiece with a handkerchief when the four of them approached. "Joey!" He put the mouthpiece back on the end of the saxophone and gave Joey a hug. "What's buzzin', cousin?"

"*You guys* are! It's sounding great!"

"Thanks." He stretched his mouth open wide a couple times, rubbing the left side of his face. "I'm hoping my lips don't fall off by the end of the night. My cheeks are already killing me." He looked at Emi. "Good to see ya. Who's the boy?"

Yoshi chuckled awkwardly. He hoped Emi would clarify their relationship when she introduced him, but she didn't call him either her friend or her guy. She didn't even react to the way Ken worded the question. She simply told him Yoshi's name. After a quick handshake, the attention shifted, and Yoshi got lost in thought as Ken and Joey reminisced about their time together in the high school marching band. Yoshi nodded and smiled, occasionally laughing when everybody else did, but in the back of his mind, he couldn't stop worrying that he had missed his chance with Emi. Though a chance to speak in private hadn't presented itself yet, he wondered if he should have said something by now. He was running out of time, and he needed to do something soon.

From behind the band's seats, a couple of the trumpeters dragged out a speaker, while the drummer propped up a microphone. One of the women from the Social Activities Department fussed with the cords. The mess hall's PA system shrieked, and everyone looked up at the roof with a grimace. Ken looked over his shoulder and asked the woman if she needed any help, but she shook her head.

"We weren't planning to have any vocalists," Ken explained to Joey. "But I caught this new tune on the radio and couldn't resist. I told my girl she had to try it out. I met her here, and boy, she's something else. She's got a voice like you wouldn't believe."

Out of nowhere, a hand with black-painted fingernails reached for Ken's face and pulled him in for a kiss. This young lady wore a red kimono with an American flag bandana wrapped around her head.

"You were saying?" she said as she let him go. Blushing, Ken took a step away from her. She playfully slapped his chest. "Aw, don't be such a fuddy-duddy. How's it going so far? I didn't miss anything, did I?" She turned to Yoshi and the others and raised her chin. "Who are these fine people?"

Yoshi's eyes shot open when he saw her; her confidence intimidated him a bit. Even though he'd never seen her before, he felt like he was in the presence of a celebrity.

Ken scratched the back of his neck, trying to play it

cool. "Here she is. Sue Fukui."

"Hey, Miss Fukui," Joey smiled.

"So formal." She extended her hand with her fingers pointed toward the floor, like she expected Joey to kiss it. "Nice to meet you, Mister…?"

"Minami," Joey answered, clasping her fingers in the strangest handshake Yoshi had ever seen. When she heard Joey's last name, her eyes widened and she froze. Then her shoulders hunched a bit, like an actress breaking character as she stepped into the wings.

"Nice to meet you," she said. Her voice was deeper now, and her blank, distracted gaze indicated she was thinking about something. Everyone waited for her to speak. "This is probably crazy," she said to Joey. "But did your dad work at Compton Elementary?"

Joey exchanged a quick glance with Emi, then nodded at Sue.

With her jaw hanging open, Sue shook her head in amazement. "Well, I'll be. What a humdinger! Talk about a small world."

Ken put a hand around her back. "You know him?"

"He tutored my sis and me after school for four years! He's the reason I speak English as well as I do. Heck, it's a little embarrassing to admit, but he brought lunches for some of us poor kids when times were getting tough. Compton was pretty tiny, and some of our families weren't so well off."

Yoshi tried imagining that gruff old man acting so warm and kind. Hearing this story made Yoshi consider how deeply the wound must cut with Emi and Joey. What do you do when the things you loved about a person vanish, when all that's left is a familiar face? Do you love the shell for its familiarity, or mourn the hollowness inside? As strange as it seemed, he felt grateful that Grandma had passed away before anything changed about her. Until her last breath, she remained the same wonderful person he always adored.

All this time, Emi kept quiet. Yoshi turned his head to her. She stood next to him, shaking a curl away from her face before looking into his eyes. Neither spoke, but a memory hid in their silence. On Yoshi's birthday, they bonded through a sad but honest vow: *it always will be hard to remember what you've lost.* She lent him this truth by the pond in October, and now, in their gaze, he gave it back to her. He could have told her not to worry. He could have promised that someday, the hurt will altogether cease. But he didn't dare to utter something he didn't believe, and he chose instead to simply stand beside her. *It's hard. I know. All I can give you is my concern, but I can't take your pain away.*

Their eye contact broke, and Yoshi felt a wave sweep over him as he came to a terrifying conclusion. He couldn't save her from anything—nor could she save him—but they kept each other from being alone, they were united in their mutual defenselessness, and in that moment, he realized he loved her.

"It's the craziest thing," Sue continued. "I was just thinking about him a couple days ago. No kidding. I was thinking, you know, what ever happened to Mr. Minami? And he's here! I can't believe it. I mean, I guess it makes sense, but…How is he? Where do you guys live? I'd love to come visit sometime!"

Joey nodded. He forced a smile, like he didn't have the strength to admit how much his father had changed. "That would be…"

Another shriek came over the PA, followed by a woman's voice saying, "Test, test."

"Sounds like they're ready for us," Ken said.

With a nod, Sue adjusted her American flag bandana so more of the stars peeked out from under the fold. Her eyes gleamed with excitement. "Good stuff. Great to meet you, Joey. I'll be seeing you around, okay?"

"You're gonna love the song, man," Ken added. "It's killer-diller. Just you wait."

As Yoshi headed back into the crowd to get out of the band's way, Sato and Emi walked beside him. Joey fell a couple steps behind, biting his lower lip and turning his eyes down toward the floor. After a second, his head shot up and he laughed. "I have to use the latrine real quick. It just hit me out of nowhere!" He scurried off between the chatting couples.

Yoshi couldn't tell if Joey was lying or not, and he glanced at Emi to see if she looked concerned. She didn't appear to be paying any attention. Her long black lashes weighed down her eyelids, and the moonlight cast a pale glow on her left cheek. When Yoshi saw how sad she looked, he said the first thing that came to mind. "We can leave if you want."

Those lashes rose. "No," she whispered. "We can't."

It took Yoshi a moment to understand her meaning. Before he could respond, Sue Fukui grabbed the microphone, and everybody started clapping. The flower design imprinted upon Sue's robe looked golden in the orange-filtered construction light. "Is this working?" she spoke into the wailing mic. The shrill feedback stopped. Beside her, Ken held up an acoustic guitar, plucking at strings to do some last-minute tuning. Once he felt ready, he gave Sue a thumbs up.

Sue straightened her back to get into performance posture. "*Konbanwa*, my fellow Americans—singles, couples, cool cats, and all you beautiful ladies. My name is Sue Fukui, and I'm here to change the atmosphere. You've all been diggin' the jive long enough, so I thought I'd *slow* things down for you." She pressed her arms out in front of herself on the word "slow," as if she were pushing a big heavy box. "So, grab a partner and button up your jackets, 'cause things are about to get cool in here."

A few singles frantically looked for a partner. One young man approached Sato, asking if she was free to dance. She looked around for a minute, wondering if she should wait for Joey. Emi gave her a little nod of encouragement. Sato hesitantly took the stranger's hand.

"This song is dedicated to President Roosevelt," Sue continued over the PA. "You're a real good man, except for when you're not. Hit it, fellas."

Ken played a short, simple hook going up a major scale, but the music was difficult to hear. Partners grabbed each others' arms as Sue started singing in a raspy soprano:

Oh, my love, you can push me away,
But don't lock me up.
Sail off; leave me at the quay,
But don't lock me up.

Emi grabbed Yoshi's left hand, and they extended their arms to each other. At first, Yoshi put his right hand on Emi's shoulder. She lowered it to the small of her back. His body quivered at her touch, revealing how new this was for him. She smiled in return, as if to tell him not to be afraid. They swayed back and forth, hardly moving their feet. This wasn't like the swing. It was a different kind of dance, softer and more intimate. No more stepping up and pulling away. This time, they stayed close to each other.

There's just one thing that makes me gripe.
Don't lock me up.
You know I'm not the marriage-type.
Don't lock me up.

Yoshi gulped. With so many unknowns already weighing on him, pursuing his feelings seemed irresponsible. He knew nothing about romance. Even worse, he didn't believe he deserved to be with someone as smart and kind and pretty as her. But despite all his uncertainties, despite his doubts and his self-consciousness, standing here in front of her was the only thing he knew was right. He didn't understand how he could feel so insecure and so invincible all at once. It was some sort of beautiful contradiction, like the warm chill tingling down his spine, or the sense of freedom he experienced while dancing in an internment camp. Emi didn't make him forget about the fence or the war or the questionnaire; if only while she smiled at him, she made him unafraid. He stared at the little dimple by her lips, at the shadows of hair curls on her moonlit face, and in that instant, she might as well have been the only thing the world refused to crumble for.

You can scoff at me and make me frown,
Starve me sick and spill my cup,
Kick me back and knock me down,
But don't lock me up.

All he had to do was ask her. All he had to do was speak the truth. *I love you*, he thought. *Just say it.* He knew this could be his only chance. If the two of them were torn apart, he would never know what might have been unless he told her now.

Yes, scoff at me and make me frown,
Starve me sick and spill my cup,
Kick me back,
Knock me down,

But don't—

He kissed her.

She stepped away from him. "Oh," she said, putting her hand to her lips. "That's not…" Her voice trailed off.

"I'm sorry," he blurted out. "I didn't mean…"

"No, it's okay," Emi said.

"I'm sorry! I wasn't thinking!" He ran through the crowd, ashamed and humiliated, disregarding the stares of the couples all around him, trying to cover his eyes while finding his way to the exit. Cold air blasted against his face as he pushed open the door. He tripped down the stairs, fumbling against the wooden handrail before thumping down onto the dirt. A puff of dust blew up and tickled his nostrils.

"Are you okay?!" One of the women from the Social Activities Department hurried over to him.

Yoshi leapt up and stumbled around the corner, leaving the woman behind. He leaned against the face of the mess hall. The support planks raised the building up to his thighs, and one of the wall's vertical beams dug into his back. In his mind, Emi was still smiling at him, and the moment right before the kiss played over and over, like the memory was mocking him. *You've ruined it!* he scolded himself. *You've ruined everything!*

Muffled cheers and applause reached his ringing ears, and Yoshi pulled up the collar of his undershirt to dab away the tears from his puffy eyes. More than anything else, his connection with Emi saved him from the depths of his depression. Longing to befriend her pushed him out of bed; developing a bond with her finally made him happy again. Whatever they had, it was special—and now, at a time when he needed her support more than ever, he lost her.

After a deep, wavering sigh, he wondered if he should go back inside. He sniffled a couple of times. The sound of crying continued like an echo. At first, he thought the night had messed with his senses, and he gazed above the distant black mountains, as if the universe was throwing his sadness back at him. But the sound kept on, and Yoshi peeked around the corner to his right. Staring down the long, shadowy back side of the mess hall, he spotted someone curled up by one of the wood planks, arms hugging knees, almost fitting into the gap between the dirt and the propped-up floor.

Yoshi took a step forward. "Joey?"

"Oh, hi Yoshi." Joey's head shot up when he heard Yoshi's voice. Streams of tears glistened on his cheeks, and his loosened tie hung lopsidedly beneath his unbuttoned collar. He smiled, showing off his crooked teeth.

"What are you doing back here?" Yoshi asked. Normally, Joey looked a little unkempt, but this was different. He wasn't just disheveled this time; he was crushed.

"I don't know. I guess I just wanted some air."

Behind the sadness, Joey's eyes were filled with fear. Yoshi approached slowly, like he was about to free a panicked deer from a hunter's trap.

"Is it something Sue said?" he asked.

Hearing the name of his dad's former student caused another burst of tears. Joey covered his face and bawled.

"He used to be so nice!" The shout filled the air. Joey wept in his hands. Yoshi sat beside him, and Joey turned his face away, sniffling a few times before continuing to speak. "But that's not even all of it. He's angry at what they did to him. He's telling me I have to answer no on the loyalty thing. He says if I don't, I'm choosing his captors over him. But Mr. Hamasaki and the JACL, they're telling me I need to answer yes. They were pushing for something like this questionnaire to happen. That's what the meeting in Salt Lake City was all about. They wanted something to prove we're patriotic." Saxophone and trumpet music seeped through the walls. Clomps of leaping footsteps resonated out of the gap under the mess hall. "My dad isn't thinking clearly. If he was, it wouldn't be like this. But I still don't want to betray him." He took a deep breath. "And I don't want to betray my country, and I don't want to betray Mr. Hamasaki, and none of them will ever forgive me if I don't do what they want!"

In the midst of Joey's desperation, Yoshi felt helpless as a friend. He searched for an adequate way to respond, and somewhere deep inside, he knew what Grandma would have said. "What do *you* want?"

Joey spun around and looked Yoshi in the eye. "None of it! I hate this! I want it all to go away!"

Neither spoke. Yoshi stared back, mouth hung open in shock. He had never seen Joey become angry like this before. Ashamed, Joey hung down his head. When he spoke again, his voice became soft and apologetic.

"I'm scared," he whispered like a shameful confession. "I'm not a fighter, Yoshi. I can't hurt another person. If I get sent off to war, I'll never make it back. It's bad to say, but I was happy when the military didn't want us. It was the only thing that saved me." He wiped his eyes with his sleeve—gently at first, then scraping the tears aggressively as the fury came back to him. "But I don't know what'll happen to me if I say no! I don't want to be sent away somewhere! I don't want me and Emi to be locked up like my dad! I don't know what's gonna happen, and I don't know what to do, and it's too much pressure to handle! I just can't take it anymore!"

Yoshi's mouth hung open. In one night, everything had fallen apart. No more jokes from Joey, no more intimate conversations with Emi, and pretty soon, he figured, no more Manzanar. It might be in a soldier's uniform or it might be in a prison suit, but a departure seemed imminent. Sometimes, you don't realize how fragile something is until it's shattered.

"*There* you are." Sato stood at the corner of the mess hall. "What happened? You guys disappeared."

"Sorry," Yoshi said. "We were just talking. Is Emi still inside?"

"Yeah. She said you went to the latrine, but that was like twenty minutes ago."

Emi had lied, and Yoshi didn't know how to interpret that. Either she was protecting him from embarrassment or trying to pretend the incident never happened. Whatever the case, Yoshi was a little relieved that Sato didn't know about the kiss. He would somehow need to explain why he couldn't spend time with Emi anymore, but the truth was too humiliating to admit. He stood up, but he didn't want to leave. Behind the mess hall, he felt hidden away from the rest of the world, and there was something oddly reassuring about shared misery with a friend.

Joey noticed Yoshi's hesitance. "Go on," he mumbled. "Sato's waiting for you."

"I want to stay here with you," Yoshi said. "She'll understand."

"No, I'd rather be alone. I mean it."

It took Yoshi a moment to believe him. As the silence continued, he knew it was the truth. With a sympathetic nod, Yoshi walked away. He reached his sister, stepping out into the moonlight from behind the building.

Sato gasped. "What happened to your shirt?"

"I tripped." He looked at the dirt stains on his belly.

"Mom's gonna kill you."

"I'll try to wash it before she sees." He knew he sounded unconcerned, and he realized how unusual that was for him. By this point, his dirty shirt didn't matter to him at all.

"Is everything okay?" Sato asked.

"We'll worry about it tomorrow. Come on, let's go."

"Don't you want to say goodnight to Emi?"

Yes, he thought. He wanted to say goodnight almost as much as he wished to tell her goodbye, but he didn't have the strength to show his face again. He shook his head, taking the first step back towards the apartment.

"Hey Yoshi," Joey called.

When Yoshi turned around, his eyes had already read-justed to the moonlight, and he could barely make out his friend's shadowed face.

"I had fun," Joey told him. "I mean it."

Looking back on the thrill and the heartbreak, Yoshi knew he would never forget this night. It was filled with passion, both exciting and devastating, and if nothing else, it made him feel alive.

"Me too," Yoshi said, before stepping around to the front of the mess hall.

He woke up at 4:30 a.m. after the deepest sleep he could remember. All the stress of the dance and the ques-tionnaire exhausted him enough for a good night's rest. Around this time, the cooks would start making breakfast, though the mess hall bells wouldn't announce the meal for another two and a half hours. Yoshi lay on his back, star-ing at the window on the wall behind his bed. The sky was still dark, and he marveled at the notion that the last time he saw the sun, none of the drama with Emi and Joey had happened yet. In a way, he still hadn't left the night behind.

But 9 a.m. would creep upon him. He needed to make up his mind about the loyalty questionnaire. After last night, he kind of liked the idea of leaving this place behind and pursuing his old dream. Answering yes would likely ship him off to the military, so he could finally become an American soldier. But he had no idea where his parents and Sato would end up, and after all the support they gave him through his depression, he couldn't abandon them.

His cot squeaked as he sat up. When they heard the springy frame, everyone else rose too. Sato pulled off the covers and sat cross-legged on her straw-filled mattress. Mom and Father sat up in their makeshift double bed, looking across the room at Yoshi and Sato. For a few seconds, nobody spoke. Another upheaval would soon be upon them, and they needed to appreciate that they were a family, a team, ready to help each other tackle whatever struggles the future might bring. This quiet moment of togetherness reminded Yoshi of their last morning at home, standing in an empty living room and wondering what was about to become of them. This time, Mom was first to speak. "How was the dance?"

"It was nice," Sato answered.

When Yoshi didn't respond, Mom cocked her head to the side, sensing he was upset about something. Yoshi wanted to forget about last night, so he just nodded in agreement.

"Good," Mom said, with a hint of skepticism in her voice. "I'm glad."

"We should answer yes," Father blurted out. "This is most safe."

"We all need to agree." Mom said. "Especially Yoshi. He's the one being asked to fight."

"He wants to fight." Father flung out his arm, gesturing towards Yoshi. "Do you not?"

Everybody stared. Yoshi answered "yes" in his mind, but he couldn't quite bring himself to say it out loud.

Father grunted. "*I* will answer yes. He can be a fool if he wishes."

Mom shook her head. "We need to stick together. Everything else may be out of our control, but at least we can give the same answers."

Father stared at Yoshi. "Tell us you want to fight."

"I…" Yoshi gulped. He didn't have the strength for this kind of pressure. "I want to take a shower."

Father stared back blankly. Mom gave a concerned nod. They quietly watched as Yoshi tied his tennis shoes, grabbed his towel, and headed for the door.

Just past the mess hall, in the break between Blocks 9 and 10, a couple of MPs scurried south. Yoshi disregarded the activity. No doubt, they were frantically preparing for a day of accepting loyalty oaths. But then, a few Japanese men from the volunteer police force rushed by too. They turned down the same path the MPs had taken. Curious, Yoshi followed them.

A group of MPs, internees, and camp police gathered near Guard Tower 6, looking out beyond the fence. Yoshi knew his family was waiting for him, but he couldn't resist walking over to the crowd to see what all the activity was about. Maybe somebody had pulled a prank to protest the questionnaire. With all the fear and frustration going around, he wouldn't be surprised at the sight of a demonstration.

The sun started rising as he reached the back of the crowd. He tried peeking over the heads to see what was going on. Some of the people wore sleepwear like him. Others were still fully dressed from the night before. Yoshi tapped the arm of the stranger to his right. "What's going on?" he asked. Just then, he noticed Mr. Hamasaki screaming at one of the MPs.

Wide-eyed, the stranger looked down at Yoshi. "You know Joey Minami? From the JACL? He's dead."

CHAPTER SEVENTEEN

SHATTERED

"Shot by one of the guards," the stranger explained. "He crawled under the fence and ran. I guess he was trying to escape."

Yoshi's mouth hung open, but not a sound squeaked out. He shook. His legs felt weak and wobbly, like they were about to collapse. His heart pounded in his chest. The air quivered in his lungs. Joey's shadowed face from last night haunted him, and as Yoshi remembered those glistening tears, those desperate sobs, and those hopeless eyes, he lost his breath. He was suffocating with guilt. *You shouldn't have left him. You should have stayed by his side!*

A couple MPs held Mr. Hamasaki back. The man was shouting—wailing—and tears ran down his cheeks. An

MP promised that an investigation would be conducted to make sure that no wrongdoing had occurred.

"That's not good enough!" Mr. Hamasaki screamed. "That won't bring him back!"

They threatened to escort him from the scene. They said something about joining the boy's sister for counseling in the hospital. All at once, Yoshi was struck with the image of Emi all alone, suffering another loss when she desperately needed a friend. He couldn't look at this scene anymore. He dropped the clothes in his hands and ran back to the apartment, stumbling, head whirling, shrieking in his mind. *You could have saved him! You could have saved him!*

He burst open the door. "He's gone!"

Everybody jumped up. He fell face-down on the empty cot by the door. Mom ran over to him and kneeled beside the bed.

"What's going on?" she said, rubbing his back. "Yoshi, what is it?"

"He's dead! They killed him! They killed Joey!"

Sato gasped. Mom and Father looked at each other in shock, a hint of terror in their eyes, fearing some kind of revolt was underway.

"Tell us what happened," Father demanded, reaching

for his suitcase, preparing to flee. "*Tell us*, Yoshi."

"He ran," Yoshi mumbled. "He got through the fence."
Father eased up a bit and let go of the bag, then started
pacing back and forth, every footstep pounding on the
floorboards. Mom pressed her hand on Yoshi's back.
Once the information settled, Sato started bawling. None
of this clamor registered with Yoshi. He was trapped in
his imagination, picturing those final moments right before the shot; how Joey crawled under the barbed wire
fence, in clear view of a guard tower, and ran from both
the future and the past.

"He knew he couldn't escape," Yoshi whispered. "He
knew they would kill him."

Mom had no words. She simply squeezed his shoulder
and pursed her lips.

Father stopped pacing. "We must answer yes," he de-
clared.

Yoshi's head shot up. "How can you think about that
right now?! They just killed my friend!"

"And if we give them what they do not want, they
could kill us too."

"Tanaka," Mom said. "We need to stay level-headed."

Father threw his hands up in the air. "They shot a
young man dead."

"For *running away*," Mom said. "You think they'll kill us all for answering—"

"You just said he deserved it!" Sato shouted.

"Sato, please." Mom closed her eyes.

"That's what you said!"

Mom kept her eyes shut. "We need to stay together through this."

"They killed him!" Sato wiped her nose. "We can't give them a yes!"

"We will do what *I* think is right." Father pointed to himself.

Mom held out her arm towards Yoshi. "Tanaka, Yoshi is the one being asked to risk his life! This has to be *his* decision."

Father froze. Aside from his fuming breaths, the room fell silent, and his gaze bounced back and forth between Yoshi, Mom, and Sato. His nostrils flared, his face scrunched up, and his chest heaved in and out. Yoshi kept his head down, the tears feeling warm against his cheeks, and when he glanced up like a dog about to be put to sleep, he couldn't tell if his father's eyes widened out of fear or pity. Father shook his head a bit, and his Adam's apple leapt as he gulped down his rage.

"He decides *now*," Father conceded. "We run out of

time."

Yoshi rose. His trembling fingers flipped back to the fourth page of the questionnaire. Grimacing, he looked down at the questions one last time, as if these papers were the novel of his life, and he was about to read the final sentence.

27. Are you willing to serve in the armed forces of the United States on combat duty, wherever ordered?

28. Will you swear unqualified allegiance to the United States of America and faithfully defend the United States from any and all attack by foreign or domestic forces, and forswear any form of allegiance or obedience to the Japanese emperor, or any other foreign government, power or organization?

He answered.

CHAPTER EIGHTEEN

GO FOR BROKE

The story of how Yoshi joined the 442nd Regimental Combat Team would always be easy to tell. How Yoshi found himself clinging to the deadly steeps of Italy's Apennine Mountains was a little bit more of a blur to him. One month after he answered "yes" on the loyalty questionnaire, a train took him to Camp Shelby in Mississippi, where he trained for a year with over 4,000 other Japanese American volunteers, and then he was sent to Europe as part of the regiment's 3rd Battalion. The first half of his journey remained clear in his head. He remembered those nighttime practice marches at Camp Shelby, where he panted and sweated as the freezing raindrops trickled down through the maple trees. He was still a little embarrassed about getting seasick on the three-week voyage to

316 · ANDREW HAYES WILLIAMS

Europe, when he vomited over the deck of the *U.S.S El-dridge Gerry*, and the gunmen aboard one of the navy's twelve escort destroyers looked up at him and laughed. And, of course, he would never forget the absolute terror he felt upon first being shot at; he'd had no time to mentally prepare because his company had accidentally stumbled on the enemy while crossing the grassy hills toward the Italian town of Suvereto. From then on, Yoshi's memory started becoming more of a blur. Some moments were burned into his memory forever, but his days blended together after a year of fighting. One battle became another, just as one mission made way for the next.

Then, on the night of April 4th, 1945, the 442nd Regimental Combat Team faced its greatest challenge yet. The Allies were about to win the war, but one major obstacle still stood in the way of forcing the Nazis to surrender. The Apennine Mountains stretched all the way across Italy, from the seacoast in the west to the seacoast in the east. The Nazis often took minorities and prisoners as slaves, and 15,000 people had been forced to build bunkers, observation posts, and machine gun nests atop these mountains. This cross-country defense was called the Gothic Line, and as long as the Nazis remained there, the war would continue to rage.

Over half a year of fighting had already occurred along the Gothic Line before Yoshi ever reached it. Though the Allies had managed to make some advances, their progress halted, and one critical area of the mountain range remained in the hands of the Nazis. Allied bombers failed to do much damage to the rock and concrete fortifications, and the Nazis could spot any approaching army from their perch atop the mountain. Germany had almost no chance of winning the war at this point, but losing this remnant of the Gothic Line would guarantee their defeat. The 442nd had proven to be one of America's great fighting forces, and their unequaled bravery was needed for this nearly impossible task. In order to reach the Nazis without being seen, the 442nd would climb three thousand feet straight up the back of the mountain in total darkness.

And so, Yoshi dug his fingers into Mount Folgorito. At this point, he was halfway to the top. With his face covered in soot to blend into the night, he kept his body flat against the rocks. He tugged at tree roots and comrades' legs to hoist himself up the sixty-degree slope. His rifle and rucksack weighed his body down, and he kept slipping a few feet back. Other than the scrape of his boots against the dirt, he stumbled in utter silence. No one was allowed to make a sound. Even his dog tags were tied together with string so the two bits of metal wouldn't rattle against each other. Every time he fumbled, he knew he couldn't look down. If he didn't catch himself, he would fall fifteen hundred feet, and screaming would alert the enemy.

He reached up and fingered around for a solid rock. His hands throbbed from clutching at shale, and he could feel that his palms had become sticky with blood. With every grip, the ache grew worse, but he knew he couldn't let go. He had to keep climbing. One hand over the other. One arm over the next. Grab and pull, grab and pull, grab and...

He slipped again. He caught the branch of a thistly bush. He patted around and found a smooth rock, then wrapped his fingers over the edge of it. He panted through his nostrils. His heart pounded like it was trying to break out of his chest. Despite the chilly breeze, sweat formed at his hairline, and his moist skin burned in the icy air. He didn't dare to wipe it away, but he stopped to catch his breath. Silent gasp, silent gasp. *Don't think of the height. Don't think of the pain. Don't think of the fall. Think of nothing.*

But he couldn't focus on "nothing." A hundred

thoughts raced through his mind at once. His instincts screamed at him to survive. One voice mocked him for believing, long ago, that war could be fun. Then, behind the terror and the scorn, way back in the depths of his imagination, he was away from all of this. He wasn't reminiscing or lingering on a memory, but fond moments from the past popped up as static images. Just by catching a glimpse of one, he knew the story behind it, and he knew what the moment meant. As he hung from the smooth stone, taking relief in the closest thing to rest he could hope for, a particular moment came back to him. The image unfolded, and the scene replayed in an instant. Even if it seemed impossible now, there was a time before Mount Folgorito, before Camp Shelby, and before his hair was cut for war.

The evening before Yoshi left Manzanar, the Yamaguchis had one last dinner together. Instead of eating in the mess hall, they brought their portions back to the apartment for privacy. They moved their cots to form a square in the center of the room, and they sat with their plates in their laps. Yoshi faced the cloth partition. Across from him, Father faced the door. With Sato to his left and Mom to his right, Yoshi felt like he was sitting around an invisible dining room table. To an outsider, the scene must have looked like a family pretending to be home. Yoshi knew better. The Yamaguchis weren't imagining themselves anywhere but here; for better or worse, they started feeling like home had never left them.

It was a quiet night. No one dared to acknowledge it, but they all knew Yoshi might never return from the war. When they found out for certain that the loyalty questionnaire had served as a recruitment tool for the military, they felt a mixture of joy and grief. Yoshi would finally get what he had once dreamed of—not only the fantasy of wearing the uniform, but also the reality of bearing the sacrifice. The Yamaguchis worried about what kinds of missions an all-Japanese regiment would be forced to undertake, and they marveled at the government's decision to draft the Nisei boys while refusing to release their families from the camps.

But Father understood the politics of the decision and didn't hesitate to angrily explain. Since June 1942, the United States had won several crucial battles in the Pacific, and as the enemy's army weakened, the small likelihood of a Japanese invasion decreased even more. Locking up Japanese Americans after Pearl Harbor never made any sense, but by early 1943, the argument of "military necessity" for internment became completely unjustifiable. Overturning the ban on Nisei soldiers was one of the first steps towards letting some internees out of camp. After all, the practicality of gaining more troops seemed more important than the principle of hating what they looked like.

Still, despite America's successes in the Pacific, the government didn't want to close the camps just yet. Father's keen speculation would turn out to be right. Ending internment was a risky political move, so President Roosevelt decided to put off any serious action until after the following year's election. Though the questionnaire was supposed to be a way to start freeing those deemed "loyal," only some college students and seasonal harvest workers were given permission to move east at first. Because Mom and Father answered "yes" to questions twenty-seven and twenty-eight, they would remain at Manzanar until the end of the war. Those who answered "no" were sent away to a camp called Tule Lake. Yoshi never learned much more than that.

As for the confusing wording of those last two questions, the problem came from simple carelessness on the part of the administration. Question twenty-seven, which asked Father about joining female branches of the military, was a silly mistake. In their haste, the administration forgot that the questionnaire they had adapted for all the camp's women would also be distributed to the Issei men. And question twenty-eight, which asked about renouncing one's loyalty to the emperor, wasn't worded strangely as a trick, but rather as a case of thoughtless writing.

But the Yamaguchis didn't speak of these frustrations on Yoshi's last night in camp. They tried to savor their final dinner together.

After taking a big gulp of the root beer Mom had bought him as a going-away treat, Yoshi felt a burp rush up his throat before he had a chance to cover his mouth.

"Sorry," he said, and Sato started laughing. Father stared across at him with a scowl, and Yoshi waited to hear a lecture about manners.

Instead, Father opened his mouth and let out a huge belch. "In the military, this is the way of burping," he said, keeping a serious face as he looked back down at his food.

On the other side of the cloth partition, the neighbors started cracking up.

Sato opened her mouth and took a deep inhale, slowly leaning forward as she tried pushing out the sound.

Father held up a finger at her. "You will run for Con-

gress. Politicians do not burp." He picked up another noo-
dle with his chopsticks, but he spoke again before putting
it in his mouth. "They vomit lies instead."

Everybody chuckled. Mom shook her head. "Only *you*
could make burping political."

Then, out of nowhere, Sato almost spit out her food as
she laughed. "I just imagined Roosevelt belching during a
speech."

Mom gasped and shook her head. "Sato, how disrespectful."

Yoshi put his hands over his mouth to imitate a fuzzy
radio. "My fellow Americans, the State of our Union
is…" He pretended to burp.

"Please, you two." Mom tried not to laugh. "That's our
president you're talking about."

"I know," Sato retorted. "He's the one who sent us
here."

"That's beside the point. He's still our president."

With a frown, Sato stared down at her plate and
pushed around the remaining noodles with her chopsticks.

"I suppose it is a *little* funny," Mom admitted with half
a grin, and everybody snickered in agreement. It felt good
to laugh again. Over the last month, they didn't have
much to smile about. Yoshi's future as a soldier worried

all of them. And, of course, there was the other thing that never left them, even though they rarely spoke of it. As it hit her, Sato's eyes watered and her lips wavered.

"Joey would have found it funny too," she said.

The room fell silent. Ever since Joey's funeral, joking around seemed inappropriate, even though the boy's legacy was making other people smile.

"Isn't that great?" Mom finally responded. "Think of how good he would feel to know that you remember him when you're laughing."

Sato wiped her eyes and sniffled.

Yoshi frowned. He took the last sip of root beer from the bottle, leaning his head all the way back and gazing at the roof beams before staring back down at his lap. He wondered how long it would be until he tasted his favorite drink again, and he tried not to consider that this might be the last soda he ever had. Being young used to make him feel immortal, like the world couldn't take his life away when he had so much left to accomplish. This fantasy no longer worked, because at some point, Joey must have felt that way too.

"You doing okay, Yoshi?"

The warmth of Mom's voice comforted him. When Yoshi looked over at her, her eyebrows were scrunched with concern. At first, he just nodded, working up the strength to tell the truth. He swallowed the growing lump in his throat and whispered his honest reply. "I'm pretty scared."

"Oh honey." Mom stepped over to Yoshi and leaned over to give him a hug. "We're all scared."

"This is good," Father added. "In the War, fear kept me living."

Mom rubbed Yoshi's back. "And just know we'll always be thinking about you. Don't ever feel alone out there, okay?"

Yoshi nodded. He may not have been a natural born fighter, and he knew he wouldn't be the strongest warrior of the bunch. But he thought about his family's support, about their love and encouragement, and if only for a moment, he felt like nothing could defeat him.

The icy shale burned his bloody fingertips. The rocks scraped his palms as Yoshi hoisted himself up. He wasn't wearing his watch, but he figured it must have been at least two or three in the morning. Panting, he shaped his lips so the breath would fill his lungs as silently as possible. Two-thirds of the way to the top, the air was getting harder to inhale. Were fear not such a powerful distractor,

326 · ANDREW HAYES WILLIAMS

he would have felt the sharpness in his lungs, the throbbing in his back, and the spasms in his limbs. But he didn't dare acknowledge the torment. All he could do was remember his training—and trust he hadn't lost his good luck charm.

Nobody understood why he carried a burned match in his pocket. Whenever he was asked about it, Yoshi simply mentioned that an old friend had given it to him for luck.

"That's gotta be the lousiest rabbit's foot I ever seen," one of the guys scoffed a few months back. "Check this out." He pointed at the Ace of Spades playing card that was tucked into the strap across his helmet. "Found it on the floor of that cafe in Suvereto. Right when I bent down to pick it up, bullets flew over my head. True story, I swear. If it wasn't for this card, I'd be dead. *That's* luck." From then on, this soldier came to be known as "Ace," earning him the most coveted nickname in the entire battalion. Sadao Munemori was given the worst one, "Spud," because at mealtime, he always chose potatoes over rice. Yoshi was satisfied with his own nickname. Whether or not the guys had intended it as a joke, Yoshi found himself fighting more passionately every time they called him "Matchstick."

However, as the young men climbed, trying their hardest to become invisible, their names no longer mattered. They were nothing but shadows on the mountain. With his left hand, Yoshi was gripping the edge of a boulder. Reaching his right arm up, he patted around and grabbed onto the branch of nearby bush. He could practically hear the strain as the branch struggled to hold his weight. It crackled, grew tauter. The leaves slipped through his clasp. Someone pulled at the butt of Yoshi's rifle, and the branch snapped.

Trying to hold the weight of both their bodies, Yoshi grabbed the edge of the boulder with both his hands and dug his boots into the dirt. The rifle strap around his shoulder weighed him down like an anchor. His fingers started slipping, grating against the rock's surface, but kicking off the soldier would be murder. *Let go!* Yoshi shouted in his head. *I can't hold on!* His grip around the rock slipped from his knuckles to his fingertips, and as he failed to get a better grasp, a question flew through his mind: two thousand feet above the earth, how long would the fatal tumble last?

The soldier let go of the rifle. Yoshi sighed with relief, and the shock of nearly dying almost caused his body to go limp. He needed to concentrate to maintain his support.

Focus on the rock, he thought, and all at once, he fully comprehended how much danger he was in. The only thing more shocking than the absurdity of this mission was the fact that none of the men had complained about it. Then again, the 442nd's slogan was "Go For Broke," an expression that meant they were willing to risk everything. With all the Purple Hearts the regiment had won, this motto couldn't have been more appropriate.

More awards were bound to come tonight. Yoshi just hoped that if he received some sort of honor, it would be for courage and not for sacrifice. Imagining his name on a plaque for the fallen made him tighten his grip on the rock. He tried to destroy the nightmare, as if picturing his own demise would somehow make the plunge inevitable. No matter how hard he tried, it kept popping back into his head: *Yoshi Yamaguchi, 1923-1945.*

He looked around to make sure he hadn't been left behind, because he couldn't tell how long he had been hanging from the rock. As he glanced to his left, the soldier climbing beside him happened to look over too. It was Ace. They locked eyes for a moment, and Yoshi took comfort in seeing a familiar face. The two of them were comrades—friends—experiencing the unthinkable together. Sensing this camaraderie inspired Yoshi, like for the first time this entire climb, he wasn't just fighting for his *own* life.

And then, in an instant, Ace vanished. Fifty feet up, someone had slipped, landing right on top of Ace's head. The card knocked off his helmet and fluttered down after him. Yoshi forced his eyes shut to keep himself from looking down, but he'd already caught a glimpse of the two soldiers being swallowed by the night. Even as they fell to eternity, neither let out a sound. Trembling, Yoshi dangled from the rock, haunted by the silence.

After having such a nice dinner with his family, Yoshi didn't want to ruin his final night at Manzanar. But he couldn't bear to leave the camp with regrets, and there was something he needed to do before he left. If he wanted to say goodbye to Emi, he needed to do it tonight.

The sun was setting behind him as he crossed the East Firebreak. He carried a letter in his hands—an assurance to himself that he would give her the words he knew he would be too afraid to speak. As for what he would say out loud when he saw her, he already felt tongue-tied just by picturing her face. Since Valentine's Day, the only time he had seen her was at Joey's funeral, but even then, the two of them didn't interact. Almost a hundred people had shown up, and the service needed to be moved from the church to a mess hall. Yoshi stayed hidden in the back of the crowd, fearing he would only add pressure on Emi by going up to her. Truthfully, he didn't know what the right thing to do was. Bothering her about his feelings seemed selfish, but he felt guilty not being around to support her when she so desperately needed a friend. As much as he wanted to pretend the kiss had never happened, he couldn't talk to her without addressing their awkward past.

Along the path to Block 2, Yoshi practiced what he would say to her. "Emi," he whispered to the air. "I just wanted to stop by real quick and say sorry. I'm sorry about the kiss. I'm sorry I haven't been there for you. I didn't want to be a bother, but I should have come by sooner. I hope you're okay. If I make it back, I'll be your friend if you want me to be." When the steps of her apartment were in sight, he froze. He rehearsed his speech again and took a deep breath. A nervous tingle warmed his belly, similar to the jitters he had felt before the dance. *Just say it, give her the letter, and walk away*, he told himself. *You'll never forgive yourself if you don't make things right.*

Once he dragged his feet to the bottom of the steps, he

cowered before the apartment door as if it were a portal to his humiliating past. *Emi, I just wanted to stop by real quick and say sorry*, he repeated in his head before taking the first step. Each time he placed his foot down on one of the stairs, he eased his weight into the wood so the board wouldn't creak. He didn't want the door to swing open before he was prepared to recite his apology, so he needed to approach as quietly as he could. Balancing on the top step, he reached his arm up to knock. *Emi, I just wanted... Emi, I just wanted... Emi, I just wanted... Emi, I just wanted...* His knuckles stayed an inch away from the door. All he had to do was gently tap.

From behind the door, Yoshi listened to Emi crying. This was the same hoarse, exhausted sob he'd heard from her at the funeral. He dropped his hand. After tiptoeing back down, he placed his letter on the bottom step and used a nearby stone to keep it from blowing off. "For Emi," the envelope said on the back. Inside, it held his last seven dollars, along with this note:

For your Senate campaign. I still believe in you.—Yoshi

He walked away.

Before going back to his apartment, he decided there was one more place he needed to pay a final visit. He walked to the other side of camp, just past the Children's Village, and entered the cemetery. A new monument for the deceased had just been built by the Buddhist Young People's Organization and some residents of Yoshi's block. Every family in camp had contributed 15 cents for the cement, and on the front of the white obelisk, three words were inscribed in Japanese letters: "I Rei To," or "Soul Consoling Tower." Yoshi hadn't been to the cemetery since Grandma's passing, and aside from this shrine in the center, the only other difference was the handful of new graves.

From the nearby guard tower, a searchlight turned toward him. Less than a year ago, this MP's scrutiny would have scared Yoshi away. This time, it didn't. Putting a hand up to cover his eyes, he disregarded the staring stranger. In a little island of light, everything around him looked like total blackness, and he let the spotlight follow him toward the wood fence in the back. This was the corner where his family had released Grandma's ashes—and, coincidentally, it was also the spot of a new grave. A mound of dirt was outlined in pebbles, and although there were no identifying gravestones, the pile of scattered flowers indicated that it must be Joey's resting place.

Yoshi knelt at the foot of the grave. He stared at the

roses on the center of the mound, which were brown on the edges and somewhat shriveled. Then, through the leaves, Yoshi caught a glimpse of something else.

"What you wanted them to know you by," he sighed.

It was the picture of Joey holding up a fish with his father: the grinning, floppy-eared 15-year-old, and the bald, half-smiling man. When the photo was taken, the two of them must have expected to be with each other forever. They couldn't have known that in a few short years, their experiences together would only exist in memory.

Hanging his head, he dropped the photograph and clenched his fists.

"You could have been so much!" he yelled at the mound. "You could have left this place! You could have been a better dad than him!" He wiped his nose. "And now you're stuck here forever. Now you'll never be anything. You used to make people happy, but now whenever anybody thinks of you, they're going to hurt. That's what you've done!" He stared at the grave, almost expecting it to disappear, almost waiting for Emi and Joey to call his name from the cemetery's entrance to ask him what was wrong. But the mound remained in front of him. Motionless. Permanent. "Why would you choose *this* for yourself?"

And then, Grandma's voice returned to him like a whispered echo. "You always have a choice," she had wanted him to know. "Even if all you can decide is whether you will still breathe."

The searchlight moved away from him. Either the guard realized that Yoshi wasn't about to flee, or something else became more important to investigate. Yoshi couldn't be sure. But when his eyes adjusted to the dark, he could see the sky. A full moon beamed in the cloudless night, and only the silhouette of the mountains blackened the mass of radiating stars. In that instant, Yoshi felt a strange sense of solace. He considered how the war that started all of this was nothing but a speck in the universe, how even in a world with tragic endings, maybe something was infinite.

Staring up at the sky, fearing the worst of a soldier's fate, Yoshi made a promise—to Joey, to Grandma, and mostly, to himself: *As long as I can, I will live.*

On the summit of Mount Folgorito, seven hours after starting the climb, Yoshi and his comrades crept toward the Nazis. Their first objective was to push the twelve machine gunners away from the big rock fortress up ahead. In the meantime, they needed to move carefully.

Once the Nazis spotted them, the 442nd would be walking straight into oncoming fire. With just a few flimsy trees surrounding them, the men had almost no protection, so they kept their bodies as low as they could without tripping over the rugged terrain. The plan was to move forward as far as they could in the dark. Then, at daybreak, they would begin their assault.

Every step Yoshi took seemed to rumble like thunder. He looked around, trying to figure out where he could take cover if the bullets started flying. From the little he could see through the black haze, nothing around him could shield him. For all he knew, a sniper might have already been watching him through the crosshairs. In a false sense of protection, Yoshi focused on the companions beside him.

Spud marched to his left. Yoshi always liked him. The two of them had something in common: their families were still living at Manzanar. Some volunteers had enlisted from all the camps, but many of these Japanese soldiers had come from Hawaii and the eastern mainland and never experienced the internment.

Something moved behind them, and Spud put out his right arm to stop Yoshi. With his left hand, he put a finger up to his lips to indicate they must stay silent. The two of them stood, frozen, staring into the blackness in front of them. Yoshi shivered. He sensed he was being watched, and he waited for the bullets. Every time he felt this way, he knew that someone was about to be shot. Scanning around, he saw nothing but his own men. Spud dropped his arm and pointed forward. They each took a careful step.

The bullets would come. He knew it. He waited for it. Any second. Somebody always fell first, and that shot was almost always fatal. Feeling his helmet itch his scalp gave him a little comfort. It told him he was protected. Of course, they all were protected. Every slain man had worn a helmet.

They kept moving forward. Into the darkness. Into the enemy's place. He couldn't believe they had made it this far. Each time he placed his foot on the rocky ground, he felt like he was walking across the top of a smoking volcano, like with one wrong step, the whole thing would erupt.

Nothing happened. *What if they aren't here?* Yoshi thought. *After all this, what if the Nazis have already left?* If the regiment had somehow lost communication during the climb, they would have no way of knowing if Germany had surrendered. As implausible as the notion seemed, considering it as a possibility gave him hope. *Maybe the war is over. Maybe the Nazis are gone. Maybe I can go home. Maybe I won't have to—*

BANG! Fiery light, shots, rips, screams. Yoshi was on the ground beside Spud. He didn't feel himself fall, but somehow, there he was, stomach on the rocky ground, hands over head, panting, heart racing, panting, heart racing. It took him a second to process what had just happened. He couldn't hear his thoughts beneath the metallic chatter of machine guns and the shrieks of "Medic!" and the squad leader calling, "Don't fall back! Don't fall back! Keep moving forward!" One of the soldiers had stepped on a mine, and the blast alerted the Nazis up ahead. In a thousand millisecond flashes of orange, the enemy's machine guns sent a tidal wave of ammunition at them.

"Grenade!"

Explosion.

"Medic!"

Explosion.

Mines blew up as the soldiers ran.

"Keep moving forward! Keep moving—" Explosion. No voice left to guide them.

"Come on!" Spud shouted before darting. Without

thinking, Yoshi started running, hoping the bullets wouldn't tear him apart, hoping he wouldn't step on a mine. Hardly aiming, Yoshi shot straight ahead. Gunfire flew both directions. Mortars whistled through the air. Something came flying towards them. It bounced off Spud's helmet and landed right beside them.

It was a grenade.

What happened next didn't fully process. Everything happened too quickly. Spud leapt on top of the grenade to cover it, and in the next instant, Yoshi was on his back. His helmet pounded against a rock. All he could hear was a high-pitched ring as the world around him turned fuzzy. Soon, the spinning faded to black. Warmness replaced the jagged rocks' sting, and he felt himself softly drifting away. Of all the places to feel a sense of peace, this one had to be the strangest. But images flew threw his woozy head, old feelings and moments, like a gentle drowning into the past.

He found himself back at Manzanar, sitting next to Grandma on her cot in the apartment. She told him about Grandpa, about the effort he spent to entertain his family, about the purpose he felt every time he made his grandkids laugh. "His dream was to make people happy," she told him. It reminded Yoshi of somebody else, and suddenly, he was on the miniature Block 2 basketball court, playing a game of H-O-R-S-E with Joey. Facing away from the hoop, Joey took a backwards shot, and Yoshi started chuckling as the ball rolled into the dirt. "I swear that worked once," Joey insisted, running after the ball. It was funny, but Yoshi cracked up even more as Sato and Joey shared jokes by the fish pond. In his hand, Yoshi held the birthday brownie that made him feel so special, and he waited to go watch the Abbot and Costello film in the firebreak, when the light of the movie projector illuminated…Emi, how she smiled at him as they danced, how he felt the small of her back on his palm, and he wished he had the courage to say "you're beautiful," but the words seemed empty when he cared so much about her. If he'd been willing to tell her the truth, if he'd been willing to appear vulnerable, he would have told her something else: "Wouldn't it be nice if the two of us could save each other?"

And then he stood at Manzanar's front gate, about to depart for Camp Shelby. He wore his soldier's cap, his light green khakis, his button up shirt with the 442nd's Statue of Liberty insignia sewn onto the left arm. His family all wore their church clothes for the occasion. Even though Yoshi had been waiting a year to step outside the barbed wire fence, he had a hard time forcing himself to get on the bus to the train station. On their walk over to the camp's entrance, the Yamaguchis filled the heavy quiet with occasional small talk. "Seems like a nice day to travel," and "I bet you won't miss the dust." They didn't have the strength to say goodbye until they had to.

Turning around, Yoshi looked back at Manzanar one last time. Thirty-six blocks stood in front of him, chunked together in groups of four and separated by giant paths of dirt. Out past the barbed wire and the guard towers in the back, purple mountains waved across the horizon. From the front of camp, everything appeared the same as it had on the day he arrived. But even if it wasn't apparent from the main gate, this place had changed since then. Those who lived here had made gardens, fish ponds, and a monument to the dead. A new hospital had been made along with the new school, and pretty soon, an auditorium would be constructed in the South Firebreak. In a strange way, Yoshi felt like he would miss this place. Of course, the good thing about Manzanar was the internees. Even after everything had been taken away from them, they refused to feel defeated. They had turned an internment camp into a community, bound together not by mutual resentment, but by a shared desire to remain optimistic about the country that had betrayed them. The Nisei and Issei had disguised their prison as small-town America—and, by now, most of them took comfort in the facade.

But he couldn't prolong the departure any longer. The Yamaguchis stared at the bus, at the highway behind it, and they knew the time had come to say farewell. Mom was first to speak.

"Oh Yoshi." He didn't want to look into her eyes, but Yoshi could tell she was crying. "It won't be the same without you here. If there's anything we can do to help you make it through, you let us know."

Yoshi nodded. He lost his breath as Sato squeezed him. "Don't die, okay?" she whispered. He chuckled through a sniffle. "I'm serious," she added. "I won't be able to handle it."

When Yoshi looked up, it took a moment for his father to speak. With a waver in his voice, Father stepped forward and gave Yoshi a one-armed hug. "This is...I feel proud."

And then Yoshi had to walk away from them. Deep down, he knew he might never see them again. He got on the bus and watched from the window seat as his family waved goodbye. *Matchstick!* The bus pulled out of the gate. *Matchstick, get up!* Leaving Manzanar once seemed

impossible. When it finally came, it didn't feel like freedom.

The roar of artillery filled his ears. Someone shook his
shoulders.

"Come on, Matchstick! Get up!"

Yoshi opened his eyes.

"There you are! Let's go! We've almost got 'em!" The
comrade ran away before Yoshi could distinguish his
face. Though everything still looked hazy, Yoshi started
coming to his senses. In a panic, he remembered where he
was. He got to his feet and started moving forward, limp-
ing at first, then pushing faster and faster until he forgot to
be afraid. Fallen soldiers surrounded him. Fewer explo-
sions and shots filled the air, but one remaining machine
gunner hid behind a line of rocks. For a second, the firing
stopped, and as Yoshi hustled toward the attacker, a Nazi
popped out from a foxhole in the ground and aimed his
rifle at Yoshi. A shot rang out, and the Nazi fell back into
the hole.

"Keep going!" someone shouted at Yoshi.

The machine gunner's assistant finished reloading.
Shots started firing again. Jumping to the ground, Yoshi
crawled toward the shooter. He crept behind the line of
rocks, saw the two Nazis, and threw a grenade before they

noticed him.

As quickly as it had started, the fighting stopped. Yoshi heard frantic shouts in German as the remaining Nazis retreated. The surviving men of the 442nd started cheering, and a few of them ran up to shoot at the fleeing enemy. All the while, Yoshi remained with his belly on the ground. When his breath started slowing back to a normal pace, he gently pushed himself up. He felt dizzy and sore; he could hardly stay standing. Once he had some time to process, he would start to appreciate how amazing the 442nd's achievement was.

In just over half an hour, they pushed the Nazis back from a position that the Allies had been trying to gain for the past five months. Even more extraordinary, the outcome wasn't much of a surprise: due to the regiment's incredible courage, the 442nd was the most decorated American military unit of its size in history, with twenty-one Medals of Honor and over 9,400 Purple Hearts. One of these awards would be given posthumously to Sadao Munemori, the boy nicknamed Spud. The notification of his honorable death would be delivered to his family at Manzanar. He had sacrificed himself to save Yoshi from the grenade, and this knowledge would horrify Yoshi forever. Amidst the trauma and devastation, it was hard not to resent the war for ever taking place.

Because the world seemed simple once. Before the fallen were sacrificed and the Gothic Line was secured, before the guard towers were built and the barbed wire fence was put up, before Pearl Harbor was bombed and Executive Order 9066 was signed, before he fought with Father, before he fell for Emi, before his good luck charm came in a birthday brownie, before the evacuation notice was taped to the grocery store window, before Ricky bought their spatula, before Gus made him cry, before Sarah laughed at the baseball game, before he lost Grandma, before he lost Joey, before he lost home, before *Pippy the Pirate* lost its humor, before he understood what it meant to be different…life could be so pretty then.

Still, Yoshi refused to succumb to cynicism. He couldn't deny that he was living through an era of suffering, hatred, bigotry, and injustice. But even in a world with men like Adolf Hitler, who commanded destruction with a twinkle in his eye, there were also people like Sato and Emi, who were dedicated to equality and peace. The same universe that had produced the Nazis was filled with the jokes of Joey and Grandpa. And even when everything seemed hopeless, Grandma had always kept a smile on her face with the promise of *Shikata ga nai*. She had learned it from her parents, and Yoshi would pass it on to his children as well. Over time, crumbled buildings would be rebuilt, and wicked men would not be fondly memorialized. When violence rages, nothing can be louder, but once a flame sizzles out, all that's left is ash. Lasting power sides with empathy and grace.

With his head throbbing and his legs shaking, Yoshi looked around at his fellow soldiers. Some lay dead on the ground, most had suffered wounds, and all of them were starving and craving an official Nazi surrender. That day of victory would arrive in a little over a month, and then Yoshi would finally get to return to his family. As much as Yoshi wanted to see Sato and his parents again, he couldn't help but wonder what life would be like once all of this was over. The reunion would be their happiest day in years, but the Yamaguchis wouldn't have their old home to go back to. Many of these soldiers' families faced the same problem, and while the new president, Harry Truman, would go on to congratulate the 442nd for their victory (against both prejudice and the enemy), life would never be the same again. Old losses could never be regained, and no executive order could make racism disappear. What would happen to them after the war? That became their new great uncertainty.

But at the moment, Yoshi didn't have the energy to worry about it. From the looks of it, none of his comrades did either. Weary of the past and anxious about the future, every man kept his focus on the present. They slouched on the rocks, waiting for the sun to rise before getting up and moving forward. Behind the screams of the wounded being treated, chatter filled the air about what had just been accomplished.

"I'm glad I shook him awake," someone said. "Maybe that matchstick is lucky after all."

For the glory was all of theirs, but the story became clear: Yoshi conquered the mountain.

Acknowledgments

I started this novel in 2015, and the four-year process of researching, writing, editing, and publishing has been a wild one. If you have been a part of this journey with me at any point, I thank you. But I would be remiss if I failed to acknowledge a few specific people.

First of all, historical fiction would be impossible without the scholarship of others. While I wouldn't have room to list every resource that assisted in the creation of this book, I do want to voice my appreciation for some of the essential works. *Years of Infamy: The Untold Story of America's Concentration Camps* by Michi Nishiura Weglyn and *Farewell to Manzanar* by Jeanne Wakatsuki Houston and James D. Houston provided helpful baseline information. For this novel's specific needs, however, I relied largely on two of Bill Hosokawa's books, *Nisei: The Quiet Americans* and *JACL in Quest of Justice: The History of the Japanese American Citizens League*. The former helped inform Yoshi's sense of cultural identity; the latter clarified the controversial politics surrounding the Japanese American Citizens League in the 1940s, and it did so while maintaining a fair and objective lens. For the day-to-day logistics of how Manzanar operated, the most helpful book was *Reflecting on WWII, Manzanar, and the WRA* by Arthur L. Williams. And for information about the 442nd, I found Masayo Umezawa Duus' *Unlikely Liberators: The Men of the 100th and 442nd* to be useful, though painting a detailed picture would have been impossible without the hidden gem that is Jack K. Wakamatsu's *Silent Warriors: A Memoir of America's 442nd Regimental Combat Team*. Aside from these books, an invaluable resource was the Densho online encyclopedia (densho.org), which has a detailed entry on just about every possible subtopic related to Japanese internment. I would also like to thank the good folks at the Manzanar National Historic Site who were happy to answer my questions and give me extra resources. (The site's NPS-run website, nps.gov/manz, also has some quality information.)

As far as the work itself goes, I would first like to thank my editor, Mackenzie Roark. Her guidance helped nudge the narrative in the right direction early on, and her enthusiasm for this story was inspirational. I also want to thank Eric Raue, who provided some essential guidance at various points throughout the long process. To my writer friends who gave me feedback on specific chapters along the way, including Daniel Gerardi, Monica Dubé, Rafael Baron, Danielle Arias, and Tim Loperfido, I thank you for your insights and your willingness to help. And this book really came alive with the beautiful illustrations of Nicholas McInvale, who took the time to know this story so he could produce the best possible visuals for it.

Finally, I would like to thank my family. My sister Allison Lindsey, a creative person in her own right, has been enthusiastic about my work in a way I deeply appreciate. My stepdad Nelson Ishii has been a force of stability and kindness for me and my family, which has no doubt aided in my ability to reach publication day. And above all, I want to thank my mom. Without her endless support, I never would have been able to see this book to completion.

Thanks to everyone involved, and thank you for reading.

A Note on Terminology

There has been some debate on whether one should continue to use terms like "internment camp," "internee," "relocation," and "evacuation." Many argue that these are euphemisms provided by the government, and terms like "concentration camp" and "incarceration" would be more accurate. This book mostly relies on the former terms; people use the lexicon with which they are provided, so it seemed appropriate for these characters to use the language they were given.

About the Author

Andrew Hayes Williams is the author of "And All of Us Go Drowning in the Loam," a short story forthcoming in the fifteenth issue of the acclaimed literary journal *F(r)iction*. His satire has appeared in *McSweeney's*, and his essay on Nathaniel Hawthorne's "Young Goodman Brown" was published by the psychology journal *PsyArt*. For contact information and links to his work, please visit andrewhayeswilliams.net.

About the Illustrator

Nicholas McInvale is an illustrator and fine artist based in San Diego. Nicholas and Andrew have known each other for many years, this book being the first time they have worked together professionally. While Nicholas' work is normally science-fiction and fantasy focused, working with historical subjects offered a chance to examine an important moment in United States history while also exploring an incredibly human and deeply emotional landscape. This would not have been possible without the extensive photo documentation of those Japanese-Americans interned in the camps at Manzanar and across the US. Chief among these is the photographer Toyo Miyatake, whose gorgeous work was a constant source of inspiration throughout illustrating this novel. Mr. Miyatake and all those wrongly interned have Nicholas' endless gratitude and admiration for keeping their minds on beauty and humanity when they were treated as less.

For more information, you may visit his website at nick.mcinvale.org or email him at nmcinvaleart@gmail.com. Thank you.

Made in the
USA
Lexington, KY